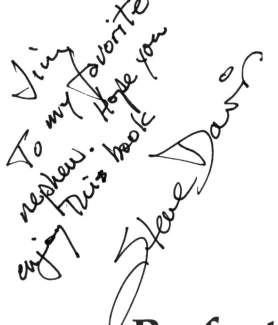

To my favorite
nephew. Hope you
enjoy This book

Steve Davis

Perfect Alibis

BY

Steve Davis

This book is dedicated to my wife, Elizabeth,
who makes my life an enduring adventure.
Here's to growing old together and remembering
families, memories, travel, and
a lifetime of laughs and memories.

And to my children,
Faith, Jeff, Greg, Karin, Chris and Carrie,
for their unwavering love and support.

Perfect Alibis was written in the memory of victims
of senseless homicides,
whose tragic and unexpected losses have left loved ones
lost and coping for answers.

CHAPTER 1

Sunday, May 26, 2013

Ryan Foster paced the floor in a tight semi-circle that seemed to get narrower each time he passed the telephone on the small table between the living room and the dining area. With each pass, he'd pause near the table, look down at the phone, run his fingers through his hair, glance first at the clock, and then at the address book in his hand. When he resumed pacing for the fourth time, Gloria spoke up.

"For God's sake, Ryan, if you don't call him, I will."

"I will," he said emphatically, "You heard the dispatcher. They aren't going to get too excited about it this early. I'm sure she is okay and she'll call if we give her a couple more minutes." Even as he said the words, the look on his face seemed to belie them, and Gloria knew it.

"I just knew it. She's too young. I tried to tell you, but no …," she said.

"Okay, okay. You've made yourself real clear on that, Gloria."

"Well, then, call him. I mean it." She got up from the chair and stepped toward him with her hand out. "Give me the phone. I'll get him out there."

Ryan held out his arm as if to block her path to the phone. He turned and picked up the receiver and dialed the number written in the open address book laying on the table. After several rings, he said, "Come on Sheriff, answer the phone, damn it."

"Hello."

"Rick. Thanks for answering. This is Ryan Foster. Sorry to bother you at home on a weekend, but we need your help. Marcy is missing over at the coast, and Gloria and I are scared. She's not answering her cell, and I can't seem to get the Mendocino Sheriff's Office excited about a missing teenager. I know something is terribly wrong."

"Sure, Ryan. What happened?"

"She went over to Big River Park with some friends for a picnic at the beach. About 6:00 pm, she went back to her friend's car to recharge her cellphone, and she never came back to the group. The others packed up and went to the parking area looking for her and found the car, but no-one was around. I understand young girls go off with boyfriends and the sheriff isn't going to call out the dogs for a 17-year-old girl who is a few hours late, but I know her, and I can tell you something's really wrong. I'm leaving to go over there now myself, and I know you and Mendocino Sheriff Dan Gleason are friends. I've only met him once or twice. I thought you might get him to have one or two deputies put in some time to help out a fellow cop."

"You are right. I remember Marcy, and it doesn't seem like her. If there is an emergency, time might be really important."

"Thanks, Rick. I hope I'm wrong and I'll owe you and Sheriff Gleason both an apology later."

"That won't be necessary. Are you going to be on the radio while you drive over?"

"Yes, and I'll have my cellphone."

Moments later, Ryan was on his way to the location his daughter was last seen, an hour-and-a-half drive to the rugged California North Coast. Since he was the Commander of the Clear Lake California Highway Patrol (CHP) Area, he was on call 24/7, and for that reason, he had an unmarked sedan for emergencies. Although this was not an official call, in his mind it was an emergency, and he turned on the red light, and urged the Crown Victoria quickly forward across the winding mountain roads leading to the coast highway.

Fifteen minutes or more passed, and the radio came to life. "7-L, Ukiah dispatch," the CHP radio blared.

Ryan quickly grabbed the two-way radio microphone from its cradle, "This is 7-L, go ahead, Ukiah." The urgency of his voice betrayed his attempt to hide his concerns.

"7-L, Mendocino Sheriff advises two sheriffs' units are en route to the location."

Ryan was relieved that Lake County Sheriff Rick Sanders had been able to get his counterpart in Mendocino County to give the disappearance serious consideration, even if only as a favor to a fellow law enforcement commander. He breathed a little easier at the thought that law enforcement help was en route and would be on the scene well before he got there.

He drove on in silence. Every time he looked at his watch it showed that he was only a few minutes closer than before, and he cursed the windy mountain road. About 40 minutes later, the radio blared again, "7-L; Ukiah."

Again, Ryan nearly pounced on the microphone. "This is 7-L, Ukiah, go ahead."

"Your current location?"

"I'm on Highway 128 two miles west of Boonville."

After a moment, the radio continued, "Mendocino Sheriff Gleason will meet you at Route 128 and Highway 1."

"10-4," he said. *I didn't expect the Sheriff himself to get involved.*

As he rolled up to the intersection twenty minutes later, there was a marked sheriff's unit in the turnout. As Ryan pulled in behind the unit, Sheriff Gleason got out of the passenger door and began walking toward his car. A uniformed deputy sat behind the steering wheel and didn't get out.

Ryan got out of his car and met Gleason between the vehicles. "Thanks for everything you are doing, Dan, but I never expected …." He stopped in his tracks when he saw the anguish in Gleason's face. "You aren't here for that, are you Dan?"

"This is the toughest thing I've ever done, Ryan." He gulped and paused to moisten his lips. "They found Marcy."

"Is … she … okay?"

"I'm sorry, Ryan. I'm so sorry. It's a crime scene. You shouldn't go there."

CHAPTER 2

Ryan's knees buckled and he leaned hard against the fender of the car. "Oh, my God, No! Not Marcy!"

"I am so sorry, Ryan. The Department of Justice crime lab is on the way and I've got my best guys called out. We'll solve this. Just give us time."

"Murdered?" was all his broken voice could force through his trembling lips.

"Yes," Gleason said in a barely audible voice."

Ryan didn't feel the need to ask for details at this moment. The look on Gleason's face spoke of facts too familiar from his own 28 years of law enforcement. Marcy's luck had simply run out. There, in that most tranquil Pacific Coast setting of warm soft sand and sea grasses caressed by gentle ocean breezes, serenaded by the tranquility of the ever-present surf, one young girl's innocence had crossed paths with the personification of pure evil.

Yes, he knew the story; he'd seen it played out dozens of times with other children and other parents; and now it was going to be his turn to cope with it … or not.

Ryan stepped away from the men and walked to the edge of the highway. For several minutes, he stood and stared in silence at the ocean bluffs in the distance as the surf relentlessly pounded the rocks below them. Gleason and the deputy, who had gotten out of the car, looked at each other, neither knowing what to say to a man who had just heard the worst news either could imagine.

Occasionally, Ryan slammed his fist into the open palm of his hand, cursing beneath his breath. After a few minutes, he returned to the other men and said, "I want to see her. Take me there, please."

"I suspected you would," Gleason said with resignation, "If you don't mind, I'll drive your car."

"Of course. Sure. I understand."

Gleason motioned at the Deputy, who got back into the patrol car and waited to lead the way. Once Ryan and Gleason were in Ryan's car, both vehicles pulled out onto the highway at a much slower pace than before.

"Ryan," Gleason said. "It's okay not to do this. If at any time you aren't comfortable, I'll understand if you want to stop or leave."

"I'll be okay on that, but I'll never accept that my beautiful daughter is dead," he said through painful tears. "Tell me what you know."

"Our first officer at the scene began to trace her steps from the beach to her friend's car, and found her body hidden in the bushes about thirty feet from the parking area. We have DOJ en route, so we didn't contaminate the scene after he confirmed she was dead."

"There's little or nothing to see, until DOJ processes the scene, so please don't contaminate the scene. You know if it was anyone else, I'd never let you near it."

"Thanks, I won't do anything. I just want to see her and say goodbye." After a few moments, he asked, "Was she …?" He choked back the words, but Gleason knew what he wanted to know.

"I was only there for a moment, so I can't be certain, but the deputy who found her said it does appear the perpetrator was alone, and probably did sexually assault her, but it looked like she fought him to the end. He should be scratched up pretty good. We will know more after the autopsy."

Ryan cringed hard, and didn't ask any more questions. He stared out the window into the darkness of the road ahead. Occasionally, he uttered, "Oh God" in a barely discernable voice. Gleason knew there was nothing he could say to ease the pain, so he just drove in silence.

Finally, he said, "Do you think you should notify your wife?"

"Shit," Ryan said, as he pondered the hell he was going to face when Gloria was told the news. "I'll take care of it afterwards. This is going to be bad. We've been having problems for a while, and this is going to send her over the edge. She is going to blame me because we had a big fight about whether Marcy should be allowed to come over here with her older teenage friends. I convinced her to let her come, and now … she's … dead." His voice trailed off into tears as they drove the rest of the trip in silence.

Ten minutes later they turned off of Highway 1 and quickly arrived at the beach parking area. Both cars pulled up to the crime scene tape that cordoned off the entire western end of the beach and parking area. There were three cars parked inside the taped off area. Ryan recognized his daughter's best friend's car, in which Marcy had ridden over to the beach, and another car he'd seen around with her daughter's friends. It appeared they were sequestered until the DOJ had the opportunity to look them over for clues.

"Nice job of protecting the scene for possible clues," Ryan thought to himself.

The third car was the marked patrol car of the first deputy on scene, who had found her body. It is also common to leave the first responder vehicle where it stopped to prevent it from wiping out possible clues when backtracking.

Ryan and Gleason approached the roped off area cautiously and gently moved under the tape barrier. Gleason led Ryan through the brush-lined path to a point where he could see the body, twenty feet from the path, covered by a yellow plastic blanket, and stopped. Upon sight of the blanket covered body, Ryan put both hands up to his face, then stood erect and wiped the tears from his eyes.

"I think this is as close as we ought to get, Ryan. We want this guy really bad, and we don't want to disturb the sand along the path. There might be clues."

"Okay."

Gleason stepped away to give him a moment to grieve alone. Ryan cupped his hands, covering his nose and mouth, took in a deep breath, and exhaled slowly into his hands. *"God, I know we don't talk much, but if you are there, you'd better fix this. I've been a righteous man ... a cop ... I've fought the battle for good over evil all my life. Why would you bring this to my doorstep? You know me. You know I'm not going to put up with this. You know this won't be the end of it for me. If you want to save my soul from hell, fix this ... NOW!"* He looked briefly upward again, then back at the body, staring at the blanket, waiting for it to move and for Marcy to sit up.

He stood there, transfixed, for what seemed an eternity, as if waiting for God to deliver on a secret pact they had just made. His eyes closed and his jaw tightened to mask his pain, as his face struggled to hide the depth of his growing pain and anger. He slowly drew in and inhaled a full breath deep into his lungs, exhaling slowly and deliberately while his face became flushed with inner rage.

Then, forced to accept the truth in front of him, he abandoned the void between faith and reality, turned and slowly walked back toward his car. "Then that's how it will have to be." he muttered as he walked away. Once inside the car, he leaned against the steering wheel, buried his face in his forearms, and sobbed uncontrollably.

As the rising moon from the east broke over the coastal mountain range, it cast an eerie glow over the Big River beach. The waves pounding the shoreline seemed to glow in the reflected twilight, illuminating the crime scene tape that now adorned the once tranquil park. And, just as the surf on that day forever changed that landscape, so too, had Ryan Foster's life changed, not for the better, and he knew that somewhere out there was a dead man walking.

CHAPTER 3

When Ryan walked into the Mendocino Sheriff's Detective's Office the following morning, his appearance announced the depth of his despair and told of the fitful, sleepless night he had just endured. There were already seven men, each of whom looked almost as haggard as he, engrossed in deep discussion in the room. Upon his arrival, all conversations stopped mid-sentence as the men stared at him, each wondering what a man would look like, or what he'd say, the morning after his entire world had ceased to exist.

To his right sat Sheriff Gleason, and the uniformed deputy who was in charge of the scene the night before, whose name he didn't recall. To the left sat Detective Darrel Atkins, the leader of the Homicide Investigation Team, and the Lab Tech who had secured the scene and evidence while they waited for the investigators from the California Department of Justice Crime Lab to get to the scene in the middle of the night.

The other two men got up and introduced themselves as detectives.

Sheriff Gleason reiterated his sorrow for the loss of Marcy, and the other men offered their condolences also.

"Thank you," Ryan said, "I'll pass your sentiments on to my wife. She is a wreck right now. I'm lucky her sister drove all night from Oregon to be with her for a few days. Thank you, men, for all your work. I know you were all up all night on this case, and I want you to know how much I appreciate your efforts, and for letting me sit in with you this morning on the progress of the case."

"No problem, Ryan. None of us can even imagine the grief you are feeling right now. She was your only daughter, and I don't know how I'd handle it if it were me."

"I'll let you know as soon as I figure it out myself. Right now, I'm just concerned about getting the dirtbags who did this to her."

"I can assure you that every man in this room will not rest easy until the case is solved. The DOJ is still on-scene processing evidence."

"What do we know at this point?" asked Ryan.

"I was just beginning to brief the investigation team," said Detective Atkins, "Please, stop me if this is uncomfortable for you at any time. We have to present this information in graphic terms for the sake of the investigation."

"Ryan, you can step out at any time and no one will think less of you for it," said Gleason.

"That won't be a problem, sir. I need to hear this information," Ryan said resignedly, "It is important to me that I know how it went down."

"Okay," Atkins continued, "It appears she was grabbed en route to the car, and she was dragged into the bushes to the scene of the assault. It looks like she put up quite a fight while the perpetrator sexually assaulted her. The perp probably has numerous scratches around his face and arms. Death appears to be by strangulation."

Ryan winced visibly and bit his lip at the thought of what Atkins was saying. He knew the details were important, but they hurt even more than he imagined, as he contemplated the suffering and indignities that his daughter had to endure before she died.

"Do you want Darrel to continue, Ryan?" Sheriff Gleason asked. "Maybe it is too fresh and you should wait a day or two until we know more answers?"

"No. I'm alright. I need to know these things. In case the asshole is ever on his knees begging me not to shoot him, I'll need to think about these things ..."

"Whoa. Wait a minute, Ryan," Gleason interjected, "You aren't serious, are you? I could understand if you felt that way, but we can't allow ..."

"No, Sheriff," he interrupted, "It's OK. I'm just talking bullshit. I could never do that. I'm one of the good guys. I'm sorry. Go on with the briefing, please."

Gleason frowned and glanced questioningly at Detective Atkins as he paused for a few seconds to size up the situation, taking the full measure of Ryan by looking him up and down, searching for a hint as to whether he was serious or not.

"No, really, I'm okay. Go on," Ryan calmly assured him.

Atkins glanced over at Gleason again, who nodded, so he continued, "There is skin residue under her fingernails, and semen samples have been obtained. We should have plenty of DNA to go from. We don't know for sure how many were involved yet, but it looks like he was alone from the footprints in the sand and dirt nearby."

He paused again to see Ryan's reaction to that statement before continuing. Seeing no visible reaction, he continued, "Of course, because it is soft sand, we can't get a foot print, but the number of impressions appear to be from one perp."

"But the evidence guys should be able to clear that up, when they come back from DOJ. They said they'd expedite it as much as possible, but we're still looking at three weeks to a month from now to be sure."

Referring to his notes in front of him, the detective continued the debriefing. "There was an unknown black substance left by the perpetrator where he touched her and when he strangled her. Smelled like paint, but, again, the lab can tell us for sure."

"Paint?" asked one of the detectives.

"Yeah. Kind of strange, isn't it?"

"Do you have any real suspects?" Ryan asked.

"Nothing concrete, but we've got a good lead, perhaps. The killer might even have left his autograph behind. There was a large amount of new graffiti in the area. All over the park, including one half-finished sign near the crime scene. Fresh black paint everywhere around the park; says 'Choco 13V'."

"Choco 13V? Street gang graffiti?"

"Yup. Apparently affiliated with a Santa Rosa street gang called the 13 Villains. Their tag is the member's street name followed by the number 13 and letter V."

"And how do we know they're connected?"

"Don't for sure. But if they are, we've got good stuff to put this 'Choco' guy at the scene and for comparison. He sprayed so much around Fort Bragg the PD even found an empty spray can with what appears to be good prints near one of the locations. We got three freshly painted 'Choco 13V' signs in the park for comparison with the paint can. One was close to where he grabbed Marcy on her way to the parking lot. In fact, it is unfinished, meaning perhaps she caught him in the act. They are going to DOJ tomorrow."

"Why would a Santa Rosa gangbanger be tagging up in Fort Bragg?"

"It's just a hunch," Atkins continued, "but we think he might have been up there for some kind of initiation; you know, tag someone else's turf, and perhaps he just crossed paths with Marcy."

"Or worse," one of the other detectives interjected, "The 13V is a bad-ass gang with some real hard core ex-cons for leaders. The PD down there says they are very violent, and that their initiation usually requires a potential member to commit a major felony, usually a robbery, to prove his loyalty to the gang. Maybe he escalated the required crime."

"Wait a minute. Let me get this straight." Ryan interrupted. His intensity increased as he spoke the words. "Are you saying that my daughter may have been raped and murdered as some kind of gang initiation?"

"We are just talking possibilities here, but you know, Ryan that we have to look at every potential scenario."

"And you think it might be this 'Choco' guy?"

"Don't know. Covering all the possibilities. The black marks on Marcy; could be spray paint from the can that got on his hands. We'll know a lot more soon, I think. When the lab tests come back. He's probably got a record."

"Anything else?"

"We're interviewing the other kids from the beach party today. And we're contacting the park rangers and other campers to see if they saw anything important. And Santa Rosa PD ran 'Choco' through their gang database. They recognized the name as a member of the Villains, but they don't have a full ID on him yet. Their detectives are already on the streets with their informants trying to get any information they will give up. Trouble is the '13 Villains' are not someone you'd want to get caught snitching on."

"I understand," said Ryan. "Thanks again for all your efforts, and for keeping me posted. Detective Atkins, can I call you tonight and from time to time to keep up with the investigation?"

"Sure, Ryan. Any time."

The forty-minute ride back home to Lakeport was a time for tears, anger, and rage. *"How am I supposed to face my wife again today? She's already reminded me in no uncertain terms that she was against letting Marcy go on this trip, and I over-ruled her, and now she holds me personally responsible for her death."*

By the time he turned onto the street he lived on, he had no answers for his wife or anyone else, but his rage was real and he began to daydream about killing the faceless Choco in cold blood while he begged for mercy.

CHAPTER 4

Each day of the next week was as bad as the day of Marcy's murder. Not a day – scarcely an hour went by – without Gloria breaking down and saying, "Why did you let her go? It's all your fault." Even her sister, who was supposed to be there to help, treated him as if he was the killer himself.

Following the funeral, her grief turned to deep depression, and the professional help the Department provided she and Ryan wasn't helping at all. She had insisted on separate counselors, so she could vent her frustration that Ryan was responsible for Marcy's death. She could barely stand to be in the room with him, and when he approached her to try to comfort her, she would stiffen up and quickly leave the room. Her nights were spent on the couch where she would cry herself to sleep late into the night.

As for Ryan, he was granted a lengthy leave of absence from the CHP, but he was not opening up to his counselor either. What could he tell him? That he also blamed himself for letting her go to Big River Park that day; or that he daydreamed every hour of the day of killing the bastard who killed his daughter? He hardly cared about the CHP right now, but he knew they would react very unfavorably if they knew what he was thinking, or that it was becoming an obsession with him.

About a week later, Gloria informed him she was leaving him and going to go live with her sister in Oregon. Ryan thought it might actually do her good, so he encouraged her to get away for a while. He knew she was going to go anyhow, so he hoped she'd get past her hatred for him if she was away for some soul searching and healing. He convinced himself she would be back home in a few weeks, and the mutual healing could finally begin.

But nine days later, Ryan got a chilling letter from Gloria, informing him that she was staying permanently. She told him that she could never get over her anger at him, and she would always blame him for Marcy's death, and with Marcy gone, there was nothing left between them. She said the only hope for her was to start a new life; to move on. She advised him that she had been to a lawyer and he could expect to be served divorce papers in the next few days. It ended with "Best wishes" and a request that he not contact her except through her lawyer.

"Best Wishes? Almost twenty years of marriage, and I get a letter wishing me 'best wishes?'" He threw the letter on the table and poured himself a drink and went out and sat on the deck and stared at the lake in the distance.

It also didn't help that the daily phone calls to Detective Atkins had not been productive, and for the last two days, Atkins did not return his calls. Nor did it help to hear that Santa Rosa Detectives were reporting that Choco, whoever he was, had apparently gone into hiding and no-one was talking about who or where he was. By the time they caught up with him, the wounds inflicted by Marcy would be healed, Ryan feared.

Even those depressing thoughts could not prepare him for the 7:00AM phone call six days later.

CHAPTER 5

BRRRING!

Ryan woke up, but made no attempt to answer the phone, deciding to let the phone ring through to the answering machine.

After three more rings, the machine kicked in, "Hello, this is the Foster residence," Marcy's voice announced, "If it's for Ryan or Gloria, leave a message. If it's for Marcy, call me on my cell phone, you know the number."

Marcy's voice made him sit up sharply. He'd forgotten what was on the phone message. He liked hearing the sound of her voice, but he knew he couldn't leave it on there forever. *"I've got to change that message, ... some day."*

His thoughts momentarily made him forget there was a call coming in. The depth of his thoughts was shattered when he heard Detective Atkins' obviously anguished voice speaking into the answering machine.

"C'mon, Ryan. Pick up the fucking phone. Ryan, this is Detective Atkins. It's very important. Call me right away. Right away!"

The anguish in his voice announced clearly that this was not going to be good news. Ryan jumped up at the first sound of Atkins panicked voice and sprinted into the front room and picked up the phone. "I'm here, Darrel."

"Shit. Good!"

"What's so important, Darrel?"

"Have you turned on the news this morning?"

"No. Why?"

"Terrible news, Ryan. I didn't call you until I could confirm this with DOJ. There was a big fire at the DOJ lab last night in Sacramento. Our evidence; it's all gone. The fire wiped out our evidence. Can you fucking believe it? We're going to have to start over. Fortunately, we can probably make a match on the paint from the signs, and we have a good description from the witnesses that day, so maybe we can…"

"That's bullshit, Darrel!" Ryan slumped onto the couch as tears streamed down his cheeks. "I'm not an idiot. We both know what it means. No fingerprints, no DNA, no semen sample …. It means all you got is a graffiti charge against Choco, whoever the fuck he is. No trace evidence means no Murder One, no death penalty, no justice."

"I know it looks bleak, Ryan, but you've got to trust me on this. Every cop in this office is going to be on the case. DOJ was very pessimistic, but maybe something survived the fire. If not, we'll rebuild it from the ground up. We'll get him yet. Trust us."

"Sure, Darrel, I trust you," he said in a very calm voice. "By the way, I'm curious, did you ever find any evidence that Choco wasn't alone? Do you think there was anyone else with him that night?"

"No, Ryan. The Rangers and other park users saw him from a distance, driving around. They can't ID him, but they said he was alone. Ryan, I know this is bleak, and I feel as bad as you, but we can put him at the park at the time of the murder. Maybe ..."

"Really? You feel as bad as I do? Bullshit, Darrel. The graffiti is his own best evidence. It shows he was there alright; to spray graffiti, nothing puts him at the murder scene, and you know it just like I do. You know what it means? I'll tell you what it means; it means that Choco doesn't die in the gas chamber; so, he'll just have to die by other means instead. I swear I will have the satisfaction of seeing him die."

"Ryan, please don't say any more and don't do what I think you are thinking. Marcy's gone, but you have to keep yourself together for her memory."

"I didn't just lose my daughter, Darrel. I lost my wife and my 'give-a-shit'. I devoted my life to the pursuit of justice, and I'm not going to see some gangbanger dirtbag asshole get away with murdering my Marcy without justice --- street justice, if necessary."

"Ryan. Stop. I don't know what to do. What you are saying is coming real close to making a 'terrorist threat', which constitutes a crime in itself, so don't say anymore. You are putting me in a bad spot."

"Let me save us both some trouble. I gotta go now."

As he hung up the phone, he said to no one in particular, "God damn it! … Looks like it'll have to be Plan B."

CHAPTER 6

It was dusk when Ryan pulled the unmarked car to the curb where he could watch the end unit of the South Park housing complex in Santa Rosa, 80 miles south of Lakeport. Soon, as he had on the two previous nights when Ryan had watched the neighborhood, a young Hispanic male, maybe all of fourteen years old, with short black hair barely visible under a black hoodie came quickly down the stairs and moved around the corner onto Benson Street. He paused for a brief moment and looked both ways, not to look for traffic, but to check for possible attackers from a rival street gang. Cautious and wary, like the rookie gangbanger he was, he satisfied himself it was clear, stuck a pair of bright orange earbuds into his ears, stopped for a moment to tune in his favorite beats, and began to walk, completely ignoring the middle-aged man in the conspicuously unmarked police sedan across the street.

Ryan started the engine and swung the Ford around the corner until he was alongside the youth, alone on the street. The young boy didn't appear to notice him while rocking out to the sounds coming from his cell phone.

Ryan accelerated and pulled into a driveway immediately blocking the path of the young man, who stopped abruptly. He stepped back and ripped off the ear buds, as he took stock of the threat he perceived from the car. But then, seeing the age and ethnicity of the stranger, he relaxed a bit, but still took up a defensive posture as he saw Ryan get quickly out of the car.

Before he could say anything, Ryan flashed his badge in front of him and said, "Joseph Quintana? ... Police Officer. Hold it right there."

"What's this?" said the young man. His first instinct was to run. Hell, he could outrun this old man in a heartbeat, but he knew he was too new to the gang to have anything to hide. Besides, somehow the cop already knew his name, so he stood there as Ryan approached. Just to show he was for real, he assumed the 'gang' posture, saying, real tough-like, "What the fuck do you want with me, cop?"

"Not much. You're going to have to come with me, Jo-Q."

"Why? What'd I do? How do you know my name?"

"We'll talk about it in a minute." With that, he pulled a set of handcuffs out of his pocket and before the young man could protest, he was handcuffed. "Get in the car. We're going to take a ride downtown," Ryan said as he opened the rear door and secured him in the rear seat.

As Ryan pulled back onto the road, the young man said, "What am I busted for, dude? You gotta tell me what you're busting me for, cop."

Without answering, Ryan turned north on Brockwood and then went east on Highway 12.

"Hey, pig, I said you gotta tell me what I'm busted for."

"You scared, Jo-Q?"

"No, man. I'm a Thirteen. We ain't scared of no cops."

Ryan didn't answer.

"Where the fuck we going? The police station is the other direction." When there was no answer, he pressed the issue, "Let me see that badge again. Are you a real cop? You're taking me out of town."

"Play along, Jo-Q, and maybe you don't get hurt."

"Who are you? You aren't really a cop. Why do you want me?"

"You scared yet, Jo-Q?"

"I told you. I ain't scared. Why you keep asking that?"

"Because you are whining like you're scared."

Jo-Q lowered his voice a few octaves, trying to sound like a seasoned gang member. "I just want to know what's going on."

"You'll know soon enough. I want some information. How I get it depends on you."

"Fuck you man. I already told you, I'm a Thirteen. I ain't telling you fucking nothing."

It seemed to take no time at all, and they were out of town in the rural area. Jo Q watched the roads intently, but didn't say anything. One minor street and a couple of quick turns later and they were at the edge of a remote wine grape vineyard. Seconds later, they were deep into the brush and among some scrub oak trees, hidden behind a vineyard, invisible from nearby homes and the highway.

Jo-Q's heart was pounding as Ryan stopped the car. "What's going on? Why are we stopping out here? What's going on?"

"You scared yet, Jo-Q? I can hear your heart pounding from here."

Jo-Q looked out the window, surveying the location and appraising the situation. After a long pause, he said, "Alright, maybe … maybe a little scared. Who are you? You working for another gang?"

"Nope. In fact, Jo-Q, I'm doing us both a favor. I am a cop. I need information, and you have it. …"

Hearing that the man might actually be a police officer seemed to calm Jo-Q's fears somewhat, and he reverted to his macho attitude. "Fuck you man, I ain't no stoolie."

"Yes, you are, Jo-Q. You just haven't figured it out yet. In a few minutes, you will tell me everything I want to know, but first let me tell you about yourself. My cop friends here in Santa Rosa tell me you could have a good future, but you seem to want to be a little bad-ass gang-banger. When I stopped you, I could have been a rival gang member, and you'd be dead by sixteen. Now here you are in a field in the middle of nowhere with a guy and a gun. I guess you could still end up dead. They tell me you are too smart to be a gang-banger, but you are also too stupid to stay alive in a gang. You're going to die on the streets and that's not what your parents came to America and sacrificed to provide for you. When we get done here, after you've told me what I want to know, I'm going to take you back home and I want you to think about it. Get out of that stupid gang while they won't miss you."

"I've heard all that shit before. I still ain't telling you nothing, pig."

"Yes, you will. But did you hear me, Jo-Q?"

"Yes, I heard you. Why are you so sure I'll tell you anything?"

"Okay, my young friend, here's why. When we get done here, I'm going to take you back to the 'hood'. Where I drop you off depends on what you tell me. Answer my questions, and I let you off anywhere you want, and no-one knows we had this conversation. Fail this test, and I'm going to let you off on Aston Ave., right by the park." He glanced at his watch just long enough to give it the proper impact. "The 13Villians will be hanging out there about this time of night. I'll pull up nearby, in sight of the gang, let you out, take off the cuffs, and pat you on the back, and drive away. Then you can try to explain to your homie buddies standing on the corner, why the cops let you go without any charges. Next time the cops bust one of your buddies, and they are trying to figure out who snitched them off, who do you think they will decide must have done it? They will remember that night Jo-Q got dropped off by an undercover cop for no reason. What do you think about that, Jo-Q?"

"You can't do that. They'd kill me. You're a cop. You got rules."

"Fuck the rules. I want information. Do you think this is in the rules?" Ryan picked up the gun on the seat and gestured toward the dark, remote location they were in, being careful not to aim it directly at Jo-Q.

"You do that and I'm a dead man."

"Dead boy," he corrected, "You are far from a man, but I don't fucking care. "You stick around the gang, and you'll be dead soon anyhow. But you'll have to figure all of that out for yourself. Now the ball is in your court."

There was a significant pause, while Jo-Q looked around and shook his head back and forth, straining in the handcuffs. "This ain't fucking right!"

"We are wasting time. We have a meeting on Aston in a few minutes. What's it going to be?"

"Fuck! ..." Jo-Q looked down, then up, shook his head from the upper left with a twist to the lower right, all the while squirming in the handcuffs. Finally, he said, "What kind of information?"

"See, Jo-Q, now you are getting smarter by the minute. I want information on the murder that occurred in Fort Bragg. A young girl ..." He choked back his emotions at referring to his daughter as if she were anonymous. "Who killed her? I know it was Choco, but I want to hear it from you."

"I don't know nothing about it."

"Bullshit, Jo-Q. We are about one question away from Aston Avenue. I didn't go through all of this to play cat and mouse with you."

"I tell you, I don't know, dude. I wasn't there."

Ryan started the motor. "I guess my friends thought you were smarter than that. While we're driving you better start to put together your story for the Thirteens waiting at Aston." He pulled the transmission into 'DRIVE'.

"Hold on man. You know I'd be dead if he found out. He's one of the baddest dudes in the Thirteens. I'm dead either way."

"Jo-Q, I'm the only person you can trust right now. I'm also the only person who can determine where we go from here. Choose wrong and you probably are a dead man, I mean 'dead boy', choose right, and none of this ever happened." He put the car back in 'PARK'. "Are you in or out?"

Jo-Q thought a few moments while he squirmed around trying to get comfortable in the handcuffs. "At least take off these handcuffs."

"There you go again, Jo-Q, acting stupid. I take the cuffs off and you try to make a run for it. No, we keep it just like it is. I'm in charge, and I make the rules. All you have to do is make up your mind; you in, or you out."

"Okay," he said in a barely audible tone. Then slower, he repeated, only slightly louder, "Okay."

He took a deep breath and let it out slowly. "I wasn't there that weekend, and I only know what I've heard some of the other dudes bragging about it. Choco wanted to show what a bad-ass he was so he went up there alone to Fort Bragg for his initiation. He tagged the shit out of Bragg; all over, they said. I guess the girl was just in the wrong place at the wrong time. She saw him tagging and looked down on him. He said something to her and I guess she told him to fuck off. So, what could he do? She dissed him, and he needed a felony to get in, so he took her down."

Ryan choked on the visual of his daughter's last minutes of terror. He suppressed the rage he felt coming to the surface. *"Easy Ryan, he's talking to you. Don't blow it now."* He took a deep breath and silently let it out through pursed lips.

"She kept scratching him, so he strangled her. You should have seen him, all clawed up. She got him good, but he passed the test, so they initiated him and he disappeared for a while. He hasn't been back yet, but the guys say the scratches are almost healed, and he'll be back soon."

Jo-Q looked out the side window. "He'll kill me. You know he'll fucking kill me."

"What's his real name?"

"You are going to get me killed, man."

"Just a couple more questions and you are a free man. His name?"

"Lemos. Danny Lemos. But you didn't hear that from me either, right?"

"Was anyone with him when he killed my … the girl?"

"No, man. He had to do it alone to pass the test. Wait a minute, did you say …"

Ryan interrupted before Jo-Q could connect the dots. "Last question. Where is he now?"

"I don't know. I heard he had a sister up in Laytonville somewhere. Word is that he went up there. He's going to fucking kill me."

"Okay, Jo-Q, you passed the test … at least for now. Where do you want to be left off?"

Jo-Q paused a few moments as if he hadn't really believed he would get let off anywhere he chose. "For real, man? We never had this talk?"

"That's right. Just like I promised. As long as it's true. If you lied to me, you'll see me again. Soon. But next time, I'll be really pissed."

"Near my sister's house. I'll tell you how to get there so no-one sees us."

Fifteen minutes later, Ryan pulled the Ford to the curb around the corner from the location Jo-Q directed him to. Jo-Q, who had been laying on the seat below the window line, stuck his head up and glanced around, then ducked down again.

"What now?" he asked.

"Okay, Jo-Q. Here's the deal. We've both got a lot to lose if anyone else finds out about this conversation. So, shut the fuck up, and play dumb when the shit hits the fan. And most of all, remember, this conversation never happened. We never saw each other in our lives, got it?"

"Fuck yeah, man. Let me out of here."

Ryan reached across the seat back and unbuckled the seat restraints. "Turn around."

Jo-Q turned quickly in the seat, staying below the window line so Ryan could take off the cuffs. Without a word, he peeked out and glanced around, rubbed his wrists, and jumped out of the vehicle. Once he was away from the car, he took a quick look to see if he was spotted, and disappeared into the night.

That night, Ryan lay in bed trying to calm down and formulate a plan, using this newly found information, to kill Choco when he found him. His heart was pounding in his chest so hard he could hear it.

Three things he knew for certain at that moment; first, his life was going to be changed forever, the extent to be determined in the next few days, and he was okay with it; secondly, he couldn't trust anyone else to even know what he was planning; and, third, and most important, he wanted to see the look on Choco's face when he killed him.

He spent most of the night talking to Marcy in his mind. She was adamantly against the plan, and she kept

Steve Davis

pleading with his mind, saying, *"Daddy, please don't do it."*
But, he woke up the next morning undeterred and more
willing than ever to see it through."

CHAPTER 7

In the morning, he called his contact on the Santa Rosa Police Department.

"Sergeant Kirkland," he said, "Thanks for the information you gave me the other day about the '13Villians'. I'm sure it will help with the case. I have another quick question for you. You got any information in your files on a member called Choco, or Danny Lemos? Could you check and see if you have information on him having a sister in the Laytonville area?"

"Sure Ryan. Glad to see you are back at work. Hold on a minute while I check the files." After a short wait, he returned and said, "Yeah, I found it on an old booking record. Her name is Angela and she lives at 13800 Vallejo Street in Laytonville."

"Great. Thanks, Sarge."

"Hang on a minute, Ryan. I'm just curious, how did you know Choco was Danny Lemos? According to the files, our detectives just found out a couple days ago."

"I'm pretty sure you told me the other day when we talked."

"No, it couldn't be me, because I didn't know until I looked at the notes in the file just now. In fact, the computer gang database says the information was only entered yesterday. And apparently they hadn't even made the connection with his sister in Laytonville."

"Well, I probably heard it from Detective Atkins at Mendo Sheriff's Office."

"No, I don't think ...." He paused as if a revelation had just crossed his mind. "Yeah, that's probably it."

As Ryan hung up the phone, Sergeant Kirkland stared at the receiver for about ten seconds. He shook his head almost imperceptibly, then picked up the receiver again and dialed a number.

"Mendo Sheriff, Detective Atkins," the voice on the line responded.

"Yeah, Atkins, this is Sergeant Kirkland, Santa Rosa PD. I understand you are lead detective on the Marcy Foster murder case, is that correct?"

"Yeah, Sergeant, do you have information I can use?"

"Maybe. Are you aware that your prime suspect, a gangbanger named Choco, has a real name of Danny Lemos?"

"No," he said excitedly. "That's great info. We've been trying to find that out. Thanks for the tip. What do you have on Lemos?"

"That may not be important right now, we've got a bigger problem."

"A bigger problem that catching Choco? How so?"

"Ryan Foster just asked me to confirm that Choco, or Danny Lemos, as he called him, has a sister in Laytonville. He already knew Lemos was Choco, and we just found out ourselves. And now Ryan knows he's got a sister on Vallejo Street in Laytonville."

"How'd he find out Choco's name before we knew it, and how does he know about the sister. Lemos has been on the lamb for 3 weeks now. No-one's giving up where he is."

"Atkins, I'm pretty sure Ryan got information somewhere that Lemos is at his sister's house in Laytonville, and he may be on his way there to kill him now."

"Shit! I was afraid he'd do something like that. Give me the address. I've got to hurry to head him off before he throws his life and career away. Got to go. Thanks for the tip."

CHAPTER 8

Ryan waited until nightfall before starting out for the address in Laytonville. While he waited, he made sure he had at least two extra clips of ammunition for his Smith and Wesson .40 caliber automatic handgun. He hoped that would be enough, because it would afford him the opportunity to look Lemos in the eyes when he killed him. Then, just in case the plan changed, he went to the gun safe and pulled out a Mini 14 assault rifle with a sniper-style scope, and a twelve-gauge shotgun, loading it full of .00 buck shot shells. *That should take care of Plans A, B, and C,"* he thought as he loaded the long guns into the trunk of his private vehicle.

At the first signs of dusk, he began the long drive to Laytonville, well over an hour north of Ukiah on State Route 101.

While en route, he again heard the voice of Marcy, begging him not to follow through with his plan. Tears streamed down his cheeks as he tried to reason with her. *"I'm sorry, baby girl. We both know I'm responsible for this. I caused it, and now I've got to fix it. I can't let him get away with murdering my only daughter and not die for what he did to you. I'm a father first and a cop second. I can't let it go."*

The time went quickly, and soon he was turning off of Route 101 onto Colton Canyon Road, which would lead him to Vallejo Street, where he would find his quarry unprepared. He still hadn't decided exactly how he would lure Lemos away from the others who might be in the home, but he knew he'd come up with something once he saw the lay of the land.

As he eased around the corner onto Vallejo, he was surprised to see the street was full of waiting marked and unmarked sheriff's vehicles, including the now-familiar unmarked car of Sheriff Gleason, and a CHP patrol vehicle. As he drove directly into the welcoming party, he could see his own boss, CHP Chief Ted Marsden, seated in the right seat of the parked CHP vehicle. The driver was a Sergeant he didn't know from the local area.

"Crap. What's the Chief doing here? How'd they know?" He stopped in the middle of the road, and Gleason and Marsden approached the driver's door of the vehicle. He rolled the window down.

"What are you doing here, Ryan?" Marsden asked calmly.

Ryan took a deep breath and looked straight ahead at his clenched fists wrapped tightly around the steering wheel. "You know what I'm doing here, Chief."

Marsden stopped his answer. "Don't say another word, Ryan. You haven't violated any law yet, so shut up and come with me. This Sergeant will drive your car home. We'll talk en route." He motioned toward the passenger door of the marked CHP vehicle.

Turning to Sheriff Gleason, Marsden said, "I can't thank you enough, Dan, for the heads up on this."

Gleason nodded and bit his lower lip.

"Are we good here?"

"We're good, Chief." With a sigh of great relief, he repeated "We're good. No crime committed, no harm, no foul. Go take care of your guy."

Marsden motioned for the CHP Sergeant to drive Ryan's car and opened the car door for Ryan to exit. Ryan said nothing as he got out of his car and walked to the marked CHP vehicle and took a seat in the right front. Marsden walked around and got into the driver's seat.

Ryan looked straight ahead at the dashboard as the two men left the scene. The first ten miles of the trip neither man spoke, until Ryan broke the silence. "You know you can't stop me. It's just a matter of time. I'll get him."

"You're probably right, but it won't be tonight."

Another long pause was broken when Ryan said, "You know you didn't take my gun away from me?"

"Don't have to. I'm not afraid of you."

Another pause, but this time much shorter than the others.

"How'd you know? And how did you get down here from Redding so fast?"

"I got a call, and we have a helicopter, remember?"

"You flew down here in a CHP helicopter just to save that dirtbag?"

"No," he said, "I flew down here in a CHP helicopter to save you, you idiot."

"You wasted your time. I'll get him some day. I don't care what it costs me."

Marsden pulled into a turnout and stopped to emphasize his point. "Look Ryan, we've been friends quite a while now. So, I'm going to be blunt. I can't begin to know what grief you are going through. Your whole life has been turned upside down. Your daughter is dead and your wife gone. I know you blame yourself, and that may be the worst burden of all. I can't begin to know what it is like, but I've asked myself a hundred times what I would do if this terrible thing had happened to me. I've got a teenage daughter myself and I had to imagine how I'd react if the roles were reversed. I don't know for sure, but I do know this. You are way too smart to throw away your life and career on *stupid* revenge when there are other options you haven't considered."

"Yeah? Like what? Forgiveness? That ain't gonna …"

"Forgiveness, my ass. You'll never forgive that bastard, and you won't rest easy until you know he's dead."

"Okay, Chief, what's your idea of another option?"

"Like I say, I've given it a lot of thought as to what I'd do, and I realize, I'm seeing it through different eyes, but I'd spend a lot of time coming up with a foolproof way of killing him without implicating myself. I'd make a challenge out of it. You know, the 'perfect crime'."

Ryan perked up at the thought, and cocked his head as he mulled over the idea.

"Now let me make this clear," Marsden continued. "I'm not condoning vigilante justice in any way, and I STRONGLY suggest against it, but you appear to be dead set to ruin your life to kill this little shit, so I'll put it to you this way. You are playing this out stupid. If you spend some time thinking about it, you might not be acting on some irrational thoughts of committing career suicide and life in prison for a moment of instant revenge. Use your head. Come up with a plan. In the meantime, maybe you'll reconsider your options."

Marsden pulled back onto the highway, leaving Ryan mulling over what he just said. "You know, Chief ...," Ryan smirked, without finishing the sentence.

Marsden stopped him in mid-sentence. "From this point on, I don't want to talk about what we just discussed ever again. Whatever you do, I don't want to hear about it, before, during, or after. And you are on your own if you get caught. Don't dare bring my name up."

Again, the landscape and the darkness passed effortlessly while Ryan stared out of the window at nothing. The silence ended when they pulled up in front of the Foster home in Lakeport.

Marsden said, "I understand you have a nice couch in your living room. I'd like to invite myself to sleep on it tonight. It's a long trip back to Redding, and there is something else I need to discuss with you."

"Sure, Chief. But you don't have to babysit me. I'm not going to try anything else tonight."

"Seriously, we need to talk about something else."

As they got out of the car, Marsden asked, "You got any Scotch in the liquor cabinet?"

By the time the Chief left the next morning, they had gone over a recovery plan the CHP put together for Ryan to keep his job. In light of his deep depression, compounded by his most recent actions, the CHP could not afford to allow him to continue in his current position as Commander of the Lakeport squad. The CHP would find a temporary replacement while Ryan underwent a prescribed psychological recovery plan. Before he would be allowed to return to work, the CHP needed to know that he was over his obsession for revenge, and once again capable of leading in the manner he had established before Marcy's death.

The prime component of the plan was that Ryan had to complete a seven-step psychological program called 'The Forgiveness Retreat', the brainchild of 'Dr. Stan' Berkeley, the famous Made-for-TV doctor who seems to have a fix for every problem. The program consisted of intense 'sharing' at a mountaintop Colorado retreat under the tutelage of Dr.

Stan, along with other attendees who were going through the same grief wrought depression.

Ryan vehemently insisted he was okay and didn't need the program, but in the end, he needed a few more years to be eligible for full retirement, and the CHP seemed to hold all the trump cards, so he agreed to participate in the upcoming Retreat, which was scheduled to start in four weeks.

In the commotion of the incident at Danny Lemos' sister's house, Lemos had slipped out the back door and escaped into the forest surrounding the residence. Again, he went into hiding and was still on the loose a week later.

During that week, Ryan was questioned by Mendocino Detectives about the case. They were particularly interested in how he found out the identity of Danny Lemos and other pertinent facts about the gang's activities. He steadfastly held back any mention of his illicit encounter with Jo-Q and the information he derived from that incident. In time, he was able to convince them that he had received an untraceable, anonymous tip which revealed Danny Lemos' identity, and he decided to act on it himself, rather than refer the information to the Detectives.

The detectives were not convinced, so he was excluded from attending any future briefings regarding the investigation, and discouraged from further contact with the Detectives working the case.

Detective Atkins was assigned to be liaison with him, offering occasional non-confidential updates, as needed. But Ryan knew there would be no further information given to him, and, besides, other things had to be taken care of first.

CHAPTER 9

And so, several weeks later, on a blistering hot California day in late July, Ryan found himself boarding a plane en route to a resort near Ft. Collins, Colorado, to attend Dr. Stan's Forgiveness Retreat.

"Colorado in July. At least you can't beat the location," he thought to himself as he settled back for the flight. *"Besides,"* he convinced himself as he pondered the upcoming schedule, *"I can use the free time to devise a foolproof plan to commit a perfect crime."*

The Forgiveness Retreat consisted of seven one-week-long sessions, each separated by a week off to work with what they learned at the previous session, then another week-long session, and so on for seven sessions. Each session consisted of sharing feelings and emotions, lectures and one-on-one counseling by Dr. Stan, and outside speakers who shared their success stories of working through their grief, depression, and hatred.

Ryan checked into the retreat and was shown to his room. He skipped the social reception the night before, staying in his room with the lights off and the TV on, but the sound muted. The following morning, for the first meeting, he dragged himself into the meeting room at the last minute, just to show his contempt for being forced to attend.

There were only two empty chairs in the room, which consisted of twelve chairs organized in a perfect circle, three feet apart. All of the chairs were black, except one larger and slightly more grandiose white one, next to the last vacant black chair. For just a moment he thought about taking the white chair, and he moved toward it. He could see a man he assumed to be Dr. Stan's retreat facilitator, standing at semi-attention near the door from which presumably Dr. Stan himself would appear. Ryan stepped toward the white chair, at which time the facilitator apparently read his mind, and quickly started walking toward him to intercept him. At the last minute, Ryan made a move to his left and sat in the black chair, causing the host to make a quick, conspicuous U-turn and go back to his post. As Ryan sat down, he caught a familiar looking face next to him smirk in appreciation of his bluff. Everyone else in the room was also trying to get a read on the new guy who had skipped the reception.

The facilitator, back at his post, surveyed the room and the full chairs, and reached over and pushed a button on the wall, apparently announcing to Dr. Stan that all were in their respective seats.

"Show Time!" thought Ryan.

Moments later, Dr. Stan made a grand entrance into the room to applause and even a standing ovation from some of the group. Ryan concluded that he and the familiar-looking stranger were apparently the only ones not star struck at meeting Dr. Stan for the first time in person.

"Thank God at least someone else is not awestruck by his Excellency. I can't place my finger on where, but I've seen or met that guy before somewhere."

"Welcome, ladies and gentlemen, and congratulations on making the best decision you will ever make in your life," started Dr. Stan.

"No arrogance there."

"You are all here for the same thing, to work through your intense, incredible, and unending grief and to welcome the 'healing feeling' that comes from finding forgiveness in your heart. Let that be our first thought as we start this journey together. Everybody say it with me, what are we here for? --- That 'healing feeling'."

"Oh, my God, it's going to be worse than I thought. I'm going to have to listen to this clown and his touchy-feely crap lectures for weeks on end. I couldn't stand him on TV, and now I'm stuck with him in person for freaking ever."

He must have been telegraphing his mood, because, once again, he heard a suppressed snicker and the familiar stranger was smiling in his direction. When Ryan glanced over, the man looked down pathetically.

"Who does he think he is, judging me? What does he know about me? He doesn't know my grief. He never met my daughter, Marcy, so how could he know anything about what I feel."

He looked around the room at the other attendees. Most of them looked pretty normal, except they all looked sad and lost, something he convinced himself he didn't look like. *"I've got nothing in common with these other losers. Forgiveness Retreat my ass. I'm going to kill the bastard who killed my daughter. Plain and simple. Forgiveness is for weaklings."*

His conscious thoughts came back to him in time to hear Dr. Stan continue in mid-sentence, "… go around the room and tell each other what tragic event happened that brought you to this incredibly low point in your life. In that way, each of us might come to realize there are others in the same boat, maybe some even worse than you. Elizabeth, why don't you start."

The room focused on a very pretty middle-aged woman seated across the room from Ryan. He guessed her age to be fortyish, but she could still be a model. Her makeup was impeccable, she was physically fit, she obviously worked out regularly, and her clothes, especially her handbags and shoes, were obviously from some very expensive women's shops, probably Louis Vuitton, Gucci, or 5th Avenue in New York, he guessed.

Surprised at being singled out to start, she said, "Oh, my. I didn't expect to go first."

"It's OK, Elizabeth. Someone has to, and I am guessing you are used to talking to clients, am I right?"

"Of course he's right. He knows everyone and everyone's story. He has to have been briefed on everyone before they got here. Probably thinks he has me all figured out. Fuck him."

"My name is Elizabeth. Elizabeth Hartman. I had a perfect life until September 5, 2011. Pausing for composure, she continued, "I was married to a wonderful man, we both had high level jobs, serving the shakers and movers of New York City. We were making lots of money, which I'd gladly give up to have my husband back."

She started to weep and dab at the corners of her eyes, as her eyeliner began to run from the edge of her eyes. "It seemed like a normal day, I had gotten home in time to prepare a home cooked meal for my husband, Travis Hartman. He had an afternoon meeting and was going to be late as he always was on Wednesday nights. About the time I was expecting him home, I heard sirens converging to a few blocks from the house, the route I knew Travis would be taking about that time. I knew it. I just knew it – right then - something terrible had happened to Travis. A little later and still no Travis, so I went down to the street and walked toward the alley two blocks away, and I saw him behind the crime scene tape."

Sobbing loudly now, she struggled to get the story out, "He had been shot and stabbed by a group of street thugs for his briefcase, his wallet, a gold chain, his ring, and watch. They killed my husband for cash and trinkets! The police said he'd already given them the money and jewelry, and they still killed him. I've tried counseling, religion, everything, but I just can't get over that they killed him and they didn't have to. My life will never be the same, all for some punks' idea of a thrill."

While the rest of the room was silent, the cop in Ryan took over and he couldn't help but ask for more information, "How many were there?"

"According to the cops, er ... police, witnesses said there were four of them."

"Did they identify them? Are they in jail?"

"No. And no. Police say there were a number of witnesses, but as soon as they were contacted, no one could remember seeing anything that would identify the killers. Police said they are known in the neighborhood, but everyone is afraid of them. I even hired a private investigator, but all he could learn was one of them, the leader, was called 'SoMel' and another was called 'B-Cat'."

Dr. Stan stopped the questions. "Those are great questions, Mr. Foster. It must be the cop in you coming out. But let's continue with everyone's stories right now. We'll talk about each case in greater detail later, but right now let's hear everyone's story."

"Mr. Foster? He's got us all pegged by name already. I wonder where he plans to go with Marcy's murder? I'm not comfortable with him talking about something I can't even talk about right now."

"I'm sure the media hardly touched upon Elizabeth's husband's murder. Right, Elizabeth?" Dr. Stan continued.

"That's right. It didn't get a mention, and that's what might have hurt the most. My life is changed forever, the greatest man in the world is dead, and no-one noticed or cared."

"Totally understandable, Elizabeth. But it can go the other way also."

Looking to the side, in Ryan's direction, he continued, "We have another attendee who endured a different kind of hell."

"Don't even go there you Bastard," thought Ryan. *"No way am I going next."*

But Dr. Stan's attention was focused on the familiar-looking man to his side. "What if every aspect of the murder investigation was front page tabloid material every day, every week, unending, and you were reminded of your son's senseless death every time you passed a newsstand? And what if your son's death is almost overlooked by the media, while the murderer is treated like a celebrity and his trial was billed as the 'Trial of the Century' on national television, dragging on for months. And, let's make it even more bizarre; what if, somehow, the high-profile celebrity murderer got off because the jury was too star struck to see the facts of the case? What does a grieving parent do then? Peter, please tell your fellow attendees your story."

Before he could continue, a light went off in Ryan's head. *"Of course. That's it."* The familiar stranger sitting next to him was Peter Levenson, whose son, Sean was killed by Terrell Rexford, the superstar athlete known as 'T-Rex', who got away with it by hiring a team of high dollar attorneys who successfully handpicked an ignorant jury, who were in awe of T-Rex's charisma, and who apparently couldn't grasp the concept of DNA evidence. T-Rex was found innocent, and continued to play pro football until he was cut after last season. He retired to Florida and now he plays golf every day, protected by his personal entourage of body guards.

Peter Levenson reluctantly proceeded to tell the group about the incident, even though anyone in the room who wasn't familiar with every detail would have to have been in a six-year coma. He ended the story by telling the group that even after he prevailed in a six-year civil suit, and he now owned everything that once meant something to T-Rex, including his Heisman Trophy, it did not bring the satisfaction he hoped, because T-Rex seemed unfazed by the loss, and he still had to watch T-Rex play football every weekend for six years, and now his every move in Florida is reported in the tabloids every week. He said he was attending this Forgiveness Retreat as a last attempt to try to heal the loss of his beloved son and to get past the injustice toward his killer.

Following Levenson was an hours-long parade of painful and heartbreaking losses, each as gut-wrenching as the one before. The common theme, in most cases, was unfulfilled justice. Ryan knew all too well that it was the latter that tears at your guts as much or more than the crime itself.

The stories ranged from Peter Levenson's epic drama played out in the headlines, and resulting in the most insulting verdict imaginable, to another young wife of a drunk driver. They had quarreled over some stupid thing, and she sent him away intoxicated and angry just before the accident in which he was killed.

Still another woman couldn't stand that a local politician in her small community got a sentence of probation and community service resulting from a drunk driving accident in which her husband was killed.

Luckily for Ryan, every time it appeared to be his turn to share, the class took a break. By Ryan's account, everyone had given their story except him, when Dr. Stan suggested the class take its last break. Afterward, just when Ryan thought he might have been forgotten, Dr. Stan called on him to give his story.

Ryan was able to quickly go through the story of the murder and the loss of evidence from the fire at DOJ, while revealing very few of the most hurtful details of the crime. He also left out the part about how he was prevented from exacting his own revenge against the murderer of his daughter.

Dr. Stan was unfazed by the omission. "You seem to have left out a very important detail which is extremely important in the forgiveness process."

"Really?" said Ryan, hoping Dr. Stan didn't know as much as he feared he did.

"Yes, Ryan. One of the phases of the healing process is dealing with anger, often extreme anger. Why don't you share with the others the level of extreme anger you felt, and how you addressed it? I think it would be a great lesson for everyone else to hear; to know they aren't alone in their thoughts of revenge."

"So that's why you called on me last. You obviously know all about my attempt to kill Choco, and you are going

to use it to embarrass me, just to get a point across to the group." He stared at Dr. Stan.

"Ryan?" he asked.

"Oh, yeah," he said as matter-of-factly as possible. "I tried to kill him, but I was 'pre…ven…ted'." He dragged out each syllable of the last word for effect, which surprised Dr. Stan.

"Yes, anger can drive a person to do things they would ordinarily never do." Dr. Stan went on to a long dissertation about anger and how it must be addressed head-on before any level of recovery can occur.

Ryan nodded in agreement, but in his mind, he thought, *"I agree, doctor, that's why I want to get through this BS; so me and my anger can go meet Choco head-on."*

CHAPTER 10

According to Dr. Stan, a significant aspect of the Forgiveness Retreat was the encouraged interaction between the attendees during the off hours. That is why attendees were discouraged from leaving the campus, and cell phones were collected at the door. Attendees, by design, were cut off from the outside world, news headlines, and most importantly, any problems or distractions they left at home.

It was hoped that this sequestration and positive interaction would free the attendees from personal problems and create mutual bonds and emotional connections that would extend beyond the week, and offer a number of options for support when each person needed it back at home.

The evenings were particularly lonesome and gave plenty of time for reflection. It didn't take long for Ryan to find his favorite place on campus to just sit and think. It was a small clearing along the trail around the edge of the mountaintop campus, with an unobstructed view of the lush valley below, and a bench that seemed to invite him to sit down and think in solitude about how he would kill Danny Lemos someday when he got the chance.

He was doing just that, on the third night when Peter Levenson came down the path and paused. "Mind if I join you for a few minutes?"

"No. Please. I was just sitting here thinking."

"About how to learn to cope with your anger?"

"No, Peter. I think I'm too far gone for that. Actually, I admire people who have learned to cope with their grief, and some can even forgive, but, no, I was thinking how nice it will feel to squeeze the life out of the dirtbag who killed my daughter." He emphasized the point by simulating choking him to death with his hands. "I've just got to figure out how to do it while being closely watched. And of course, I will be the first guy they come to when it happens. I'm trying to figure out the perfect crime, but don't tell Dr. Stan. I need for him to think I'm cured."

Looking up and seeing the surprised look on Levenson's face, he continued, "I'm sorry, Peter. Don't let me distract you from the forgiveness program. I'm sure it's probably a good program, but I'm not a very good candidate for forgiveness. Maybe six more weeks of this bullshit will get to me, but I'm not ready to forgive yet; I'm ready to kill."

"You may have me pegged wrong, Mr. Foster."

"Call me Ryan."

"Okay, Ryan. You may have me wrong. I HAVE to work at this because I've run out of options. I wish it was as easy as driving up to T-Rex's door and killing him. I'd do it and gladly face the consequences, but I can't get anywhere near him. He's too well guarded and I'm also constantly watched by the police and the media. If I got anywhere near him, they'd be on me like stink on you-know-what."

"It's called shit, Peter, 'stink on shit'."

"Yes, I know. But you get my point, right?"

"Yes, I get your point. I've already tried that, but my cop friends got there first, and that's why I'm here instead of jail. I'll bide my time, then find a way to kill him without implicating myself."

"You're lucky. He's probably not guarded 24/7. You know, I've never told anyone this, but I even tried to hire a guy to kill T-Rex, but when he found out who I wanted killed, he became more interested in blackmailing me than taking that job. I out-bluffed him because he was too stupid to tape the conversation and he was on parole with warrants out, so he just went away. But it scared me to death. I never tried that again."

Ryan's thoughts were far away by the time Levenson finished his story. "You don't seem like the kind of person who could kill someone point blank."

"If it was T-Rex, you bet I could. But probably not someone else I didn't hate. I just want to kill T-Rex."

"What did you say you did back in Hollywood?"

"I am the head of the Makeup and Styling Department for American Independent Studios. I also supervise the unit which creates props for the movies we produce. We almost won an Academy Award two years ago. Now everything is monsters and werewolves, and I just never got into that. But I oversee a staff that is into it."

"You know, Peter, I just had an idea about my case, but I need to think about it a lot. I hope you'll excuse me, but … how about we meet here tomorrow right after the last class of the day. Okay?"

"Sure, Ryan. See you here."

The men shook hands and went their separate ways toward their respective cottages for the night.

As soon as they were out of sight, the bushes parted nearby, and out stepped Elizabeth Hartman. Seeking solitude, she had walked off the trail and was sitting on a rock looking out over the valley within earshot of the bench when they came down the path and sat on it. She maintained her silence because originally, she didn't want to appear to be eavesdropping. As the conversation progressed, she began to listen intently. Once they left, she walked over to the bench they had been sitting on, and sat down where the men had been, *"Damn. Imagine that,"* she thought to herself.

CHAPTER 11

All the next day, Ryan paid little attention to the class lectures. He even seemed to escape the ever-present gaze of Dr. Stan, who tried to keep his attention from wandering. He even tried to trip him up by asking, "So, Ryan, you seem pretty absorbed today in deep thought. What has you so distracted?"

He wanted to say, *"Dr. Stan, I was just thinking that, instead of listening to you, I'd rather be thinking of how I could choke the crap out of the dirtbag who killed my daughter, without getting caught."*

That was what he wanted to say, but instead, he said, "I'm sorry Dr. Stan, I was absorbed in what you have been suggesting, and I was just trying to figure out what it would look like if I embraced your 'healing feeling', and actually forgave Danny Lemos and got on with my life."

"That's great, Ryan. I wasn't sure you were getting it, and I'm very pleased to see that it is coming through and forgiveness is on your table."

After that, Ryan continued contemplating his perplexing problem. Did he really want to get involved with Levenson in a conspiracy to commit murders? The plot could work if it was done right; a reciprocal murder pact. Each of the men could not get away with killing their child's murderer, but they could probably get close enough to kill the other's quarry. While Levenson killed Choco, Ryan would have set up a perfect alibi. And vice versa, when Ryan killed T-Rex.

Levenson was a makeup artist. He could easily get to and kill Choco if they could devise a foolproof plot to get him close enough. But could he trust Levenson to be strong enough to do it, since he didn't have that personal hate-connection with Choco. And then could he be trusted enough to NOT cave in later, to his conscience, or during questioning, if it got to that? Could he live with himself if Peter was killed in the attempt?

And what about himself? He was a twenty-five-year cop, dedicated to preventing crimes, not committing them. He knew he was fully prepared to kill a person in self-defense as part of the job, but could he actually kill a man in cold blood, even a man as despicable as T-Rex, since he wasn't involved personally? Lemos would be easy for Peter to get to, but T-Rex would be much harder. Could he transfer his hatred to T-Rex in exchange for Danny Lemos' death? And would that even be good enough; to not see Lemos' eyes, or hear his pleas for mercy?

Yet another complication was this. If he, himself, killed Lemos outright, perhaps a sympathetic jury might understand his grief and find 'temporary insanity' and he'd be free on that technicality. But if he got caught killing T-Rex, that wouldn't be a possibility.

The risks of the unknowns were too great. By the end of the day, he had decided not to approach Levenson about a possible reciprocal murder plan. There were far too many variables dealing with Levenson's unknown or weak personality, as he saw it.

As the last hour was coming to a close, no-one noticed that Elizabeth Hartman excused herself from the group and headed for the ladies' room just outside the door. And, of course, they couldn't have seen that she walked right past the ladies' room and scurried down the path toward Ryan and Levenson's meeting point.

Peter Levenson was already sitting on the bench when Ryan, who paused at the men's room, arrived. They exchanged pleasantries and Levenson jumped right into the conversation. "You had a thought about your case yesterday afternoon when we left. Any progress on that thought."

Ryan wasn't prepared to unveil his plan quite yet. He wanted to give it more thought, so he decided to play it down. "It wasn't important after all. It was nothing."

"I'm going to be blunt, Ryan. You asked about my work. I think I know what you are thinking. The answer is yes; I could kill someone I didn't have a personal hatred for. Say for example, if he was a rapist murderer of a beautiful young daughter of a friend who couldn't kill him himself. Like the asshole who killed your daughter, for example. It would allow you to set up a foolproof alibi. Then, if, someday, someone familiar with guns, like a cop for instance, took out T-Rex with a sniper rifle on the seventh green of Castle Dunes Golf Resort, where he plays every Tuesday and Thursday, I could be in Hollywood on the set of a movie with a hundred witnesses."

"You were quicker on that than I thought. Are you sure you could kill someone in cold blood? It is a hard thing to do even if you have trained to do it for twenty-five years."

"How about you, Ryan. You ever killed a man in cold blood?"

"No, but I …"

"Then how do I know I can trust you not to freeze up and not do it?"

"Point well taken, Peter, but I'm still not convinced. It isn't as easy as just shooting him and getting on with your life. You've got your conscience to contend with, and if T-Rex gets shot, they'll still come straight to you first. How are you going to stand up to intensive grilling by professional investigators?"

"Remember the alibi? I was three thousand miles away." I've been around some of the best actors of our lifetime; do you think I haven't picked up a thing or two?" To try to lighten things up a bit, he continued, "Obviously, you've never seen my two-minute walk-on in 'Serpents from the Black Sea' in 1989."

"Okay, Peter, let's leave it at that for now. We can't be seen too much together, or Dr. Stan might get suspicious. Let's think on this tonight, tomorrow we go home after the session, and we can give the matter great thought over the next week and confirm or dissolve the idea when we come back next time. I want you to think about it and all the possible ramifications, and if you really want to risk life in prison for revenge. Either of us can just say we aren't interested and it dies on the vine, okay?"

"Okay, but let me leave you with this. He killed my son, my best friend. I've spent six years trying to hurt him back. I went after him in civil court, and now I own everything he used to have, but it hasn't stopped the pain for even one day. I'd have killed him myself, and turned myself in, if I could have gotten close to him. Just the thought of it … this is the first time I've smiled inside for years. I'm all in, and I hope you'll team up with me to commit two perfect crimes.

"Tomorrow at the ten o'clock break, just say, 'I slept well last night', and I'll know we're still good until the next session. Now, here is the deal from now on. No buddy-buddy at the Retreat. We need all the other participants to remember later that we barely talked to each other. No phone calls either way, when we are apart, and especially no texting, tweets, or e-mails to each other. We both have to be careful not to tip anything off to Dr. Stan. From now on we are model campers, fully engaged in the 'healing feeling of forgiveness'. Agreed?"

"Agreed."

Once again, as the night before, the men parted company and walked in separate directions to their respective cabins. And, once again, the nearby bushes parted and Elizabeth Hartman stepped into the clearing. She looked both directions, then set out toward her own cabin, humming to herself.

The following day was the last of the first session. The mood of the group was extremely upbeat in anticipation of going back to their respective homes and lives. The objectives of the first session seemed to have been met and bonds and allegiances were already beginning to develop between willing participants. Dr. Stan was visibly pleased that everyone, including Ryan Foster and Peter Levenson seemed to be really getting it.

As discussed, Ryan and Levenson were cordial in the group, but did not give the impression of closeness beyond classmates. At the ten o'clock coffee break, Levenson walked up to Ryan at the coffee machine and said, "I'm telling you, this forgiveness stuff must really be working, I sure slept well last night."

Before Ryan could respond, from immediately behind them, Elizabeth Hartman walked up and said, "I agree, Peter. I slept well last night, also. How about you, Ryan?"

Ryan looked over at Elizabeth, who smiled and walked away. Ryan and Peter looked at each other with a perplexed look.

"You don't think ...?" Peter whispered.

"Nah." But as he said it, he looked and watched Elizabeth walk away. She seemed to have an air of confidence he hadn't noticed before.

CHAPTER 12

During the next week back at home, it seems everyone he knew called Ryan to inquire how the first week went. Everyone except Gloria, that is, but that was probably going to be addressed in the half-inch thick packet he received during the week postmarked from an attorney's office in Salem, Oregon.

He left the packet on the table, unopened.

To everyone who asked about the retreat, he gushed about how much he enjoyed the camaraderie among other attendees, and how Dr. Stan was so effective at getting everyone pointed in the right direction.

Through Detective Atkins, he was brought up to date on the progress, or lack thereof, of the investigation. Danny Lemos had returned to the area, scratches healed and their attempts to question him were intercepted by his attorney, who refused to allow him to be questioned. He was frequently seen around town, almost arrogant to the police, knowing he was virtually prosecution proof.

There was one good tidbit of information that Ryan learned by listening to Atkins. It seems Danny Lemos got his nickname Choco from the fact he loved chocolate; especially Chocolate Coffee Mochas; Starbuck's Coffee Mochas to be exact. In fact, he had a habit of going to a nearby Starbucks almost every day at 11:00AM and ordering a Vente Coffee Double Mocha.

"Unusual behavior for a gang member, for sure. But everybody is entitled to their little quirks. This quirk just might give me and Levenson the opening we need, and could cost Choco his life."

Ryan spent most of the next week thinking of various ways to kill Choco and get away with it. Choco might be easy, just kill him outside the Starbucks. But he'd have to come up with a foolproof plan to pull it off without arousing suspicion, injuring someone else, or getting caught.

His end of the bargain, killing T-Rex in Florida, might be even riskier. How would he manage to get into position to kill T-Rex, surrounded by his 'posse', on a golf course he'd never seen, in a state he had little knowledge of?

The Saturday night before he was to return to the Forgiveness Retreat, he was relaxing at home watching the prelude to the upcoming NASCAR race at Iowa Speedway, when he began to formulate a bizarre idea. Ryan was a big NASCAR fan, and he knew that T-Rex used to attend every Daytona 500 in February upon his return to Florida after the Super Bowl ended the pro football season. Perhaps in the crowd and excitement of a NASCAR race, he could kill T-Rex with a silencer equipped gun, and get lost in the crowd during the confusion that followed. He'd have to give that one a lot of thought, though, before doing it in a large crowd surrounded by T-Rex's bodyguards.

CHAPTER 13

The twelve attendees arrived Sunday night for the beginning of the second session the following morning. At the evening mixer, they all renewed acquaintances and there was a buzz of shared progress evident in the room.

Other than the normal, expected pleasantries, Ryan and Levenson didn't show any unusual interest in each other. Ryan retired early and went to his room to look over the handouts for the second week of classes, and to plot murders.

The next morning, Doctor Stan began the session with a rousing pep talk, mentioning that some of the attendees had already made lasting friendships, which have already paid early dividends during the week-long break as some attendees reported mutual calls of support among those who needed it most.

Ryan paid little attention during the day, in anticipation of the meeting that night to see if Levenson was still in for the collaboration of murder plans.

Eventually they broke for the day and ate dinner at the cafeteria, then retired to their rooms. Just before dusk,

Ryan started down the path toward the clearing and the meeting with Levenson after dark.

When he arrived at the meeting point, Levenson was again already there. Ryan sat down beside him.

"How was last week, Peter?"

"Long, … agonizing. I can't stop thinking about our deal. I'm still all in. You?"

"Yes, but we need to talk about it."

Their attention was diverted to their right, by the approach of another member of the group out for an evening stroll. They sat in silence as Elizabeth Hartman approached, but instead of passing by, she walked up and sat down on the bench next to Ryan.

"Good evening, Elizabeth," Ryan said, "Out for an evening stroll?"

"Not exactly. I'm not the type to beat around the bush, gentlemen. You guys don't know it, but I was sitting on the rocks overlooking the valley, just past that bush over there, when you had your meetings last session. I know all about what you are planning."

Ryan was clearly caught off guard by Elizabeth's bluntness. "What do you mean?" he said, but his attempt to feign ignorance was amateurish at best.

"The conspiracy to commit reciprocal murders," she said in a low voice, "But don't worry. I don't want to stop you; I want in."

"In?"

"You heard me. I want in. I want justice for Travis, just like you two want justice for Marcy and Sean. Let me say it again, I want IN."

Levenson sat there dumbfounded that the plot was so easily compromised.

"Absolutely not!" Ryan said, "It's not quite that easy, Elizabeth. I don't know what you think you heard, but you've got it all wrong. There's nothing illegal going on here."

"Don't be stupid, Ryan, and don't make me play my trump card – telling Dr. Stan what I overheard. Hear me out. I've been thinking about it all week and I am 100% committed to your plan. In fact, you need me to make it work."

"We need you?"

"Yes." With that, she reached into her purse and pulled out a thick envelope and dropped it on Ryan's lap. "Go ahead, open it."

Ryan and Levenson looked at each other and Ryan opened the envelope stuffed with twenties, fifties, and one hundred dollar bills. "Where did this come from? There's got to be five thousand dollars in there."

"Ten," she said casually, "Unmarked, untraceable, and out of circulation for four years."

Levenson whispered to Ryan, "I think she's serious. What do we do?"

Ryan said, "Elizabeth, even if what you thought to be true was true, you couldn't just buy your way in. It's much more complex than that."

"You're an idiot, Ryan. How'd you get so high up in the CHP? I'm not buying your favor. And I'm not hiring a hit man. I'll do my part, too. Here's what you are missing. It is going to cost thousands of dollars for travel, lodging, and meals while you scout out your plans. Or were you just going to show up, use your credit card and shoot people."

"Of course we weren't." Ryan said defensively.

"Well, here is the money to pull it off. And there's more if it is needed."

"Where'd you get this kind of cash?"

"In addition to his day job as a stock broker, Travis was a hell-of-a poker player, in demand for some of the biggest games in the city. This is some of his winnings."

"How do you know they aren't traceable."

"I know the poker players, some of the richest, most secretive men in New York. They don't want publicity either. It's all clean. Now listen to me, to pull this off, you'll need a score of untraceable cell phones. None get used twice. You'll need good quality fake ID's, that's got to cost a fortune for good ones; they'll have to get by TSA and maybe Customs. You'll need costumes, disguises, and untraceable handguns and rifles. Are you getting the picture? And another thing. You need a woman to be able to do the things only a woman can do, like get a man to stop thinking with his brain and start thinking between his legs."

"How do we know you aren't a plant?" Levenson asked.

"Simple. I'll do the first murder. I've already thought about it. We'll do Marcy's killer first. He should be easy, as long as he stays out of jail and available."

Levenson said, "Ryan, you know she's right. We need lots of money to pull it off, and a woman might make it easier in some cases."

"Hey. This isn't some kind of college prank we're talking about. We are talking cold blooded murder; maybe as many as five or six murders, in fact. It's almost impossible to pull off a 'perfect crime', and we are talking about six perfect crimes. And, when you get down to it, what we are doing is really no better than what was done to our loved ones. Walking up to someone you don't know and killing them. Even with the best alibis, we are talking about intense questioning by people who are pros at breaking people down. We're talking about another Trial of the Century when T-Rex is murdered. The racial angle alone is unfathomable. Three white people conspire to kill a black athlete, a Hispanic in California, and several mixed-race youths in New York who will be portrayed as choir boys when they are dead. I'm only in this because a month ago I was willing to throw it all away to kill that bastard. I'm not convinced you two are willing to risk everything you have … or ever will have … to taste the sweetness of revenge. And even if you are, I'm not sure I'm willing to bet it all on your ability to tough it out and stick together. One folds, and we all go to prison for life."

Elizabeth looked directly at Peter, and he looked at her in return. No-one said a word for maybe five seconds, so Ryan continued, "This is serious shit we are talking about. The commitment has to be TOTAL, irrevocable, and unshakable."

When he finished, Elizabeth looked at him with hard, calculating eyes, and said, "Are you done talking, Ryan?"

"Yeah, I guess."

Okay, I'm IN! Let's get started."

Peter was looking down at the ground with great consternation on his brow. Ryan mistook the look for hesitation, and started to say, "Look, Peter …," but he was interrupted by Peter's hand held up in front of his tear stained face. Before anything could be said, Peter said, "Hold on Ryan. I know you think I'm the weak link, but I'm all in. I've dreamed of this for six years. I always thought the heat would die down and I'd just walk up to him on the golf course and shoot him and take the consequences. It never did. I certainly never thought I'd have the chance to see him die under conditions that I might not get caught. You've given me hope for the first time that I might actually see justice for Sean, and live to smell the sweetness of it. I'm absolutely in, and

I'll promise you this. If it turns to shit along the way, I'll never give you two up. Ever."

"Same here," said Elizabeth.

"Okay. We're all together on that," said Ryan. But I still need to think about it. Let's meet tomorrow night at the same time, in my room. Anyone wants out, that's okay with me. But we've got to be together or not as of tomorrow night. Get some sleep on it tonight. Oh, and don't let anyone see you come into my room. That is important. Everyone okay with this?"

"Yes," Levenson said.

"Of course," Elizabeth said.

CHAPTER 14

Elizabeth Hartman was the first to slip into the room the following night after dark. "Been a long time since I slipped into a man's room after dark," she said.

Two taps on the sliding door, and Levenson eased through the door. "Is this a private party?" he joked.

"Okay, we might as well start with the rules," Ryan began as he motioned the others to sit around a small table. With only two chairs in the room, Elizabeth sat on the end of the bed.

He took several sheets of toilet paper out of his shirt pocket and spread them out on the table. Each had copious notes scribbled in ink.

"Seriously, Ryan? Toilet paper?" Elizabeth asked, "You should have said something, I have some resort note paper in my room I could have brought."

"Let's start with that. From this point on we have to think like the military Black Ops teams you've seen in the movies. Rule 1 – No paper trail. Nothing gets written down except on toilet paper for immediate notes, then it is destroyed. Do you know how to destroy notes written on TP, Peter?"

"I get it, Commando Major."

"Okay, let's get serious. If we get caught, it probably won't be while we are committing the crime, it'll be some stupid detail we forgot, like throwing away a piece of paper, or leaving a print behind. We are trying to commit the rarest of crimes, a perfect crime, but we have to do it three or more times for this to work."

"Rule 1 – Repeat. No paper trail. Rule 2 – We have no reason to overly-fraternize. We will be friendly in the group during the Retreat, but must be clandestine in our meetings. When we are not here at the retreat, no meetings, contacts or phone calls. No visits to each other's areas. Remember, EVERYTHING is traceable nowadays, travel, rental cars, private phones can be subpoenaed to show all numbers called, cell phones are traceable both directions to the nearest tower, pinpointing your location at any time. Security cameras are everywhere, and their footage is available for law enforcement. We have to be very careful about fraternizing. When these dirtbags start dying, and they find that we have an alibi, they are going to look at who we hung out with. I don't even want Dr. Stan to notice we might be overly friendly."

"Sounds clear," Elizabeth said, glancing at Peter, who was nodding his head.

"Okay, Rule 3 -- After the murders are accomplished, each of us will go our separate ways and never contact each other again."

"Really? Never," said Peter.

"Yes. None of this ever happened, so there is no reason to get together to discuss the 'good old days'. Unless Dr. Stan has a reunion."

"I guess it makes sense. But even 'Black Ops' teams get together once in a while," Peter said.

"Black Ops aren't illegal murder co-conspirators. I like you both, but it's never or nothing. If we are friends, we might end up enemies, and I don't want to cross anyone's path down the road for any reason."

"Okay," said Peter.

"Okay, it makes sense that way." echoed Elizabeth.

"Rule 4 -- No innocent persons are endangered. Each plan must be calculated so that only the target is hit, and no innocent bystanders, family, witnesses, etc., are jeopardized. Clear?"

"Absolutely," they both chimed in together.

Reading from his toilet paper notes, Ryan continued, "Rule 5 --Each person must be a full participant so no-one can burn the others later."

"Rule 6 – Each of us must come up with an ironclad alibi for both the crimes they do and don't commit. Alibis must be foolproof. There has to be an alibi paper trail and other reputable, uninvolved people must be available to substantiate the alibi without knowing about the crime. Ironclad and unalterable, like on a cruise, or a vacation out of the country."

"Rule 7 -- Money, travel, trips, locations, hotels, meals, cars, weapons, and phones must be untraceable. We must be especially careful to use our own credit cards for the alibis, but the 'Cash Pool' money for the actual crime expenses."

"You just said there is no such thing as untraceable," Peter said.

"You are right. Cell phone calls, and even when you are not calling, for example, cell phones are traceable, but we will buy disposable phones that are not traceable to us. I'll work on those details and get back to you."

"Elizabeth, you are the money person. You will be in charge of the 'Cash Pool' money. Each of us will start with a couple thousand dollars for untraceable incidentals. It's going to take more than the $10,000 to be foolproof. How much do you have to put in?"

"I've got $100,000 in cash at the house. Like I said, Travis was probably the best poker player you never heard of. It is all available, if needed."

"Okay, but remember, the money is where we could get screwed up. We have to use cash for anything related to the crimes, and we have to use our own credit cards for expenses we want them to know about, like alibis. And, under no circumstances do you mingle the cash with your own accounts. Got it."

"Yes," said Peter.

"Yes," said Elizabeth.

"Peter, you will be our disguise expert. We'll need good ..., no, make that foolproof, disguises. I assume you can get your hands on all that without leaving a paper trail at the studio?"

"Piece of Cake."

"Okay, if we are all clear, I have some paperwork to flush."

For the rest of the week, the trio met clandestinely in Ryan's cabin, which was the most remote on the campus, and could be entered and exited with the least likelihood of being seen. They worked in subdued light with curtains drawn so the room appeared dark from the outside. They limited their planning sessions to two hours each night so they could be in their own rooms by 10:00PM. By the end of the week, the trio had developed a rough game-plan for the murder plots.

It was agreed that Danny Lemos would be the first. He would be the easiest, and would be the best test of Elizabeth and Peter's commitment and 'stomach' for the job.

Each conspirator was given assignments to have ready for the next meeting, nine days from Friday.

CHAPTER 15

During the week following the Forgiveness Retreat session, Ryan checked in with CHP Chief Marsden, a condition of his psychological retraining program, and he checked in with Detective Atkins on the progress of the Lemos investigation.

As for the latter, an arrest warrant had been issued for Danny Lemos, charging him with felony vandalism with regards to the tagging in Fort Bragg. They found him a few days later at a local Starbucks and hooked him up. The arrest allowed them to search his house and car for anything that would support that arrest, and hopefully they would find something, anything, that would link him to the Marcy Ryan murder. To everyone's dismay, nothing was found to help establish that connection.

Lemos pled guilty to the vandalism charge, and was sentenced to 120 hours of community service cleaning up gang graffiti in Fort Bragg. The Marcy Foster murder case remained cold.

The following day, Tuesday, using cash pool monies, Ryan got up early and drove two hours north to Eureka, a mid-sized town on California's far north coast. Using the name Harry Smith, he checked into the Surf View Motel, where they don't get excited about names, and cash is an acceptable form of payment. He drove south on Highway 101 to the Seafood Grotto, where he had a bowl of clam chowder and fresh seafood jambalaya.

After dinner, he stopped at Wal-Mart, south of town, bought three cheap computers with unmatched carrying cases, and a half-dozen untraceable no-contract 'throw down' cellphones with cash pool funds supplied by Elizabeth. He then went back to the motel and settled into his room for the evening.

Ryan used the hotel's Wi-Fi internet access, which couldn't be traced to him, to go online on each computer and logged onto Twitter.com.

Using aliases he made up for that purpose, he opened a bogus Twitter account for each member of the team. Using the alias Sally Jones, Elizabeth became '@SeahawkSally'; Peter, as Bridget Brown, became '@SassyInSeattle2'. Ryan used the name Harry Smith to sign himself up as '@Smitty41414'. A fourth account, '@Sequimsquatter' was set up to be used for emergency messages, if needed.

The aliases, names, and numbers selected held no significance to the conspirators, but, if somehow they came to the attention of the authorities, they had the potential to keep police busy for months trying to identify them from the tantalizing name clues.

All four accounts were then linked as followers of each other, and Ryan then signed them all up as followers of the television soap-opera "General Hospital", and the Seattle Seahawks Football Team.

He then posted generic 'Tweets' from each of the computers and accounts to the General Hospital page, jumping into conversations as a test, discussing whether one or more characters in the drama had done one another wrong during recent episodes.

CHAPTER 16

During the third week of the Forgiveness Retreat, the conspirators were ideal students the first two days, and then they met, as agreed, in Ryan's room on the second night.

Ryan opened his suitcase and retrieved the three computers he had purchased the week before. "Here are your new identities and the only acceptable methods of contact away from the retreat from now on. From this point on, our mantra is simple; 'Admit nothing, deny everything, and demand proof'. And above all, never, EVER, give up the others. Agreed?"

"Yes," they said in unison.

"Okay, let's get started." He handed Elizabeth and Ryan each a computer and carrying case, which also contained two untraceable cell phones. "If you believe, for any reason, that your identity might be compromised or if you misplace or lose any of these, destroy what you can and move on."

"I feel like a secret agent," said Peter.

Steve Davis

"You are," said Ryan. "Remember this. We haven't broken any laws until we put the plan in motion. Until then, we just bought new computers to play on the internet anonymously, like 50 million other people do every day."

"Smart," said Peter.

"Right now, while we're still talking about it, is when mistakes are made that will undo us later. This is also the time to have cold feet and decide this is real, you can go to jail for life. So, if you have any second thoughts, this is the time to tell us."

"We've already covered this. Let's move on," said Elizabeth. As she opened the laptop she had been given, several sheets of scribbled toilet paper fell out into her lap. "Really, Ryan, toilet paper again?"

Peter opened his laptop with the same result. "Wow. Self-destructing instructions. I really do feel like a secret agent. Your mission, should you choose to accept ..."

"Our mission ... is to not get caught, not leave any incriminating evidence behind, and live happily ever after. For that reason, we have to think like secret agents and leave no trail to be followed."

Peter glanced at the top sheet of toilet paper. "Who is Bridget Brown?"

"I'll get to that in a minute. After you've memorized the notes in front of you, well, you know what to do with toilet paper."

Elizabeth rolled her eyes as she glanced at Peter.

"Okay, here's how it works. The Twitter accounts will be used, as needed, to leave vague messages among ourselves. To an observer, the messages will be lost among the hundreds of thousands of Seattle Seahawks fans, and the legions of 'General Hospital' followers. You probably know that General Hospital fans are known for their fanatical ravings and involvement in the soap-opera storyline. Log onto that site, and you can say almost anything and won't raise eyebrows."

"Now, let's go over your identities," Ryan continued. "Elizabeth, you're Twitter name is Seahawk Sally, '@Seahawk Sally'. You love the Seattle Seahawks and you are a big fan of Alexis Davis on the soap opera 'General Hospital'."

"I'm a Giant's fan. I hate the Seahawks and I hate soap operas."

"Not anymore," said Ryan. "Besides, you are therefore the last person anyone would suspect of being Seahawk Sally. Get it?"

"Please don't make me a '49ers fan," said Peter.

"Nope. We all love the Seahawks. It's part of the ruse. Speaking of 'the ruse', Peter, you'll be Bridget Brown, Twitter name '@SassyInSeattle2'. Bridget is a flirty fan of Russell Wilson, and a fan of General Hospital's hunky Mafioso character, Dante Falconeri."

"I'm a flirty girl?"

"You can pull it off, Peter. You're from Hollywood. I'm sure you've seen some of the best."

"You're going to explain all of this to us soon, I hope," said Elizabeth.

"Yes. I will be Harry Smith, '@Smitty41414', a Seattle fan and fan of General Hospital in general. And, perhaps the most important twitter account is '@Sequimsquatter'. Sequim is a town in Washington state in the Seattle area. That account, '@Sequimsquatter', is to be used only for a full-on abort signal. Any message to either the General Hospital or Seahawks pages from '@Sequimsquatter' will show up in your account, and means to abort everything immediately and destroy all evidence."

"Why all the secret agent stuff, Ryan?" asked Elizabeth impatiently.

"Why? Because we need the ability to converse when we are away from the retreat. By leaving a notation on the Seahawks or General Hospital Twitter pages, we can alert each other of possible dangers, completed tasks, send 'abort' or 'call me' messages, and other things we need to know. For example; the comment 'the Seahawks may be in over their heads this year' would mean 'I'm getting cold feet, let's abort the mission'."

"Why those pages?" Peter asked.

"Simple. General Hospital has over 180,000 rabid, sometimes eccentric followers on Twitter. You never know what they are going to say. We may need to prey on that passionate naivety to make pointed remarks. The Seahawks have almost a million followers. In either case, any messages left by us will be lost among the others. I have pre-programmed your laptops with direct links to these Twitter pages, so that any message any of us leaves on either one of those pages will send a copy to all of us."

"Why Seattle?" asked Peter.

"In case the whole plan goes awry, the authorities will devote their initial attention to the Pacific Northwest, away from all of us." Then he chuckled and said, "Maybe they will even blame it on D. B. Cooper."

"The parachuting hijacker," Peter mused. "Pretty smart, Ryan. Remind me to never mess with you."

"Now let's go over the rules for these devices; One, remember, whenever you log into the internet from home or work, you leave a trail the authorities can follow back to your internet provider, and then to you. Therefore, use these laptops only on anonymous Wi-Fi connections, such as fast food and coffee shops, away from your home or work. So, obviously don't use it here this or any other week, not even to test it."

"Two, the same is especially true of the phones. Wherever you go, if it is on, it is bouncing off the closest cell tower. Any call or other use of the phone leaves a permanent record of the closest cell tower. If your location is compromised, wipe the phone clean and drown it into a water source; even a nearby toilet tank will work. Use the 'throw down' phones for urgent or coordinating phone calls. Use the phone marked #1 first. As the name implies, if you use it for anything that implicates the phone to a plot, destroy it and go to your throw down phone #2, and so on. We'll get more as we need them."

CHAPTER 17

As the reality of the task at hand, only two weeks away, began to settle into Elizabeth's consciousness, she tried to avoid thinking about it altogether. But after a long and sleepless weekend, she knew she couldn't run from it any longer. She had to confront the matter head-on.

She cancelled her Monday appointments and walked from her apartment to the alleyway where Travis was murdered. She turned over an abandoned milk crate and sat on it. *"Talk to me, Travis. If I don't do this now, I'll never have another chance to see justice ... ever. It's almost as if Ryan and Peter are the answer to my prayers. I miss you so much I'm willing to risk it all to see those bastards pay for taking you away from me. Yes, I know ... I know... I've got it made and I should concentrate on my successful life and comfortable surroundings, but ...I've tried for two years, and it isn't working."*

She sat motionless for several minutes, as if waiting for a sign or reply from Travis, then got up and walked to the nearby Prospect Heights subway station, continuing the silent conversation, as she boarded the 'A Train' to Central Park, where she and Travis used to go for their occasional Sunday strolls.

Soon she was at the park, where she walked to the same hot dog cart they always frequented on those outings, which now seemed so long ago. She sat on the same nearby bench they always sat on, and ate the hot dog. It tasted terrible to her – just as they always did - but Travis loved them - so she always pretended to enjoy them, as she did this morning.

When she finished, she threw the trash into an adjacent trash receptacle. She then buried her face in her hands and began to cry. As she did, she said softly to herself, *"What have you gotten yourself into, Elizabeth? You're not a murderer. You don't even jaywalk."* A moment later, she changed to the first person to answer herself, *"I know why I'm doing this, for Travis, but how do I prepare myself to actually kill another person, no matter how despicable that person may be?"*

She got up and, as they had done a hundred times together, she began to walk slowly around the park. Lap after lap and hour after hour, she talked to herself in a subdued, but animated, conversation, sobbing at times and consumed with anger at others, all the while attempting to focus that anger on the atrocities of the acts perpetrated on Marcy Foster.

She had no trouble conceptualizing Danny Lemos being executed for his crimes, along with the hoodlums who coldly and deliberately killed Travis, but could she accept herself in the role as their executioner?

In the end, she knew there would be no justice for Travis if there was no justice for Marcy, and justice for Marcy required her to follow through with the plan she demanded to be a part of. As dusk fell over the park, she fatefully accepted her role in the upcoming plan to murder Danny Lemos.

At the same time, in Northern California, Ryan was having no such problem with his conscience. For most of the week, he sat on his deck overlooking Clear Lake, sipped on a glass of 16-year-old Glenfiddich on the rocks, and meticulously planned what he hoped to be the trifecta of perfect crimes, with no more remorse than if he were setting out poison for cockroaches.

Six hundred miles to the south, Peter was working late into the night, every night, ostensibly to make up for lost time on prop designs and make-up plans for the studio's upcoming Sci-Fi horror movie "The Ontario Experiment."

In truth, he was working on a travel bag of disguises to take with him for the Lemos murder plot. He was also using the studio's prop making equipment to create technically accurate false passports and drivers' licenses, for future use, using the aliases and information provided by Ryan.

CHAPTER 18

"One week from today, we are going to put Operation Number One in motion," said Ryan when they assembled in his room the following Monday night at the retreat. "Everyone had a chance for it to sink in? Anyone can stop this today, right now, if you are having second thoughts."

"Nope," said Peter.

"None," said Elizabeth, "I won't deny I had some reservations, but I am 'all in' now."

"Okay, Peter …" He motioned for Peter to take over.

"Here is your costume, Elizabeth." He handed her a paper bag as he winked at Ryan. She emptied the contents into her lap and stared in disbelief at the two huge life-like breasts that were staring back at her. "What is this, your idea of a joke?"

"It was Ryan's idea," Peter said sheepishly.

Elizabeth looked at Ryan. "Ryan?"

"Trust me. It is an integral part of the disguise. If you play this right, when it's all said and done, those are all the witnesses will remember. Now, trust me and go try them on."

She stared at him for a few moments, then looked at the breasts in her lap and smirked. "I guess you haven't steered us wrong yet. Plus, I've always kind of wondered …" Her voice tailed off as she got up and headed for the bathroom.

Elizabeth soon emerged from the room. "It's hard to walk with these things."

"As long as they fit right enough to look convincing, you need to learn to walk like they belonged to you all along," said Peter.

Elizabeth gave them a jiggle and everyone burst into laughter.

"Now here is the tough part. Not the fit, but the attitude. You've got one week to transform your personality to match those puppies. Now you two need to go over the plan together one more time and after Friday night, you are on your own, so you have to have it right. I will be sitting on a tropical isle sipping Margaritas. Good luck."

As they turned to leave, Elizabeth said, "This might be kind of fun. I've never been close to this big before. I'll get to see how the other half lives." As she was closing the sliding door behind them, she said to Peter, "Do I get to keep them for later?"

"Hell, no," she could hear Ryan say from inside the room as the door closed.

The next few days were busy for Peter and Elizabeth as they met clandestinely in Peter's room and went over the details of the impending murder in Santa Rosa, California. By Wednesday morning, Peter, in particular, was very comfortable with the plan. The following morning, as he stood behind Elizabeth at the coffee table, he leaned forward and whispered in her ear, "Good Morning, Ms. Juggs, sleep well last night?"

Elizabeth turned and looked damningly at him, and Ryan, who overheard the comment, was aghast. "Peter," he whispered sternly, "We need to talk … outside … now." He lightly pulled Peter's elbow, nodding with his head toward the door, and led them outside to a quiet corner.

By this time Peter realized he had screwed up and started to say, "I'm sorry, Ryan, I just …"

He was cut off by Ryan. "Peter, are you out of your fucking mind?" he said in a stern whisper, "That's the exact kind of screw-up that can put us all in prison for life. That comment is called a 'clue' when detectives are looking for a woman with big tits for the murder of Lemos."

"This plan is far from fool-proof," he continued in an even lower whisper, "Don't be the fool who proves that. You need to get your head out of your ass and realize this is murder we're talking about. You have to get your head in the game and you have to do your part perfect. No mistakes allowed in murder. Got it?"

"Yes, of course. I just got carried away with how well the plan was going, and …"

"You can do this, Peter. And Elizabeth and I will do our parts, too. Think like a cold-blooded murderer and you'll do fine. Work on it before Monday. Now let's get back inside. Act like I just told you a dirty joke."

Peter and Ryan laughed, Ryan slapped him on the back and they returned to the conference, which was just restarting.

CHAPTER 19

Santa Rosa, California; Monday Morning

Donna Summer was belting out "Bad Girls", selection number 3 on "Best of Disco", the Starbucks' featured album of the month, in the background when Peter walked in the door of the Santa Rosa Starbucks. *"Bad Girls? Now that is righteous,"* he chuckled to himself.

He was hardly recognizable even to himself, with a bushy mustache neatly trimmed to the edge of his mouth. Dark eyebrows were clearly visible behind the wire frame designer glasses. He was neatly dressed in beige Dockers and a nondescript pastel green polo shirt. Black medium-length hair protruded from a sun-bleached S F Giants ball cap. Although he was shaking like a leaf in a breeze inside, he strode confidently to the counter.

"What can I get you this morning," the young male barista asked.

"I'll have a Vente Coffee Mocha, Double Mocha," he said in a clear low tone; clear enough to be heard, but low enough to not be heard by others around.

"Very good, name on the cup?"

"Danny," he said.

"I'll have it right up for you, Danny," he said as he walked toward the coffee machine.

Just behind him, from the other direction, Elizabeth stepped inside the front door. She looked twenty-five years old, thanks to the makeup job Peter did earlier that morning. A flowing strawberry blond wig hung below her shoulder blades from an oversized sun bonnet, and she wore a tie-dye skirt gathered above the waist. She wore a one-size-too-small thin white 'T' shirt over the fake breasts, which quickly announced, by jiggle and bounce, to anyone who might be interested, that she was not wearing a bra and she was very well endowed.

Another patron seated nearby turned to his companion and whispered, "…like two bobcats in a burlap bag." While the companion laughed and elbowed the man, Elizabeth overheard the comment, and smiled to herself. *"Nice job, Peter."* That was just the type of impression she was looking for.

Directly behind her, Danny Lemos walked in, true to his daily routine. Elizabeth paused, blocking his path to the counter, and bent over as if to read a sale sign adjacent to the waiting line. He looked down at her breasts, obeying the laws of gravity and filling the too-small 'T' to capacity. His eyes locked on her protruding nipples, and he took full measure of the sight. Elizabeth slowly stood up directly in front of him and her eyes caught him looking at her breasts. She giggled, and said, "Oh, Hi. How you doin'?"

"Hello, back, mama. I'm jus' fine, ... and so are you."

"You low-life pig," she thought. But instead, she said, "Oh, thank you." She quickly turned away, with a jiggle and a bounce, and approached the counter. "Small, ... I mean 'Tall', Chi Latte, please."

"Any extra shots?"

"No, thank you."

"Name for the cup?"

"Danielle," she said as she wiggled and jiggled her way to the side to wait for her order. When she got to the waiting area, she glanced quickly at Peter, just as the male barista said to him, "Danny? Your Double Mocha." Peter picked up the cup marked 'Danny' and stepped to the side, putting it on the side counter, out of sight of the other customers. Shielding his body from view, he opened the cup and poured a whitish-yellow substance into the cup, mixed it quickly, and put the lid back on.

While he was doing so, Danny Lemos stepped up to the next barista, a young female, and said, "I'll have the usual, Vente Coffee Mocha, Double Mocha, honey."

The girl said, "Oh sure, I remember you. Double Mocha. I'll have it ready for you right away. Danny, isn't it?"

"You got it, sweetie," he said with a wink.

Lemos stepped over to the wait area where Elizabeth was waiting, while Peter stood nearby, supposedly admiring the artwork on the wall.

Elizabeth turned to Lemos and said, "So, … I heard the girl say your name. You're a Danny, and I'm a Danielle. They're almost the same. Those are nice tattoos on your arms, Danny. You work out, don't you?"

Lemos was pleased that the pretty hippie woman with the big breasts appeared to be coming on to him. "Yeah, sweet thing, we're almost like twins. You're new around here, aren't you?"

"Yes, I'm just here for a couple days. What do you do around here for fun?"

"Before he could answer, the barista said, "Danielle, your Chi Latte is ready."

She said, "Wait just a second." She scooted over and grabbed the drink and went right back to Lemos. "So, Danny, you were about to tell me what you do for fun around here."

"Danny, order up," the barista said as he placed the cup on the counter.

As Lemos turned toward the counter to pick up his drink, Elizabeth glanced at her watch and said "Damn, I forgot my sister is waiting. Say, if you'd like, write your phone number on this paper and I'll call you later today. Maybe we could find something fun to do later."

"Sure," Lemos said. He wasn't about to pass up the opportunity in front of him. He took a moment and wrote his phone number on the paper. At that moment, Peter, who was anticipating the arrival of the order, had moved back to the counter. As soon as the waitress turned away, with his back to Lemos, Peter scooped up the cup and deftly replaced it with the other cup marked 'Danny' and moved quickly away from the counter and out the side door.

Elizabeth said, "I'll talk to you later, Danny." and quickly walked away toward the front door. Peter had already gotten into the rented minivan, and drove to a point near the front door with quick access to the driveway exit. Elizabeth got into the sliding side door of the minivan.

Lemos picked up his Double Mocha, and smiled about his unexpected rendezvous a little later. He headed out the door, smiling to himself, as Peter pulled out of the driveway and headed for the nearby freeway.

Moments later, everyone in Starbucks was startled by a loud scream, followed by a hysterical woman running inside, yelling, "Call 911! There is a man on the ground outside, and he's having convulsions!"

CHAPTER 20

Once out of the driveway, Peter headed for the nearby freeway entrance and drove south. In the back seat, Elizabeth began removing her disguise. As she untangled the wig from her own hair, she paused to lean her head back and consider what had just happened. After a few seconds, she looked up and locked eyes with Peter in the rear-view mirror. They stared at each other briefly, as if for a signal as to how each felt about the deed they had just done.

She sat back in the second seat and cocked her head fully back and took a big breath and released it with a heavy sigh. She smiled, then frowned, as she caught herself. "I don't know what to do first, high-five, or throw up, because for sure I want to do both right now. Part of it was as hot as sex, and part of it is vile and disgusting. And I didn't even see him die, but I think I heard him start convulsing as I closed the car door. I suppose I'll never get that out of my head."

"We just killed a man in cold blood," she continued, "We are murderers, Peter." Her voice went up one or two octaves. "When we were talking about it, planning it, and putting on the makeup, it made a lot of sense, and it seemed like the right thing to do, but it's all pretty conflicting right now."

Peter looked back at her in the mirror and said, "The person we just killed murdered a beautiful seventeen-year-old girl so he could get into a street gang. In my eyes, he was also T-Rex and the same gangbangers that murdered Travis to steal his cash and jewelry. He didn't give a shit about the consequences he left for me, Ryan, you, and Travis' friends and family. If you can't see it that way, we're both in trouble."

"Don't worry about me, Peter. If this is the price to see Travis' killers pay for the crime, don't worry. I actually feel good about it. I'm sure I saved someone else's life down the road by taking Lemos out of the picture."

They continued to drive southbound for about five miles, when Peter pulled off the highway and pulled into the parking lot of a large mall they had scouted out earlier. On the outskirts of the parking area, he parked and turned off the engine. The routine coming and going of mall parking lot traffic would pay no attention to them as they began to remove their makeup for the trip home.

He removed his fake mustache, eyebrows, glasses, and hat, and turned in the seat to put them in a black gym bag they had brought along for that purpose. As he did so, he glanced at Elizabeth, who was removing the tie-dyed T-shirt, exposing the fake breasts beneath them. He turned back to the front, but couldn't resist a glance in the mirror as Elizabeth removed the fake breasts, revealing her own naked bosom.

"Very nice," he thought to himself, as he stared into the mirror like a small boy peeking at his first naked woman.

Elizabeth reached for her bra, but hesitated when she caught Peter staring out of the corner of her eye. She slowed down so that Peter had a chance to watch her for several seconds. She put the bra across her lap and glanced up at Peter in the mirror.

"Oh, Sorry," he said as he realized he had been caught staring. He looked forward out the windshield again. "I, uh, just …"

"You don't have to quit looking, Peter. In fact, I kind of like it."

Peter looked back at her in the mirror.

She placed her right hand across her left breast, then slowly opened her fingers, revealing the nipple between her fingers.

Peter paused in mid breath as she slowly pulled her hand across both breasts. Glancing up at Peter's gaze in the mirror, she said, "It has been a long time since I've had a man look at me that way. I've missed it."

"Beautiful," was all Peter could say.

Elizabeth reached under her left breast and pulled it upward, caressing it, as she ran her right hand down into her underwear until the fingers disappeared under the cloth. As she did so, she let out a long sigh. "Would you like to come back here with me, Peter?"

"You're Goddamn right."

"Then get back here."

Peter scrambled over the console and sat on the rear seat to her right. She turned to the left and leaned back against him and took his right hand and placed it under her breasts and pulled them upward across the nipples, as if to show him what she wanted him to do. Then she took his hand and shoved it down into her underwear as she put her head back against his neck and let out a long, low moan.

Peter required no further coaxing, pulling her back onto the seat, kissing her neck and caressing her body as she tore his shirt off and unbuckled his belt and unzipped his pants. For the next half-hour, they both rediscovered the thrill of passion and lust that had been missing in their lives for several years.

Forty minutes later, they pulled back onto the freeway, for all practical purposes just another normal middle-aged couple cruising down Highway 101 to San Francisco, perhaps for an evening in the city.

"Ryan is going to be really mad," Peter said. "He was real clear about not getting involved with each other."

"Are you sorry you made love to me, Peter?"

"Absolutely not! You were incredible, and I'd do it again in a heartbeat."

"Then I guess he'll have to get over it, won't he?" Before Peter could answer, Elizabeth said, "But that was a good idea you just had."

"What idea?"

"Doing it again." She looked across at Peter. "Pull over into that parking lot, Peter, I want to do it again."

Steve Davis

Peter obediently hit the turn signal and headed for the adjacent off-ramp.

A few hours later, the rental car was safely returned to SF Airport, and using the same phony identification that they come to the Bay Area with, they were both en route to their respective homes, Peter to Burbank, and Elizabeth to New York. The gym bag, containing all of the disguises, was safely stored inside Peter's checked luggage to be safely disposed of hundreds of miles away.

Murder number one was actually pretty easy for Elizabeth and Peter. They never saw Danny Lemos writhing in pain before he died, and their respective local news outlets had no coverage of a man who died of mysterious causes in faraway Santa Rosa, California. They both knew the other murders would not be so easy.

The next morning, Elizabeth and Peter woke up in their own homes, and could almost convince themselves that the murder never happened; it was just a bad dream. Yet each of them thought about the other and wondered how they were doing, having just murdered a man, albeit a dirtbag, much too easily.

The intense passion of the sex the night before also left them both wondering and a bit confused. How would they look at each other on Monday? Was the attraction real, or just passion from a situation more real than they had ever felt?

As hard as it was, they were true to the pact, and resisted the temptation to call each other, except for the Twitter post the next morning from Seahawk Sally saying, *"Big fireworks at the game last weekend. Seahawks scored early and often."*

CHAPTER 21

Ambergris Caye, Belize; Tuesday

Ryan raised his eyes from the novel he had been reading and he leisurely scanned the Atlantic Ocean in front of him. He turned the book over in his hand so he could see the title again. *"'22E ... Officer Down!' Pretty good mystery for an unknown author. I'm glad the last guest left it in the room. It's hard to put down."*

He got out of the cozy deck chair and walked over to the barbeque on the veranda of his hotel suite on Ambergris Caye on the Caribbean coast of Belize. He carefully turned a dozen or so jumbo shrimp, basting them with his own thrown-together concoction of Old Bay Seasoning and garlic butter, then grabbed another Belikin beer and headed back to the hammock and the book.

He had arrived at the Bay View Hotel and Marina three days ago on a six-day Scuba Diving Vacation Getaway Trip sponsored by a local Santa Rosa dive shop. The group made two dive trips each day on the dive boat Reefer Madness to the Blue Hole and other sites along the Belize

Barrier Reef, the longest reef in the world outside the Great Barrier Reef near Australia.

As he passed in front of the open doorway, he noticed the red light flashing on the telephone by the bed. He went in and picked up the receiver and called the front desk. "Did you have a message for me?" he asked.

"Oh, yes, Mr. Foster. A Mr. Atkins called from the states and asked for you to call him as soon as possible. The call came in at 11:45 a.m. this morning. It seemed important to him."

"That would make it about 7:45 a.m. California time. That's pretty early for Darrel. Thank you, senor."

Ryan was embarrassed that he called the desk clerk 'senor'. He had a hard time not thinking of Belize as a Hispanic speaking country, due to its location between Mexico and Guatemala. This was the third time he had done the same thing in three days.

Ryan looked at the clock. *It's 7:00 p.m. now, that makes it 4:00 p.m. back in California.*

He hung up, grabbed his wallet and pulled out an International Calling Card. After three attempts to enter the correct combination of thirty-one numbers, he finally heard

the phone ringing and hoped he had correctly dialed Atkins'
cell phone number.

"Hello."

"Hello, Darrel. This is Ryan. You left a message to
call you?"

"Yes, Ryan. Thanks for the call. Are you really in
Belize?"

"Yes, of course. Why do you ask?"

"Santa Rosa P. D. is trying to track you down. Danny
Lemos was murdered yesterday."

"No shit." He had to play this straight. "Choco is
dead?" He paused a few seconds, as if to let the 'shock' wear
off. "How? A gang hit? Drive by? Shot pulling a robbery?
Any way is fine with me."

"None of them. Somebody poisoned the son of a
bitch. Outside a Starbucks Coffee Shop of all places. I always
figured he'd die on the street, but I figured it'd be in a hail of
bullets, not from poisoning on the sidewalk in front of
Starbucks."

"The plan must have worked perfectly," Ryan
thought. Then he said, almost disappointedly, "So somebody

got to him before I could. But why does Santa Rosa want to talk to me?"

"They just want to account for your whereabouts because of the threats you made before. Pretty routine, I'm sure. But you can probably expect to hear from them as soon as you get home."

"Thanks for the heads up, Darrel. You can tell them I get back on Saturday night, and I'm supposed to fly out Sunday afternoon for the Retreat. Are they serious enough to want to see me on a Sunday?"

"I'll contact them and see if they want to do it on a Sunday or wait a week."

"Great. Thanks for the good news, Darrel."

"Boy, it sure was lucky that this went down while you were out of the country. Otherwise, we all might have thought you were involved."

"Yep, Darrel, they say timing is everything."

CHAPTER 22

Ryan threw his windbreaker over the chair and put the KFC three-piece dinner - dark meat with mashed potatoes and cole slaw - on the table as he arrived home from the Belize dive trip. He hit the 'on' button for his stereo as he passed it on the way to his bedroom. The Elvis Channel was belting out the end of 'Suspicious Minds' on the XM radio, as he changed into his Saturday-evening-sit-around-and-vegetate comfortable attire. The radio moved on to one of his favorites, 'Kentucky Rain' by the time he re-entered the front room. "In the cold Kentucky Rain…," he sang along, as he walked toward his fine-dining chicken box.

The flashing lights on his answering machine beckoned him, and he walked over, pushed the playback button and turned back to the kitchen and his now lukewarm dinner box.

"You have two recorded messages; First Message;" the machine said.

"For God's sake, Ryan, what have you done now?" the familiar voice of his estranged wife barked from the machine.

"Great welcome home, Gloria," Ryan said aloud, "The first sound I hear is my estranged, hateful, soon to be ex-wife chewing me out."

The machine continued, "I just got off the phone with a Detective from Santa Rosa PD, who wanted to know where I was on Tuesday, and if I had someone to verify my alibi. My alibi! It seems the asshole that killed my daughter got killed on Tuesday in Santa Rosa, and she wants to know if I have an alibi. I know you did it, Ryan, and I told her so. You're trying to make up for letting her go to Big River and getting her murdered. Don't even try to drag me into this. For God's sake, she even wanted to know my bra size. My bra size! What's that got to do with it, Ryan? Don't even call me back, just get me the hell out of your crap. You hear me, Ryan?" You could hear the phone slam down, even on the recording.

Ryan pushed the Save Message button. *"Message saved. Second Recorded Message;"* the machine continued.

"Ryan. Darrel Atkins. I just got off the phone with Santa Rosa PD. They want to talk to you before you go back to the Retreat on Sunday if possible. Call the Detective's Office, you've got the number, and tell them if you can't make it at 10:00 a.m. on Sunday. If they don't hear from you, they'll assume you will be there. A female Detective named Lawler is the lead investigator on the Lemos murder investigation. I don't recognize the name. She may be a new Detective. I told them I would sit in since we are friends and it involves our murder case."

The following morning, Ryan showed up at the Santa Rosa Police Department Detective's Office fifteen minutes early. Detective Atkins was already there as he promised. The primary investigators were SRPD Detectives, led by a short, slightly stocky female Detective who introduced herself as Delfina Lawler. While he was looking at her short cropped bleached blond men's haircut combed perfectly in place, and the single ear ring, she stared back at him with a *'Don't think for a moment that because you're a cop you're going to get special treatment from me'* sneer.

"Before we start, I want to make one thing clear, Ryan," Lawler began, "You are not a suspect at this time, but I think we need to talk just the same. We need to tell you that if you are involved in any way, we can't help you, cover for you, give you a break, or anything else. As soon as we think you might be involved – in any way – we have to treat you the same as any other suspect."

"With all due respect, ma'am. it sounds like …"

"With all due respect, Ryan, I don't like 'ma'am'. You can call me 'Detective'."

Ryan paused long enough to look at the others as if to say, *"Is she kidding?"* Their glances at the floor told him she wasn't kidding, and this was apparently Lawler's standard procedure. He could see that Lawler was looking for someone to solve a murder, and everyone was a suspect.

"Of course, Detective. And you can call me Lieutenant Foster, or just Lieutenant, if you prefer. As I was saying, Detective, it sounds like you are already considering me a suspect, interviewing me on a cold case on a Sunday morning, even though you know from Darrel here that I was on tropical island thousands of miles away at the apparent time Choco was killed. So, just to cover yourselves, aren't you supposed to advise me of my rights?"

"We're not close to that point, Lieutenant Foster," Lawler said, implying a strong 'yet'. Then she cocked her head to the side and said, "Do you think we're at that point, … Ryan?"

Her deliberate return to his first name was an old interrogation trick, using the first name of a suspect to imply an apparently superior position for the interrogator, like in a parent/child relationship. Ryan decided to play the game in return, "No ma'am," he said, as if addressing a kindly old lady.

"You are a new Detective, aren't you?" Ryan continued, "In fact, I'm betting this is your first murder case, and you are going to use every trick you learned last month at DOJ School to find the killer, even if it means ignoring the obvious, playing hardball, and trying to intimidate everyone you question."

She winced and started to say something, raising her pointed finger, but she was cut off by the other Detective, "I can see why you'd be offended, Lieutenant. After what you've been through, it is understandable. You've lost your daughter and, I understand, your wife, over this. Detective Lawler just wants to clarify where we have to stand. I understand the Mendocino Sheriff kind of covered for you the night you went after Lemos in Laytonville. We are on your side. We just want to be clear."

"We are clear. And you can forget that 'black hat – white hat' shit. I've been using it before you were a cop. Now do you want to tell me why you are even considering a

134

guy who was on vacation on a Caribbean island when the murder occurred, instead of focusing on Choco's enemies right here in town? He's got plenty, you know."

"It's easy," said Lawler, who inserted herself back into the lead interrogator role. "One, you tried to kill him once already, but were saved by Mendo S.O."

"He murdered my daughter and I was distraught. I'm okay now. I'm becoming a forgiving man, thanks to Dr. Stan's retreat."

Lawler continued as if Ryan hadn't said a word. "Two, your alibi is just a little too convenient. Three, it wouldn't be the first time a murder was farmed out to a hit man. Four, if you wanted it to look like a gang hit, when was the last time you heard of a gang hit using poison?"

"Poison? So, you think I gave him a slow acting poison before I left on vacation?"

"Don't be a smart ass. We might not hit it off well," Lawler continued.

"Really? Does this hard-ass approach really work for you? You mean we might lose this close relationship we've forged during the ten minutes since you identified me as a suspect."

"You aren't a suspect."

"Okay. Now I have a question for you. Have you done any actual police investigation into this? Do you have any leads on who killed him? Suspects? Witnesses?"

"We can't share that with you, you haven't been cleared as a … person of interest."

"You mean suspect? Is that how you plan to solve your first unsolved murder, Detective Lawler? Instead of going into the gang, digging for answers, which might be dangerous, you accuse someone who was nowhere around, just because he threatened him in the past? Not very professional, Detective Lawler."

"For the last time, Foster, no-one is accusing you of anything at this time."

"Really? You just said, and I quote, 'If you wanted to make it look like a gang hit.' Not 'if someone'…, not, 'if the murderer', you used the word 'you'. That's pretty accusatory. I think you crossed the line and better Miranda your suspect, Detective."

"That's not what I said."

"Really? Check the tape. If I'm not a suspect, I'll be leaving now. It will give you a chance to find Choco's real killer from among the thousand or so suspects who had a reason to kill him, and who were within a thousand miles of the murder. And, by the way, I want a copy of this recording before we talk again. Are we clear?"

As he got up and left the room, Atkins followed him out the door. "Ryan. I'm sorry. She took it way further than she was supposed to. I wouldn't have been a part of it if I'd known."

"I'll believe you for now Darrel. But I'm not sure who's playing 'white hat' and who's playing 'black hat' right now. If you are looking for a reaction from me, here's what I've got for you. I'm glad Choco is dead, and I don't give a shit who killed him or how. I've still got to get over the fact that whatever happened to him, my daughter is still dead and I'll never see her again." They turned and continued down the hallway, and Ryan changed the conversation, "Do they have any real suspects?"

"Not really. A couple witnesses saw him talking to a late twenties attractive hippy-type woman. All they could remember was the bright tie-dyed skirt she wore, shoulder length reddish-blond hair in a bonnet, and huge tits." He laughed, "All the witnesses remembered was the big tits and no bra. There's actually no sure connection with her, but witnesses saw her talking to him just before he died, and they just want to talk to her."

"Maybe she's not even involved, said Ryan. "Maybe a Ft. Bragg gang banger came down to get even for Choco tagging their territory. I think they better start looking at his gang activities again. Thanks for your support, Darrel. You've been a friend throughout this ordeal. Let me know what happens, will you?"

"Sure. And you take care of yourself. By the way, how's that Forgiveness Retreat working out?"

"Must be working. I feel better already."

CHAPTER 23

The Sunday morning interview caused Ryan to have to re-schedule his flight to Colorado, which, in turn, caused him to miss the Sunday night pre-session reception.

Had he been there, he probably would have noticed the casual flirtatious glances between Peter and Elizabeth at the mixer, and he certainly would have noticed that Elizabeth slipped out of the room earlier than usual, and Peter left a short time later and wandered off in the direction of Elizabeth's room.

The following morning, Ryan entered the meeting room and walked straight to the coffee urn and poured himself a cup of coffee before the first session. Dr. Stan approached him as he was reaching for a jelly doughnut.

"Aha. So, it's true what they say about cops and jelly doughnuts."

"Yeah, I guess you got me on that one, Doc."

"We missed you at the reception last night. It's a shame. I really think it is an important part of the seminar;

networking with your classmates. And I think you are going to be one of the leaders in this group, Ryan."

"I'm sorry, Doc, I planned to attend, but something pretty important came up and I had to change my flight to the red eye."

"Yes. Actually, I got a call from a Detective Lawler a few days ago. She told me that the fellow who killed your daughter was murdered this week, and she wanted to know if I thought you might be behind it. She doesn't seem to like you for some reason. You'd probably be wise to be careful around her."

"Thanks for the tip. We met, or should I say we crossed paths, yesterday, and yes, it was apparent she would like to think I'm involved."

"I told them of course you weren't involved. Plus, it appears you had a perfect alibi. How was Belize?"

"Beautiful. There is nothing like deep sea diving to take your mind off of your depression. The Belize Barrier Reef is spectacular, the fish are beautiful, and the seafood is cheap and fresh."

"Tell me, Ryan, since your daughter's killer is no longer around, I hope you will continue with the Retreat. There is still some great benefit in going through it with your fellow attendees, and, as I said, I consider you one of the leaders of this class."

"I absolutely agree, Sir. I am happy to stick around and see if I can be of assistance to others in need of healing."

"Good. Thank you for staying. Well, we might as well get started. We'll probably start with your case today and see how some of the others feel about it."

"Yes, Sir. I'm rather curious about that myself."

For the group in general, the morning session was mostly a discussion of the death of Marcy's killer and its impact on the grieving/forgiveness process. But for Ryan, Peter, and Elizabeth, it was about furtive glances and invisible reassurances that the murder was not going to be a burden or impediment to the overall plan. And for Elizabeth and Peter, there were additional casual glances, with an occasional raised eyebrow.

At the morning break, Ryan sidled up alongside Elizabeth at the coffee pot, and asked, "Good morning, Elizabeth, how have you been lately."

"I've been fine, Ryan. Peter and I were talking at the reception last night, and we agreed that we can all take solace in the fact that one less murderer is around to prey on young girls. We all share your relief."

Ryan looked around to see if anyone was nearby and whispered, "Tell Peter. After dark, my room, tonight, we'll talk it all out. Well done and thanks."

That night, in Ryan's room, they quietly toasted their success and discussed details of the Lemos murder, analyzing it in detail to see if anything might have tripped them up.

They also discussed how each felt about the murder conspiracy to see if anyone felt they couldn't continue with the plot. Each of them was committed to finishing the job they started by moving onto murder number two, the New York street gang.

Satisfied that the crime was committed to perfection, they stopped for the night and agreed to discuss the next crime starting tomorrow.

Elizabeth and Peter left Ryan's room and began walking up the path toward their respective rooms. When they reached the fork in the pathway, Peter said sheepishly, "Would you like to come to my room for a nightcap, Elizabeth?"

She stopped abruptly. "Wait, Peter, we need to talk."

He stopped, then stepped back when he saw the serious look in her eye. "Yes, I suppose we do."

Elizabeth motioned for Peter to follow her over to one of the park benches along the trail. Sitting down, she patted the seat next to her, and Peter sat down obediently.

She looked all around to make sure they were alone, which prompted him to give an *'oh yeah'* nod, and look around himself.

"Peter … what we did the other day, … after the thing we did …," she paused awkwardly and glanced over her shoulder again, "It was wonderful, and I think we both needed it. I know I did. It was a wonderful moment, or should I say moments, for me."

"I felt the same way," he said.

"I'm glad, but I need to finish, please. I don't regret it for a moment, and I hope you won't either, but it wasn't love, or even lust. It was a euphoric high, like I hadn't felt in years, and I wanted you close to me."

"I think I understand. I've never made love to such a beautiful woman."

"I was so high, so fulfilled. Revenge can be sweet. I felt like I had just killed Travis' killer, instead of some stranger."

"I felt the same way."

"The thing is, we can't let it go further than that. It can create some real problems if we let it go any further. We need to get back to the original plan, no involvement. Does that make sense?"

Peter paused. He hadn't expected Elizabeth's response, but he knew she was right. "Yes," he said, the disappointment evident in his voice. "I'm sorry. Of course, I wanted it to go further than that. I mean, you're a beautiful woman and it was incredible. But I understand. We've still got work to do and we agreed …."

Elizabeth reached over and kissed him gently on the cheek, then she stood up, holding his hand until he was on his feet.

"Let's leave it at that, Peter."

She smiled and walked briskly down the path toward her room, without even a glance back at Peter. He stood and watched her until she was out of sight, then let out a sigh and walked slowly in the direction of his cabin.

CHAPTER 24

At first it was a bit awkward, especially for Peter, as the conspirators met several times during the week to discuss the details of the plans for the remaining murder plots. Ryan sensed the uneasiness in the room, but assumed it was because they were having a difficult time reconciling that they crossed a forbidden line and were now murderers.

By Friday night, they were keenly focused on the plan to murder the gangbangers who killed Travis Hartman.

"So, Elizabeth, did you make the arrangements with your sister, like we discussed?"

"Yes. I'll be in the Los Angeles area all next week, so you'll have several days to pull your plan off."

Peter abruptly interrupted the discussion of Elizabeth's alibi. "Let's talk some more about this so-called plan. Now, if I understand you correctly, you and me are going to go to New York, lure four or more murderous gang members into a dark alley and just gun them down?" Peter asked incredulously.

"Yes."

"And they'll never suspect anything and will let us do it?"

"Yep."

"And we won't get hurt or killed?"

"Nope. Not if you do your part right, Peter."

"No way. You are crazy, Ryan. We'll end up in a shootout and probably both get killed. There's just no way it can work. I've never shot a gun in my life and you think I will just turn into a gun-slinging killer?"

"You won't have to shoot anyone, Peter."

"Really? You're going to kill them all and I just stand there? Why am I there in the first place, then?"

"That's easy. You are the bait."

"Bait! Did you just say 'bait'? You know what usually happens to the bait, don't you? It gets eaten."

Ryan chuckled. "Don't worry, Peter. Gangsters don't usually eat their victims. You got a better plan, let's hear it."

"Me? A better plan to murder four experienced murderers?"

"Then let's go over it again. Your job is easy. Just don't turn around."

CHAPTER 25

New York to Los Angeles flight; Sunday Morning

Elizabeth Hartman returned to New York only long enough to clear some leftover paperwork on Saturday, then pack for her next trip. The next morning, she caught a cab to La Guardia and flew to Los Angeles for a quickly improvised family vacation. Upon arrival, she rented a new, bright red Mustang convertible from Los Angeles International Airport, and headed for her sister's home in nearby Glendale.

"Elizabeth! You are really here," her sister, Cassie, greeted her with a long hug, "I was so excited to hear from you that you wanted to come to LA for the week. But, I thought for sure you'd cancel again. You're really here, and we're going to have so much fun."

"Yes, Cassie, I'm really here this time. Thanks for letting me stay with you on such short notice."

"Forget it. I'm thrilled to spend a week with my big sister. Please tell me that life is getting better and you aren't still going through hell every day."

"Not much better, Cassie. I still miss and grieve for Travis every day."

"I'm so sorry, but I still pray for you every day. How is the Forgiveness Retreat thing working out? Dr. Stan seems to be a sincere fellow on TV, is he as genuine in person?"

"He's really trying to help, but it's a tough trick to pull off. He'll help a number of people in the class before we're through. Hopefully I'll feel better soon. I've talked to a couple other men with similar situations and talking to them seems to be helping."

"Single men?"

"I'm not even going there, Cassie. Travis was the one and only for me. They are just helping me find ways to address my grief and hate."

"Maybe that will change some day. You deserve more love in your life."

"Hey, let's change the subject. Did you get the tickets?"

"Yes, I did. For the next week, we are going to be Hollywood junkies. We are going to one television show taping every day, just like you asked, for the next week. I even got the Tonight Show like you asked for Wednesday night. Curious, why was Wednesday so important?"

"No reason, he just always seems to have the biggest name celebrities on Wednesdays."

"Really? I hadn't noticed. I'll have to pay more attention."

"How about the daytime excursions?"

"We're scheduled for the Brea Tar Pits on Tuesday morning, and Universal Studios Thursday. I don't remember you as being such a tourist groupie, Elizabeth. What's up with that?"

"Just trying to take my mind off of things, and I don't know when I'll get out here again. Thanks again for letting me stay here all week."

"My pleasure. We are going to have so much fun this week. Just like when we were going to High School."

"What say we get this party started tonight with dinner at Roxy's, my treat of course."

"Oh boy. Let's do it."

CHAPTER 26

The Red Eye Flight to Munich, Germany, Saturday night.

Just after 9:00 p.m., on Saturday, the wheels lifted off the ground and shortly later, Lufthansa Flight 459, nonstop to Munich, left the friendly airspace of San Francisco.

The Flight Attendant approached the man seated in seat 6A. "Can I get you something to drink, Mr. Foster?"

"Thank you. I'll have a scotch and soda, please. Can you make it a double; I don't sleep well on these long flights. And keep them coming, please, as long as I'm awake." Ryan sat back to enjoy the comforts of First Class. After all, it was Elizabeth's money – actually, he corrected himself, - it was Travis' money they were spending. When the drinks arrived, he made an imaginary toast to Travis Hartman.

Some thirteen hours later, at 5:15 p.m. Sunday, Munich time, he was met at the airport by his distant cousin by marriage, Klaus Harbusch. Over the years with Gloria, they had visited Klaus and Ilona Harbusch and their family in the northern German hamlet of Besse many times, and he and Klaus had gotten pretty close through the years. He was glad they didn't give him up when he and Gloria split up. In fact, they were in full support of Klaus meeting him here in the south of Germany for a brief vacation to Oktoberfest in Munich. They hoped returning to the scene of one of their happiest trips together would get his mind off of Marcy's death.

Klaus was a German to the bone, which included total and complete trust and loyalty. He also carried a hearty disgust for law breakers; especially one who would commit such a senseless crime as to murder and assault a young girl like Marcy. He took the crime personally, and was happy to help Ryan in any way possible, without questions, if it helped ease the pain of Marcy's death.

Klaus had been briefed by Ryan on the basics of the plan by phone, and he agreed to participate in the plot and, most importantly, to keep it a secret from Ilona and the rest of the family. He happily obliged Ryan out of disgust for the American justice system he saw as deeply flawed for releasing a known killer on 'technicalities'. And Ryan needed to believe in Klaus' loyalty, because his life, and to a lesser degree, those of Peter and Elizabeth, were going to count on it.

As they drove an hour to their rented chalet in Schliersee, thirty kilometers west of Munich, Ryan went over the full details of his plan for his alibi, explaining just enough so that Klaus could not be implicated, and Klaus again agreed to participate in the elaborate cover plot.

"Ryan," Klaus said as they drove into the night, "What you are going to do will put you in great danger, and you will be totally by yourself in the plan. Are you sure this is what you wish to do? I will worry for you, and I don't know what to tell my family upon my return, if you are killed or arrested."

"Just remember that you don't know anything. If something goes wrong and the authorities talk to you, you will tell them you understood I was just meeting a woman somewhere and you were just covering for me."

"What is wrong with your justice in America that you have to kill Marcy's murderer on your own?"

"It's hard to explain how it got to this point. Do you have the real passport?"

"Yes. I just got it in the post a week ago, I was worried it wouldn't get here on time. I felt funny checking the mailbox every day of an empty house in our town."

"Good. Now I can get rid of the fake one Peter gave me as a backup. The legitimate German passport is surely better than trying to use a phony. I didn't want to implicate you in any way. It was smart to have it delivered somewhere it couldn't be traced to you. You've been a big help. You had no trouble with the information I sent you?"

"No, the birth certificate was a very good quality false German birth document. I mailed it in with the application and the photo you sent, and got the passport quite quickly."

Klaus had come to Munich from his home near Kassel, allegedly to spend the week partying with Ryan at Oktoberfest, Germany's premiere party extravaganza.

"And you had no trouble getting away alone to come meet me?"

"No. Ilona wanted to come, of course, and see you again. But I convinced her it had to be men only so you could talk freely. I told her you'll be back soon and she can visit then with you. And of course, I had to promise a trip to the Canary Islands this winter."

"You Germans are always trying to chase the sun. You like going there, and we both know it."

"What if the police look up your Hans Wasserman passport and see your picture?"

"There is no reason they would consider Hans Wasserman as a suspect in their investigation. He's just one of tens of thousands of tourists who fly in to New York, stay on business or pleasure a couple days, and fly home again."

Once they checked into their room, they went over the details of the alibi scheme Ryan devised. Ryan gave Klaus his personal Debit/ATM card and a sample of his signature. Starting the next morning, they would attend Oktoberfest, the world's greatest street and tent party, where for the next fifteen days, a half-million visitors a day would enjoy the best beer, bratwurst, sauerkraut, pretzels, and fraulein watching in the world; except that Ryan would not be there for most of it.

Klaus would spend freely, buying two of everything, using Ryan's card to access ATM funding every other day, being careful only to access temporary ATM's without video recording capabilities. He would even buy two tickets each day for the train ride to and from their Schliersee chalet. He would order two breakfasts each day in their room, calling as Ryan sometimes to put in the order.

The paper trail would prove Ryan was there the entire week, and the ATM withdrawals would substantiate his continued presence. Any hotel employees would attest they talked to Ryan frequently on the phone during the stay.

CHAPTER 27

Los Angeles to Washington, D.C. flight; Sunday.

"Stewardess, may I have another Jack and Coke, a double, please?"

"Certainly, Mr. Levenson."

A few moments later, she returned with the drink and placed it on his tray table. "Thank you for flying United, Mr. Levenson. Can I get you anything else?"

"No, thank you. You've been very kind."

Peter took a large swallow of the drink, took in and exhaled a huge breath of air, finished the drink in another swallow, and tilted his head back into the pillow of the First Class seat from Los Angeles to Washington, D.C.

"How did I ever let Ryan talk me into this crazy scheme? I'm not a cold-blooded killer." His subconscious quickly reminded him of his role in the Lemos murder. *"At least not when they are armed and dangerous and can shoot back at me. I don't even squash spiders. Danny Lemos was easy, I never had to look at him, but now ... now here I am flying across country to help Ryan kill some young subway*

*punks in New York City. Hell, we don't even know if they'll
be there. If I hadn't already taken part in one murder, I'd
quit and forget this revenge bullshit once and for all. Now
how do I get out of it? How'd I let him talk me into it? It'll
never work and we'll all end up dead or doing life in
prison!"*

As he twisted and squirmed in the chair, suddenly a
voice said, "Don't worry, Mr. Levenson. It'll all be over
soon." The words jolted him from his private thoughts,
causing him to jump nearly out of his skin.

He jerked to his left at the Flight Attendant standing
at the aisle over him. "Was I talking out loud?" he asked,
wondering how much of the plot she had overheard.

"No, of course not. I meant the flight. I can see you
are extremely nervous about flying, and I just wanted to let
you know we're almost there and the flight will be over
soon."

"Oh, the flight." He was relieved to know he hadn't
said anything out loud. "Yes. Thank you. Yes, I am quite
nervous. Can I get another Jack and Coke to settle me
down?"

"Maybe one more, but this will be your fourth, and we're supposed to limit it to three, but I can see it might help you. I'll be back."

Once he got the last drink, he took a long drink, then leaned back to go over the plan. *"Okay, I use my own money to rent a car in Washington, with unlimited miles, my own money to drive to Baltimore, and for the hotel room at the always crowded, five-star Chesapeake Bay View Hotel. Then in the morning, I go to Camden Yards and use my credit card to buy bleacher seats for the Orioles entire home stands against the Rangers and the Angels. I go to the first game, and make sure I get on camera, if possible. Then I buy some souvenir shirts and get out of there. Then, the next morning, I disconnect the odometer and drive to New York through York and Allentown, avoiding toll booths and cameras, using cash from the 'cash pool' to buy gas and food."*

He took another drink and took a deep breath. *"What was the name of that deli we are to meet at? Oh, yeah, Beni Hoffa's. And I only use cash and only use the throwdown phone if I have to."*

His hand fingered the untraceable phone in his pocket marked '1'.

"Crap. What a dumb idea. I wish I'd never let him talk me into this. Anything can go wrong! What if the street thugs don't show up all week and we wasted this time, money and grief? Hell, what if they <u>do</u> show up and they shoot back and kill me or Ryan? What if the cops find us in New York with guns? Does Ryan really think he's going to kill four guys in a shootout, and he and I don't get hurt? Crap! Damn you Ryan!"

"It's almost over, Mr. Levenson," the Flight Attendant reassured him again as she passed by, putting her hand on his shoulder as she passed.

"If you only knew, Honey. If you only knew."

CHAPTER 28

Munich, Germany; Tuesday

Ryan and Klaus were at the Main Gate when Oktoberfest opened for the day on Monday. They spent the day at the Festival, taking dozens of photos of each other, periodically changing the date stamp on the camera and wearing different shirts they brought with them in a backpack. They asked strangers to take several pictures of them around the various tents, carefully avoiding clocks and calendars in the background.

Just before midnight on Monday, they drove to the Munich airport in time for Ryan to catch Lufthansa Flight 355 to JFK, paid for with cash pool monies, under the false German passport in the name of Hans Wassermann.

"Good luck, Ryan, … I mean Herr Wasserman, …, be very careful and good luck."

Soon Ryan, as German citizen Hans Wasserman, boarded the Lufthansa jet to New York. He settled into his First Class seat, ordered a Warsteiner Pils, and went to sleep thinking about the plans he had crafted for the murders of the subway gang.

Upon arrival in New York in the morning, as Hans Wasserman, he used cash from the cash pool, caught a cab to Midtown, Manhattan, and rented a room at the Midtown Hotel. After a short nap, he awoke and walked to the Beni Hoffa's restaurant near the hotel.

At 4:00 p.m., Peter walked through the door and joined Ryan at a corner seat in view of the entrance. The look on his face was one of pained anguish, and told of two days of flying across country, baseball in the sun, a fitful night's sleep and driving five hours. He grimaced at the sight of Ryan, which meant the plan was still a 'Go'. He made no attempt to conceal that he would have preferred that Ryan was a no-show, thereby cancelling what he considered a suicide mission later that night and all week if necessary.

After pleasantries and a recap of Ryan's flights to Germany and return to New York, the conversation waned. During lunch, Peter kept fidgeting in his seat uncomfortably. Ryan said, "Relax, Peter. We'll talk about it in the room. Remember, I'm the one who's going to do all the work."

Peter glared at Ryan with contempt in his eyes. After dinner, they paid the tab with pool money, and walked to the room.

"Jesus, Peter, when you took out Lemos, were you this nervous? Elizabeth never said anything about you wigging out on her?"

"Hell no. But we caught Danny Lemos out of his element. These guys are going to be armed and will be shooting back."

"If they do, we'll just have to shoot straighter than they do. Now if you'll excuse me, give me the keys to your rental car. I've got to go 'shopping'."

"Shopping? What for?"

"Firepower."

"Firepower? You mean a gun? You don't even have a gun? How are you going to kill a bunch of gangsters without a gun? Where are you going to buy a gun today? I heard New York has the strictest gun laws anywhere."

"You just sit tight, have a drink and get some sleep. You're going to need it for tomorrow night. Leave the little details to me."

"Little Details? Going into a gun battle with no gun isn't a little detail, Ryan."

CHAPTER 29

Ryan drove the rental car to the north edge of the high-crime Brooklyn Heights neighborhood, near the East River docks. The plan was simple; drive around in a strange town, in an area you've researched to be a high gang and crime location, until you find a drug deal going down, break up the drug deal by pretending to be a task force of cops, steal the bad guys' weapons, and get away. At least it sounded simple to Ryan.

He began to drive around the warehouses in hopes of encountering one of the many drug deals that occur nightly in the city. He knew what he was looking for, and after an hour or so, he found it as he drove around the corner of a building with his lights out.

There, in a back corner of the parking lot, just over three hundred feet away, he saw the shadows of two cars parked facing each other in a dark area of the dockyard. The area was totally dark, the result of lights which had been broken out some time ago for that very reason. The little moonlight that existed made the shadows come to life.

One of the vehicles was a newer white Toyota Camry. Standing in front of it was a man who appeared to be Caucasian, mid-twenties or older, maybe 6' tall, wearing business attire.

"There is my buyer ...," thought Ryan.

The other vehicle, parked facing to the left at a slight angle, its wheels pointed to the right for a quick exit, was a brand-new Mercedes sedan with a 'lowrider' suspension and blacked out windows. The man who was talking to the businessman in the dark between the vehicles was a light skinned mixed-race man about 5' 9" tall who looked to be in his early twenties. He wore dark pants, an expensive black leather jacket and a New Jersey Nets ball cap.

About ten feet away, standing in the background, was a large man, looking to be 6' 4" or more and heavy set. He wore a three quarters length leather trench coat and kept his hands in his pockets as he watched the other men. The driver's door of the Mercedes was open, offering some illumination of the people, until the big man closed the door when he saw Ryan's car moving into the other end of the parking lot.

"... and there is my dealer and his bodyguard."

The bodyguard immediately pointed Ryan's car out to the smaller man, who stopped and turned toward him. This caused the businessman to also look, and he took a nervous step backwards toward the door of the Camry.

"Showtime," Ryan said as he got out of the car, as casually as a man who wanted to look like a cop could look, making sure the badge on his belt was visible in the reflective light from the direction of the men. He held his cell phone up to his mouth as if it were a police radio, and looked east and pointed twice in that direction as he spoke into the imaginary radio. He hoped to the men, it looked as if he was directing an unseen posse. He then pointed in a sweeping motion to the west, as if directing others to move around to that side.

The two men Ryan suspected were drug dealers looked at each other and walked quickly to the side of the Mercedes away from Ryan and bent over at the same time.

The Camry driver had already gotten into his car and started the engine, but paused to see Ryan's next move. Ryan made an animated motion as if he were talking on the radio and waved again behind the men as if directing officers into the scene.

The Mercedes occupants made a furtive movement toward some nearby broken wood pallets, got into their car and drove away in one direction, while the Camry went in the opposite direction.

Ryan got into the car quickly as if to give chase, which caused the Mercedes to drive faster onto the adjacent road and disappear around a corner.

As soon as they left, Ryan drove to the site where they had been standing and walked to where they had ducked down. As he suspected, he located a baggie of whitish grey powder, and laying under a discarded tree branch, he found a large automatic handgun. He picked it up, assured himself it was loaded, and put it in his waistband.

He ripped the Baggie open and poured the contents on the ground. As he turned to leave, he noticed another handgun, a revolver, lying next to the pile of broken pallets, about six feet away. He picked it up and got in the car.

He then drove around the back of the building, away from the direction the Mercedes had fled. Three quick turns and he was on the Brooklyn Bridge heading toward Lower Manhattan.

He was entering the borough at the east end of the bridge, when he saw a pair of headlights overtaking him from the rear at a high rate of speed. As it got closer, he could see the outline of the lowered Mercedes as it pulled in behind him.

"Oh shit. I didn't think they'd come back so quick."

Traffic was light on the bridge as it approached the area where both lanes merged in preparation for the end of the expanse. The Mercedes pulled out to the left and sped up to come alongside Ryan's car. The smaller man, in the passenger seat, leaned forward and looked intently toward Ryan, trying to decide if he was really a cop or not, and trying to figure out what was happening. Ryan sped up enough that the other driver had to do the same as the lane ended at the end of the off-ramp. Then, he timed his next move until the last moment, and drove hard into the 180 degree turn at the end of the sudden off-ramp at the end of the bridge. The Mercedes had to slow to a near stop to avoid the guardrail, which allowed Ryan to pull away on the connector road to FDR Drive.

As Ryan merged onto FDR Drive, he had a one block lead on the rapidly accelerating Mercedes. As Ryan took the next exit, he went through the corner smoothly as the Mercedes had to brake hard, losing another half block. Ryan made a quick right turn, and another right turn behind an abandoned pier building, where he made an intentional power turn, spinning around, tight against the curb. He jumped out with the automatic pistol aimed at the corner where he could hear the approaching Mercedes.

Suddenly the car appeared as it turned the corner in hot pursuit. The men found themselves facing Ryan in a combat crouch pointing the gun at their windshield. The driver ducked and swerved to the left, jumping the curb and continuing until it struck a light stanchion at a low speed, stopping abruptly. The front seat airbags exploded, filling the car with smoky powder. The men inside were dazed but otherwise uninjured as they bailed out of the powder filled car.

Just as quickly, Ryan was back in his car and drove quickly from the scene onto FDR Drive heading toward the hotel. In the distance, he heard sirens heading toward the location of the Mercedes.

Ryan smiled. He was comfortably assured the men would also be gone from the scene when the police arrived, and though they might report the car stolen in the morning, he was confident they would not report the theft of their guns and drugs to the police. In fact, it would simply look like an accident caused by excessive speed.

Ten minutes later, he was back at the hotel. He entered the security code, which opened the gate. He drove around to the rear of the hotel's underground parking garage and parked the car.

He sat in the car and looked closely at the guns in his pockets. The automatic was a Glock .40 caliber equipped with laser sights. The magazine was loaded with 10 rounds of half-jacketed hollow point ammunition. *"Sweet. Nice piece."*

Then he picked up the second gun, a common 6-shot Smith and Wesson revolver, also loaded with half-jacketed hollow point ammo.

When he got upstairs into the room, Peter woke up and sat up. "What happened? Are you okay?" he asked.

"Yes. Everything worked out as planned," Ryan said as he laid the guns on the table.

"What the …," Peter began.

"Don't ask," Ryan interrupted. "Get some sleep. We've got a busy week ahead of us."

CHAPTER 30

Peter, wearing a gray striped business suit and tie, looked every bit the part of a commuting businessman, as he stepped into the third car from the rear of the Red Line #2 train from downtown to Brooklyn and sat down in a solo seat near the door. He didn't have to fake nervousness as he clutched his briefcase closely on his lap and looked around furtively. There were few passengers on the car at that time, 7:28 PM, the exact time, station, subway line and platform from which Travis Hartman began the last subway ride of his life two years earlier.

The plan was for them to ride the same train every day for the week, hoping to encounter the subway gang on one of those nights, at which time they would put their plan into action.

Peter looked at his hands, and was relieved to see they weren't trembling as much as he thought they were. He stared at the gaudy imitation gold ring on his hand, and the fake Rolex on his wrist. His hand reached up and touched the gold necklace that hung loosely around his neck. His disguise, he knew, was perfect, but wouldn't the robbers, if there were any around, recognize it as an obvious trap. The jewelry, hat, the suit, the shoes, even the Bluetooth in his ear, all said man of means. *"Who'd fall for this obvious ruse,"* he thought, but his thought was interrupted when he noticed he had, in fact, caught the attention of a young black hoodlum-type sitting in the back corner of the car.

"Shit, the guy at the end of the train looks like a street thug, and he is watching me. He might be one of the killers right there," Peter whispered into the Bluetooth microphone hidden under his lapel.

"Relax. That's a good possibility and a good start. But let's keep our eyes open for the others. Remember, they don't have the balls to operate alone, there will be four or five," Ryan responded.

He and Ryan had gone over the details a hundred times, but he never thought it would go down the first night and the first time they set the plan in motion. Yet the young black male, he guessed around seventeen years old, but very tough looking, was trying not to be obvious but was eyeing him closely. Peter took a deep breath, held it a few seconds, and let it out, and glanced back at the youth. He was relieved to see the boy was now standing in front of the door as if to get off at the next stop.

"Looks like he's getting off. I guess it's a false alarm," he whispered.

"Atlantic Terminal, Barclay Center, next stop," the train's garbled and barely audible announcement said. Soon the doors opened and the young man stepped out of the train and walked down the platform toward the back of the train. Peter swallowed hard and took another deep breath and sat back for a moment in relief.

That relief was short lived, however. The train had barely begun moving again, when the rear door of the train opened and the same youth returned through the connecting doors from the car behind, followed by a foursome of even more menacing companions, the youth casually nodded toward Peter and stepped back to the rear of the group.

The apparent leader, a man in his early twenties, had a hard look about him, covered with prison tattoos that looked Riker's Island fresh. He looked over and scowled at a young Hispanic couple who were seated in the end chairs, gave an almost imperceptible sideways jerk of his head, and the man and woman literally jumped to their feet, as if they had been through this drill before, and headed past Peter and left the train car toward the front of the train.

The gang members then sat in the now-vacated seats at the rear of the train, and kept watching Peter while they talked among themselves.

Peter's heart was beating like it was out of his chest, and he could feel his carotid artery pounding in his neck. "Shit, Ryan, they are all here now."

"Easy, Peter. Remember the plan and stick to it."

Peter began to seriously doubt whether Ryan's plan was going to work. Before, they had talked about four nameless young 'street gangers', but these were grown men watching his every move. Not just men, but hardened, prison tattooed, just got out of Rikers Island bad-ass-mother type cons, and there were five of them, not four. And he knew they were going to try to kill him, just like Travis Hartman, when he got off the train, maybe even before. Ryan's plan wasn't going to work if they tried to kill him on the train. To make the plan work, he was going to have to get off the train, clear the platform and escalator, walk a full block without getting murdered before Ryan would be in position to help. *I should have never agreed to this stupid plan. I hardly know Ryan Foster, and I let him talk me into this dangerous plan that will surely get me killed. What the hell does he know about what a New York street gang will do.*

When he looked up again toward the men, there were
only three. Startled, he looked around and saw that two of the
men were now positioned at his end of the train, not eight
feet away. *"Maybe if I just give them the briefcase and
jewelry while I'm still here, they'll get off the train and let me
live."*

"Look at that watch, 'So'," the smaller of the two
whispered, barely loud enough for Peter to overhear.

"Shut the fuck up, 'Cat."

*"'So'? That would be 'SoMel', and 'Cat' was surely
'B-Cat'."* Those were the two names Elizabeth had given
them from the police report as possible suspects. "These are
the killers, Ryan. They're practically right in my lap," he
whispered, covering his mouth with his hand as he looked
down.

"I know. I'm watching you now. All that 'bling'
you're wearing has done its job, now we have to do ours."

Peter looked at the doorway between his rail car and
the car to the front of him and saw Ryan casually standing in
the shadows between the cars. It made him feel a little better,
but not much.

"Now shut up or you'll give us away. Just follow the plan at the next stop, just like we ran through it this morning. You'll be fine. Just give me thirty seconds to get in place."

"Bergen Street, Prospect Heights, next stop," the automated recording announced.

"Oh shit. We're here already. This is the station Travis got off at, and the one where the plan is supposed to happen." Bergen Street is the first stop for the nearby affluent townhouses of Prospect Heights, but it is also just a short walk from the high crime neighborhoods along Fulton Avenue, making commuters an easy target for muggings and robberies once they leave the subway station, especially at night.

Peter reached into his jacket pocket and fondled the revolver Ryan had given him to defend himself, if the plan went wrong. He'd never fired a real gun before, only stage guns on movie sets. He wasn't sure if he could do it, shaking as he was.

He looked back in Ryan's direction, but he was gone. He would be on his own now, and he was flat out scared to death.

Before he knew it, the train had come to a stop. He pulled on the left glove he brought along and grabbed the briefcase, then shoved his right hand into his pocket, where he fondled the revolver. He took a deep breath, and got his shaking knees to move enough to step off the train and onto the platform. He began walking toward the front of the train, which was now pulling away again. He didn't even have to look back to see if he was being followed, he could hear them talking, maybe fifty feet behind him. He looked up ahead to see if Ryan was there as planned, but there was no sign of him.

He covered his mouth and Bluetooth and said, "Where'd you go? What happened?"

"Relax, buddy. I'm ahead of you and I'll be in position. They won't do anything until you get away from the businesses on the street and turn into the alley. Act scared, glance back every once in a while, and they'll back off a little till you get close to the alley. Then walk fast until you get in the alley, they'll catch up quickly in the alley. Keep walking, and run if you hear gunshots, no matter what happens behind you. We'll meet where we planned. If I don't show up, follow Plan B as we discussed. Relax, you can do this and it will work."

"Okay, I will, and I won't have to act scared. I'm shaking."

"10-4. Toughen up, Peter. It's too late now to do anything but do just as we discussed. No time for fear now, it'll just distract you from what you have to do."

"Okay. Okay, I got this," he said unconvincingly.

As Peter traversed the business section surrounding the Metro Station, he turned up a darkened street and glanced back. The gang was following about 40 feet behind, not saying a word. He had to go over two blocks before the service alley in which Travis and numerous others over the years had been mugged or robbed. He could hear them closer now, so he clutched the briefcase closer and pulled the revolver discreetly from his pocket and held it under his open coat near his stomach.

Sensing his fear, the gang backed off a little, not wanting to spook their prey, and Peter relaxed only slightly until he approached the alley entrance. As he turned the corner, they were now only twenty or so feet behind him. It was totally dark, since all the lights in the alley had been broken years ago by the gangs that preyed on the neighborhood. A faint light came from the far end of the alley, silhouetting the fact that there was no-one waiting to save him. "Shit, Ryan, where are you?" he whispered. There was no response.

He quickened his pace in the alley and suddenly he heard the leader, not ten feet behind him say, "Hey, you. Hold it right there." He was still fifteen feet from the nearest object - a dumpster - large enough to hide behind. If Ryan was there, he was now in the crossfire if Ryan came out now. He ignored the order to stop, and heard the ominous click of a cocking handgun behind him. "I said hold it right there. Now!"

Peter stopped and began to turn around, still deciding whether to comply or start shooting, when Ryan swung swiftly and quietly into the open alley from around the side of the dumpster. Kneeling in a combat firing position, his movement was almost undetectable, as he was virtually invisible in the dark alley, wearing black levis, a dark ski mask, black gloves, and a black jacket.

A red dot briefly appeared on the face of the gang's leader, who had a revolver aimed at Peter. A second later, the man was dead, from a laser-directed accurate shot to the head. Ryan's second and third shots hit the second man in the group, who was also holding a gun in Peter's direction, before he could even react and turn to face the new threat. The next two shots, in rapid succession, followed the red dot to the third man in the group, striking him in the middle chest, knocking him straight to the ground. The fourth man, still confused as to where the shots were coming from, turned to run, firing one shot wildly as he spun around. Ryan's next shot followed the red laser dot and hit the man in the middle of the back, and he lunged forward and collapsed face down, writhing in a rapidly forming pool of blood.

Ryan spun around to face the last robber, who was crouched down groveling with his hands out as if to block the bullet he knew was coming. It was the baby-faced youth, certainly not over fifteen years old, who was the lookout for the gang on the train. "Please mister, don't kill me. I don't want to die."

As Ryan contemplated what to do with the youngster, he heard two quick shots ring out behind him. He wheeled around, and saw that the third man he'd shot, in the chest, had propped himself up and raised a pistol, poised to shoot Ryan, but Peter had shot him first.

Ryan looked in disbelief at Peter. "Thanks," he said. "Now get out of here, stick to the plan. Go."

Peter turned and scurried out the end of the alley and down the street as planned. Residents were beginning to open windows and look out to see what happened. Peter hurried that much quicker. Around two corners and he was in a quiet neighborhood, as he heard sirens in the distant background.

He walked normally to the parked rental car, got in and drove off in the opposite direction, as they had planned.

The alley was dark and quiet again, as house lights began to illuminate the side streets on either end of the alley. Returning to the youngster, Ryan asked, "How old are you?"

"Sixteen. I'm sorry, mister. Please don't kill me."

"What's your name?"

"Reginald, Reginald Bennau."

"Okay, Reginald, listen carefully. Here's what is going to happen. When I leave, you go around and pick up all these weapons to be sure they don't disappear before the cops get here. Then you sit on them, no matter who comes into the alley, and wait for the cops with your hands in the air and give yourself up. You give the cops the guns and tell them to run them against unsolved murders in this neighborhood, then you take whatever they give you for being here. I don't care what you tell them, but the descriptions of us better not be even close to accurate. Double cross me and, well, you've seen what I'll do to you. Got it, Reginald Bennau?"

"Yes, sir ... yes sir."

"Don't fuck this up, Reginald. You just saw what I do when people piss me off. Don't piss me off. It's your only chance."

"Yes, sir. I got it, sir. … thank you for not killing me, sir."

Ryan turned and ran out of the alley in the opposite direction from Peter. He turned to the right, and in a calculated move to draw attention away from Peter, he ran down the road yelling, in his best African-American ghetto slang, "Help! Call the po-lice, they shot me. They shot me."

Soon the NYPD emergency switchboard was lit up with calls. After describing what they had heard, most described a black man in dark clothing running south and west from the scene, yelling he'd been shot, while a few described another man possibly white or light skinned, walking briskly away from the scene to the northeast carrying a briefcase. The first responding officers headed toward the former, thinking it was more likely to be involved, and that the man needed emergency assistance.

Two blocks away, outside of earshot of the gun battle in the alley, the neighborhood was much quieter, and Ryan slowed to a walk and slipped unnoticed into a stoop leading to a downstairs apartment. He removed the ski mask which had made him appear to be a black man to the witnesses. He removed his black jacket and turned it inside out, now showing Dodger blue with the team logo in white on the chest. He put the gloves and mask into a fanny pack he wore under his jacket and again stepped out onto the sidewalk. A half of a block later, he walked up to a parked bicycle chained to a light pole, which they had placed there earlier in the day. He unchained the bike, got on and rode off, avoiding the streets with oncoming sirens.

Ryan was able to avoid the responding police cars by ducking in and out of stoops and alleys as they approached. Once he got to the meeting point a mile away, Peter was waiting with the rental car. Ryan carefully wiped down the bike handlebars and leaned it against a railing in front of an apartment complex, knowing it would be stolen by daybreak.

En route to their room on the other side of town, Peter said, excitedly. "My God, Ryan, you did it, just like you planned it. I was scared shitless. They did everything exactly like you said they would. You did it, you killed them all; bam, bam, bam-bam, bam. You are fuckin' Rambo, Ryan!"

"We had some luck, Peter. First time out of the gate and we get the same bastards who shot Travis. And, I'd be dead back there if you hadn't stuck around to cover me. You shot pretty straight, too. Thanks."

"Yeah, I did, didn't I?" He slightly grinned as he paused in thought for a moment, then said, "I had to. That's how you roll when you're with fuckin' Rambo!"

CHAPTER 31

NYPD Detective Sergeant Tony Delarosa was sitting in his T-shirt and underwear, on his overstuffed couch in front of a giant screen TV. The apartment he shared with his current girlfriend Alecia was long and narrow, so much so that the TV filled the side wall like a movie screen when viewed from the sofa on the opposite wall. He held a fresh Pabst Beer, which he had just opened. Alecia, sipping on a glass of Merlot, was wearing nothing more than one of Tony's old T-shirts. "This is my favorite part," he said as his hero, Rocky Balboa entered the ring to fight his nemesis, Apollo Creed.

"I love this," Alecia said, "I can't believe you are off and you're not even on-call tonight."

The words had scarcely left her lips when Tony's cell phone began to vibrate wildly on the table ten feet away. They both looked at the phone dancing on the countertop, then each other, as if to question whether her words had cursed them.

"No problem, baby," Tony said as he lifted her from his side and slid off the sofa. "I told you. It's my night off and the lieutenant promised me no call-out tonight."

He stopped to hit 'pause' on the DVR, then picked up the still vibrating phone and looked at the caller information. "God Damn it. Why is the office calling me? The dispatcher probably didn't look at his note before she called. I'll tell them to look at the damn schedule."

"Don't you do this, Tony!" Alecia said adamantly. Her Brooklyn accent was clearly heating up.

Without flinching, he hit the button. "Delarosa," he said into the mouthpiece.

"Tony, we need you right away to get to a shooting in Prospect …"

"Hold it, Lieutenant. Remember? Night off. No call-out. You're getting pretty forgetful, sir, that was only today."

"I remember, Tony. But this is going to be big news in the morning, and we need to be on top of it tonight. I need the best I've got on the case. When can you get here?"

"Big, huh?" Delarosa lived for the big cases, and he was immediately intrigued. "Who got snuffed? Politician? Sports star? International diplomat?"

"None of those. Four young black hoodlums from a foiled robbery attempt."

"Wait a fuckin' minute? You're cancelling my night off for a gang shooting?"

"Not just a gang shooting. You remember a guy named Bernard Goetz, don't you? Well, think bigger. Think four dead gang bangers. It's all you are going to hear about for months. Dark alley. Two blocks east of the Bergen Street Station, near Barclay Center. Do you know how many tourists go to events at Barclay Center? Get here quick."

Tony hung up the phone and looked down at the table top. Before he could even turn around, he knew it was going to happen again.

He could feel Alecia standing not two feet behind him. He knew she had her hands on her hips and the most disgusted look he could imagine. He could feel the heat from her stare. Finally, she spoke, in what could only be described as a full Brooklyn boil. "You're going to do it again, aren't you? I swear, Tony, if you do it again, I'll be gone when you get back!"

He could mouth the words by memory, he'd heard them many times before from different girlfriends. How many would this be since he became a Detective Sergeant?

Five? Six? Trouble was, he really liked Alecia and thought it would be different this time. He swore the next time he'd stand up to the Lieutenant when he said, '*Sorry, Tony, but you're the best I've got. It has to be you. No one else is good enough.*'

But he knew himself, too. And he knew, if this was going to be big, he wanted 'in'. Somewhere out there, in a dark alley between Bergen Station and Prospect Heights, there was 'action' to be had and enjoyed, and, like the lead wolf in the pack, he had to answer his own 'call of the wild', and he knew, just like the others, Alecia would be gone when he returned.

"Baby, I'll make it up to you, I swear. The Lieutenant says this is going to be big, and he needs me."

"Did you ever think that, just once, someone else might need you, too? Or that someday you are going to need someone else?"

Tony stammered a moment.

"See?" She threw her arms up into the air, turned and walked into the bathroom and slammed the door. Tony quickly grabbed his clothes from the bedroom and walked toward the door with his shoes still in his hand.

Through the bathroom door Alicia yelled, "I mean it, Tony. If you go through that door, I'm gone."

He eased the door open and slowly and quietly closed it behind him. He slipped on his pants in the hallway, and his shoes as he walked, and, halfway down the hallway, he heard the loud crashing sound of one of his belongings breaking against the back side of the door.

"I hate this shit," he said as he hurried toward the elevator as if drawn by some invisible force, but his mind was thinking, "I wonder what I'll find when I get there?"

CHAPTER 32

Back in their motel room, Ryan and Peter turned on the television and scanning the news channels. Finally, the 11:00 pm news had a 'breaking news' lead-in about the murders, including speculation that they appeared to be in self-defense, or vigilante style murders.

At 11:35, they switched to the Tonight show.

"And now, here's Jay Leno!" As Jay came out onto the stage, a number of the audience members crowded around to shake his hand or give him a high five.

"Look Peter. There she is. She did it."

Peter jumped off the couch to get a better look. There was Elizabeth, shaking Leno's hand and glancing over her shoulder toward the camera and smiling, as if she knew Ryan and Peter would be watching. Considering the time zone changes, she now had an indisputable perfect alibi.

"You are a genius, Ryan. I'm with a fucking Rambo genius!"

CHAPTER 33

Tony Delarosa stooped under the crime scene tape in one smooth motion, demonstrating he'd done this a hundred times before. Without breaking stride, he flashed his badge at the patrolman who was rapidly heading him off. "Okay, sir," the patrolman said and returned back to his post.

Delarosa carefully made his way to the middle of the crime scene, careful not to disturb even one of the many expended cartridges littering the ground. He looked around, surrounded by dead bodies on the ground. "This was done by pros," he said to Detective Lieutenant O'Reilly, who approached. "It is certainly not a gang shooting. Too well planned and well executed. Almost Mafia-like."

"Well executed, you say. Good police work, Delarosa. I knew there was a reason I called you out," acknowledged Lt. O'Reilly.

"We'll talk about that later. Any survivors?"

"Yeah. He's in that squad car over there. Singing like a bird."

"Then what's the problem? Should be simple to wrap up."

"If it was that simple, you'd be home shagging that hot new girlfriend you've been bragging about. It's getting complicated."

"I'm afraid you blew it for me with Alecia. One too many call-outs. She'll be gone when I get back."

"Probably for the better. I know you, Tony. She'd been around too long, and you were probably getting tired of her anyhow."

Delarosa shot a stern look at O'Reilly. "What do we have so far?"

"Depends on which version you want. Witnesses at the south end of the alley heard a bunch of gunshots and when they looked out, they saw a black man in a dark jacket running out of the alley yelling he'd been shot and running down the street westbound. Some thought he might have been limping, one thought he was holding his arm like it was shot. Witnesses at the other end of the alley saw a white man, nicely dressed, walk out of the alley with a briefcase, stride casually but quickly down the block and disappear into the night."

Tony looked at O'Reilly, "He could be a well-armed and well-trained vigilante, and one of the guys was just wounded and got away, or maybe the white guy just witnessed the shooting and got the hell out of there."

O'Reilly continued, "Then there is Reggie's side of the story."

"Reggie?"

"The surviving robber in the squad car."

"Wait a minute. What's he even doing here? Why didn't he run away like every other young punk would have done?"

"Good question. When the cops arrived, he gives up, hands them all the guns at the scene and describes the shooter as a lone businessman they followed off the subway. They tried to rob him, only he turns around and shoots them all, except Reggie. Reggie says he was a thin white man, at least 6'4" or more with a big scar on his cheek. He says he was like a military special forces guy, Bam, bam, bam, everyone is dead and only one of them got a wild shot off."

"Why isn't Reggie dead? What else did he say?"

"Yeah, get this. He tells the officer that the shooter didn't kill him, walks over to him and tells him to stay here and tell the cops they should have the lab compare the guns against all the unsolved murders and shootings in the area."

"Sounds like revenge. What does the scene tell us so far?"

"Reggie is right. The shooter has obviously had some tactical training. He knew what he was doing. He lured them into exactly the location they would have chosen for the robbery. When he went into action, all of his shots were dead on, all 'kill shots'. Casings on the ground are all .40 caliber."

"Wait a minute. What about the black man running down the street yelling that he'd been shot?"

"Reggie says no-one escaped, and no-one else got shot. He says it didn't happen, the witnesses said it did. Maybe it was unrelated. Anyway, there's no blood trail like you'd expect if the guy was shot."

"Maybe the witnesses got it wrong or misunderstood the guy yelling. Seems if someone else was shot, we'd have gotten a call on that one by now, too." He pondered the information he'd been given. "Reggie. Something not quite right about Reggie's story."

"I agree. But everything else he said seems to have been borne out by facts, evidence, and witnesses."

"Okay, that's quite a bit to start with. We should be able to wrap this up. A military-ops trained vet with a big scar for his troubles, probably brags about vigilante justice, likely lives in this general area, and we've got a good description. He's interested in previous murders in the area, probably a previous victim, a relative of a victim, or a witness to one. As for the running black man, have a patrolman check all the hospitals tonight for a gunshot victim, and we'll have someone check all doctors' offices in Bed-Stuy tomorrow morning. I think we'll have the guy before the press can blow this vigilante thing out of proportion.

CHAPTER 34

The next morning, Ryan and Peter walked down to the Deli Llama and sat down to breakfast. Picking up the paper, they were surprised to see the murders were already on the front page.

VIGILANTE MURDERS NEAR BERGEN STATION

Four young men, whom police described as young thugs who apparently preyed on subway riders on the Red Line #2 near Bergen Station, were gunned down, reportedly by a single gunman in a deserted alley near the Subway Station. Police say five as yet unidentified well-armed street robbers lured the man into a dark alley with the intent to rob him, but the victim apparently got the drop on them and shot four of them in a shootout. The unidentified shooter, or shooters, escaped into the night, apparently unharmed.

A fifth would be robber witnessed the murders and survived by hiding behind a dumpster nearby. In an odd circumstance, police report that the fifth alleged robber did not flee and was waiting for police when they arrived. He gave himself up and admitted details of the planned heist, and gave police the shooter's description;

a white man, thin, very tall, at least 6' 4", black hair with a scar across his cheek, and wearing a dark coat.

Other witnesses, who saw a man they believed to be the shooter walk from the scene, didn't remember him as being that tall, but their perspective was from a second story window. Additionally, a black man seen running from the scene, yelling for help, was originally thought to be a person of interest, but it appears he has been ruled out by the surviving robber.

Police Detectives on the scene recovered at least three handguns from the dead robbers, and hope to use them for comparison to previous unsolved murders and assaults in the same vicinity by gang members matching the description.

Only two years ago, a Bed-Sty businessman, Travis Hartman, was the last person murdered under similar circumstances in the same alley. That case has never been solved.

"I do all the work, and you get the credit," Ryan mocked, as he handed the article to Peter.

"It's too bad Elizabeth can't see this this morning. It won't get a mention in California."

As if on cue, the disposable cell phone #1 rang. It was Elizabeth. "It's me. I'm on a cash only pay phone miles from my hotel room. I have to tell you, 'Thank You.' I'm walking on air this morning. I know Travis is giving us a thumbs up with a big smile from heaven. Fox News is all over it this morning, even out here. Apparently, the New York talk radio shows are going crazy on this. They say it's better than Bernie Goetz, and they are hoping no-one ever gets caught. Some callers are saying this is how a neighborhood watch should work."

"Wow. Even in Los Angeles? Now listen, the press will be calling you, Elizabeth. They've already mentioned a possible connection between the gang and Travis. Be careful what you say. Don't overdo it. Remember that the police will probably want to talk to you also. The less said, the better."

"Got it. I know Peter is a disguise genius, but how did he turn his little five-nine body into six feet four inches tall?"

"Long story. Gotta go, now. My phone marked Phone Number 1 will be destroyed and is out of service."

Turning to Peter, he said, "I have a plane to catch, and you have a long drive ahead of you. Don't forget: Don't get caught speeding or on a red light camera where you aren't supposed to be. Drive extra careful, and don't forget to re-connect the odometer about fifty miles out of D. C. on the trip back. Since we got lucky the first night, enjoy the rest of the Orioles' home stand against the Angels. And try to get on camera again."

On the way to the airport, they stopped behind a deserted riverside warehouse, wiped down and dismantled their handguns, throwing the parts into the East River, their gloves and clothing went into a double black garbage bag. They poured in a bottle of bleach and fish oil fertilizer to dissuade anyone from claiming them from the trash, and threw them into a dumpster at the curb behind a busy Chinese restaurant. Ryan removed the battery and SIMM card from the phone, drove their car over it, crushing it, and scattered the pieces into yet another dumpster.

Peter then drove Ryan to the airport, dropped him off outside, and began the road trip back to Washington, D.C.

Before the flight home to L.A., Peter memorized the key points of the box scores from the Wednesday night Orioles game, in case anyone asked about it.

As Lufthansa Flight 96 took off for Munich, Germany, Ryan, as Hans Wasserman, sat back in his First Class seat.

"Hello, Mr. Wassermann, did you enjoy your stay in New York?" asked the flight attendant.

"It was a little hectic at times, but I accomplished everything I'd hoped to. Now I'm just happy to be heading back home."

"What can I get for you to drink?"

"What German beers do you have?"

"Beck's and Warsteiner Pils."

"I'll have a Warsteiner Pils. I've been drinking nothing but watered down American beers and now it's time for a real beer."

"Very well. I'll be right back with it."

CHAPTER 35

Dr. Stan leaned against the wall watching the attendees intermingle at the Sunday night welcome reception. He was quite pleased with himself as the group neared the end of the seven-week course. Each of the group had appeared to make great strides in their quest for acceptance or forgiveness.

He began to walk around the room engaging the attendees in casual conversation when he overheard a woman speaking to another in the group, "I've been hearing a lot in the news about that vigilante who gunned down four robbers in an alley in New York near a subway. I shouldn't feel good about murder, but isn't that cool. I wish someone would have done the same to the dirtbag who killed my boyfriend, Lonnie."

"Do you think they were the same robbers who killed Elizabeth's husband? Wasn't he murdered near the subway in New York?"

"New York is a very big city. I'm sure they aren't related or Elizabeth would be high-fiving everyone."

"I hadn't thought about that," Dr. Stan thought. *"Both murders were in Bedford-Stuyvesant. I wonder if Elizabeth has put the possibility together?"*

He walked over to where Elizabeth was standing, chatting with another client. "Elizabeth, may I have a word with you?"

"Sure, Dr. Stan."

"Can we step over here," he motioned as he walked about ten feet away from the crowd. "Say, Elizabeth, I've been hearing about that vigilante who shot those robbers in New York. Do you think they are the same ones who killed Travis?"

"Absolutely. I'm sure of it. I've been following the story all week, and it looks like the same descriptions, same location, everything matches. I'm sure it was them, and I shouldn't say so, but I'll be thrilled if it turns out to be them."

"Have you called the police to tell them your thoughts, or to ask them if they think so too?"

"No, I haven't. I understand they have already put some of it together. There is nothing I could add."

"I'd think if you thought the killers of your husband were gunned down in a similar situation, you'd be jumping up and down about it."

"I'll bet she is, inside," said Ryan as he walked up and interjected himself into the conversation. "I think she's just more subdued than someone else might be. Excuse me for interrupting your conversation. She was just telling me a few minutes ago how happy she is that maybe the assholes, --- excuse me --- the alleged robbers, seem to have gotten their just dues. I know the relief of knowing that the killer of your loved one is not going to be out there to hurt anyone else. You want to jump up and down, but it is a human life, and you have to temper your happiness or you might appear to be … shall we say, ghoulish. Right Dr. Stan?"

"Yes, Ryan, I suppose that's true. If so, then you two are very fortunate to have shared that mutual joy. I'm happy for both of you. We've never had anything like this happen during a retreat. That will be a particularly good topic for the opening discussion in the morning."

"By the way, what did you do over the week off, Ryan?"

"Actually, it was an eventful week for me. I flew to Munich and went to Oktoberfest with my German cousin."

"Munich? Germany? Wow. That's quite a trip for a short vacation."

"Well, as you know, I'm single now, and I have a lot on my mind, so any distraction is welcome. I'm sure you've heard of Octoberfest? Europe's biggest party? I'm just trying to adjust to the new 'forgiveness and get on with your life' lifestyle you are teaching us about."

"You are certainly getting into the concept. Belize? Munich? Very interesting. Now if you'll excuse me, I need to spend some time mingling with the other guests."

"Sure," said Ryan.

Once Dr. Stan was out of hearing range, Elizabeth said, "Thanks, Ryan. He caught me by surprise. How am I supposed to act?"

"Innocent. At all times, innocent."

After a few minutes with the other guests, Dr. Stan stood off to the side and contemplated the conversation which had just occurred. He noticed Ryan exchange pleasantries with Peter, then leave the room a short time later. A short time later Elizabeth slipped out the side door.

"Ryan and Elizabeth. They seem to be friendly, but not openly so. Strange. Ryan's daughter's killer is murdered, possibly a female was involved, while he is on a dive trip in

Belize. Now, Elizabeth's husband's murderers are gunned down by a trained killer, while she is on national TV in Los Angeles and Ryan says he was in Germany. I wonder if he has witnesses to back him up. The alibis are perfect. Maybe too perfect. I wonder ..."

Meanwhile, Ryan, Peter, and Elizabeth met in Ryan's darkened room and went over the weekend murders, and began to plan the next, and final murder of T-Rex.

Outside the room, they couldn't see Dr. Stan walk up the pathway and pause outside the small veranda near the room. He heard Elizabeth laugh from inside the room, so he stood there for quite some time, trying to discern the conversation from inside. He could hear Ryan's voice and Elizabeth's voice, but couldn't make out what was being said.

After a few minutes in vain, Dr. Stan gave up and moved further down the path and sat in the dark, waiting. Soon, the sliding door opened and he heard Elizabeth say, "Good night," as she slipped out of the sliding door and began the walk to her own cabin. She glanced back at the path behind her and turned back to find herself almost face to face with Dr. Stan, who was now standing directly in front of her in the shadows on the pathway.

"Hello, Elizabeth."

"Aaack," she screamed in surprise. Regaining her composure and breath, she said, "Dr. Stan, you startled me. What are you doing here?" Her voice was louder than normal, loud enough she hoped, that Ryan or Peter could hear from his cabin.

Ryan heard the scream and peered out of the doorway and saw the two shadows on the pathway. He held up his arm to prevent Peter from exiting the door also.

"I was just out for a stroll, Elizabeth. It's such a nice night for a stroll, isn't it?"

"Yes. Yes, it is." She wasn't sure if Dr. Stan saw her leave Ryan's apartment, so she decided to play it safe. "I thought I'd walk down to the edge of the property and see the moon."

"Is that Ryan's cabin?"

"Uh, yes, I believe it is."

"Well," Dr. Stan said. "I didn't realize you two had developed such a close bond, but now I see …"

"Please, sir, don't mention it to the others. We've tried so hard to keep our little affair a secret."

"Affair? Oh. Yes. Well, we do encourage our attendees to get to know each other and to use each other for support …That's funny. Actually, I thought … oh never mind; it was a silly thing."

"What?"

"It was just … I thought … never mind. I'd better get on my way. Good night, Elizabeth, and don't worry. Your secret is safe with me."

Back in the room, Ryan had been listening and breathed a sigh of relief. "Quick thinking on her part. Our affair. Boy, Peter, I'm glad it wasn't you that got caught leaving."

They both laughed, then Peter said, "I'm not convinced that encounter wasn't planned. We need to be careful about Dr. Stan. He is on to something."

"I think you may be right."

After a few minutes Peter slipped out the door and went to his room.

For the remainder of the week, they used the charade of the affair to their advantage. Peter would secretly slip into the room early, while Dr. Stan was occupied, then Elizabeth would enter the room a little later. After going over the plot for the last murder, upon leaving, Elizabeth would leave first and be a lookout for Peter's exit.

During the daytime, Elizabeth, in particular, was under the watchful eyes of Dr. Stan, who enjoyed winking at Elizabeth knowingly every time she left the room or cafeteria.

CHAPTER 36

Even though Dr. Stan was now convinced of an affair between Ryan and Elizabeth, he got up every morning with one troubling thought on his mind. He couldn't shake the fact that Ryan and Elizabeth, who seemed to hardly acknowledge each other for the months before he caught them together, seemed, in retrospect, all too familiar with each other now. He wondered how he had missed it, and how long it had been going on. The affair obviously didn't begin that night; it had to have been in place weeks before. And then there was the other, unshakable, coincidence: the murders of their loved one's murderers. It was too curious to be happenstance, and he didn't know how the pieces might fall in place, but he felt compelled to share his suspicions.

And besides, he figured, if there was something to his hunch, there might be a huge story and some free national publicity in it for himself.

On Friday morning, he couldn't stand it anymore. He pulled a business card out of his desk drawer, reached for the phone, and dialed the number of Santa Rosa Homicide Detective Delfina Lawler.

"Detective Lawler," said the voice on the phone.

"Detective Lawler, this is Dr. Stan from the Forgiveness Retreat. Do you recall that we talked about Ryan Foster and the murder of that gangster who killed his daughter?"

"Of course, I do. How are you, Doctor? Do you have something for me?"

"Nothing specific, but I don't know. Is your case still unsolved?"

"Yes."

"Did you say there was a woman involved?"

"Actually, we don't know that for sure. He was apparently distracted by a flirtatious woman, described as a 'hippie-type' with big breasts, just before he died. We have found nothing to pursue in this case. We are at a dead end, so we'd just like to identify her and talk to her as a 'person of interest'. Do you have someone you suspect?"

"Suspect? No. But there is a curious thing going on here. We have an attendee named Elizabeth Hartman whose husband was murdered by a gang in New York City. Well, she and Ryan have certainly 'hit it off' recently, if you know what I mean."

"Yes, I think I know what you mean. Continue."

"Here's the curious part. Ryan's daughter's killer was murdered, in your case, and a woman might be involved, and wouldn't you know it, Elizabeth's husband's murderers, four of them, were murdered in New York City this last week by a robbery victim or a vigilante; a white man who got the drop on them and killed four of them before they could shoot him."

"Whoa, that is a big coincidence, isn't it? I've been watching that developing story out of New York out of curiosity, but didn't know about the connection with Ryan's girlfriend. Hmmm. Ryan is known to be a crack shot. Tell me more about Elizabeth Hartman."

"I can tell you now, Detective, Elizabeth doesn't come close to the description you give. She's a very proper professional businesswoman, and she isn't that well-endowed, either.

"Well, they can do a lot with disguises and makeup nowadays, doc."

"Disguises? Did you say disguises?"

"Yes, why?"

"Something else just occurred to me. Let me tell you about this other fellow going through the Retreat. In fact, you probably already know his name, Peter Levenson."

"Peter Levenson? Isn't that the guy whose kid was killed by that famous football player who beat the murder charges?"

"Yes, but that's not half of it. He is also a famous design and make-up artist from Hollywood, and ...," he paused for effect, "he has gotten friendly at the retreat with both Ryan and Elizabeth."

"No frickin' way."

CHAPTER 37

Detective Sergeant Tony Delarosa cruised effortlessly into the Office of Detectives, twenty minutes late, which was actually early for him. The open center of the Detective squad room was crowded with desks and the din of twenty phone conversations at once filled every nook and cranny of the room, which must have been quite elegant when it was built in 1959, but it was a dirt infested pigpen by today's standards. Private glass-walled offices of the Chief of Detectives, Lieutenant O'Reilly, and a dozen or more Sergeants and senior Detectives surrounded the open area.

"Tony," a clerk said when she saw him. The chief and lieutenant are waiting for you in the conference room. He said to get you in there as soon as you walk into the door. Must be big, there's some FBI with him, and a dike detective from California. Get in there and find out what's going on."

Tony walked into the room while the conversation was already underway. Detective Bureau Chief Gerald Moran and Lt. O'Reilly were seated on one side of the long table, while opposite them were two 'suits' – obviously federal officers, - he guessed they were FBI, and seated alone on the same side was Santa Rosa Police Detective Lawler, who wore a dark blue business suit. Her short-cropped hair and the scowl on her brow told him she was probably the aforementioned California Detective.

One of the 'suits' was speaking as Tony slid into the seat next to O'Reilly.

"... the governor sees the potential of this vigilante mania growing out of control, and he has asked the President to help him 'nip it in the bud'. So, we are here to assist you in any way possible. Right now there are just the two of us assigned, but we can get more if needed."

Delarosa held up his hand in a half wave, "And you are?"

"FBI Supervising Agent Eric Chilcote, and this is my partner, Agent Jim Logan."

Chief Moran spoke up, "Agent Chilcote, NYPD has handled these types of high profile cases before, remember Bernie Goetz and Son of Sam? And I have every confidence in Lieutenant O'Reilly and Sergeant Delarosa, here, and I think we can handle this one too. We appreciate the FBI's generous offer, but ..."

"Chief, I assure you Agent Logan and I would like to be working closer to home and working on our own caseload, but, maybe you didn't hear me; President Obama, and your Governor, have directed us to be here. Here's the bottom line for the President and your Governor. It's been over a week since the murders, and you have no suspects. As you were saying, it's happened before in New York and there has already been two more 'vigilante' type murders in the region. It appears that with the news media making these guys - and it looks like three unrelated killers, so far - with the media making these guys out to be heroes, there will certainly be more. Here's the bottom line; vigilantes killing street thugs, guess what minority is getting killed? Four black youths killed by a white vigilante in the streets of New York ... Do you think President Obama is not going to get involved?"

Agent Logan picked up the conversation on cue, "Reverend Al Sharpton and Jesse Jackson are here already to feast on the publicity and stir up the black communities. We, you and us, have to stop this before New York is portrayed as the KKK north. Let's work together on this."

"Okay," said the Chief, "We'll give it a try. But we work together as an NYPD task force, share all information, and when an arrest is made, we do it together, not like you guys usually do, where you jump in and take the credit. Any information you hold back from us, and your desks will be cleaned out for you. Agreed?"

"Yes." Chilcote reached his hand across the table to shake hands with the Chief.

"I have a question," Delarosa said.

"Go ahead, Tony," said Moran.

"Who is this young lady?" he said, motioning to Detective Lawler, who cringed at the description.

"Before she could speak, Agent Chilcote said, "Excuse me. This is Detective Delfina Lawler, she is the lead Detective on a case in Santa Rosa, California, that may be connected. Ms. Lawler, why don't you tell these men what you have."

"Very well, sir. But first, I don't like 'Ms.'. Or ma'am. I'm a Detective just like you all, and I'd prefer to be called Detective Lawler."

Delarosa looked at O'Reilly, who looked down and rolled his eyes. Delarosa scratched at his temple to hide a look of consternation. "R-i-g-h-t," he said, dragging the word out for several seconds."

"I'll start at the beginning," she said. Shooting a quick glance at Delarosa, she continued, "and I'll talk slow. Danny Lemos, my murder victim, is a dirtbag gang member from our town who raped and murdered CHP Lieutenant Ryan Foster's 17-year-old daughter. Foster tried to kill Lemos but was stopped by the Mendocino Sheriff's Office. Foster was going to lose his job with the Highway Patrol, but he got a reprieve if he attended a 'Forgiveness Retreat' put on in Colorado by renowned Psychologist Dr. Stan Berkeley."

"Isn't he that wacko fake Doctor on TV who claims to be able to solve every ailment known to man? I think 'renowned' might be a little stretch," Delarosa said.

"He's a real doctor and is highly respected for his work. But he's not the point here."

Delarosa turned to O'Reilly and whispered loud enough for all to hear, "Berkeley? I got five bucks that's not even his real name; he probably picked it from the college."

"University," Lawler corrected Delarosa. "Berkeley is a University, not a College."

"Whatever," said Delarosa.

"I don't care if it is his real name or not. Can I continue with the story?"

"Can we fast forward to the part where it has something to do with our case?"

"I'll get to that. Ryan Foster is a suspect in the murder of the punk who raped and killed his daughter, in Santa Rosa."

"Do you have evidence or witnesses or anything that puts him at the crime scene?"

"No, actually he has a foolproof alibi. He was diving in Belize."

"But you still think he did it?"

"He may have orchestrated it, while he had a perfect alibi."

"Wait. And we are here talking about this California murder because ...?"

"Dr. Stan has developed a theory that there is a good chance Ryan Foster may be the shooter in your vigilante case, and the cases are connected."

"Do tell? Go on. I want to hear more about how you're going to pin the murder of the dirtbag who raped and murdered his daughter on Foster, while he was on a Caribbean vacation. Then I can hardly wait to hear how you've connected him with the subway murders in New York. Then, if that doesn't work, there's always the Boston Strangler murders. They've never been officially solved, either."

Lawler looked imploringly at the Chief in an effort to shut Delarosa up, but Moran was actually enjoying the repartees, so he just said, "Well, that is kind of funny. We try to take ourselves less seriously than maybe you do out in California. Go ahead, tell us more of your theory, Detective Lawler."

"Okay, so I got a call from Dr. Stan the other day, and he says Foster appears to be having an affair with a woman at the Retreat who is also seeking counseling to get over her husband's murder. Her name is Elizabeth Hartman and her husband is Travis Hartman. Does his name sound familiar to you? They should. I understand his murder was your case, Delarosa, and now it's being tied to the 'vigilante' murders of the four youths who killed Travis. Here is where it gets interesting. Both Elizabeth and Ryan Foster each, conveniently, have elaborate perfect alibis for the time of the murders they are connected with. Dr. Stan thinks they might have done reciprocal murders for each other."

"You're here because a wacko TV Doctor, hungry for a ratings boost, told you he has a theory? Boy, sounds like you really bit at that lure. What about your own investigation? Do you have a suspect in the Lemos murder?"

"Not per se, but a woman of interest was seen with him shortly before he was poisoned."

"Where was he killed?"

"At a downtown Starbucks in Santa Rosa."

"Can I ask a clarifying question or two?" Delarosa asked, dipping his neck as a mocking gesture.

"Yes, sure."

"A dirtbag gets poisoned at a Starbucks, in front of, I presume, dozens of customers, and you find out he was talking to 'a woman'," Delarosa gestured with imaginary quote marks to illustrate his mockery of Lawler, "while he was in the Starbucks, and you immediately decide it must have been Ryan Foster's girlfriend from New York? That seems like a stretch. But I'm sure you have more evidence than that. Tell me she is at least a good match for the description of the murderer?"

Lawler took a deep breath. "No. Not exactly."

"What do you mean, 'not exactly'? I remember Elizabeth Hartman. What is the description of the woman who was seen talking to him?"

"She was described as young, shoulder length blonde hair, wearing tie-died clothing," then as if she knew she was serving up a huge mistake, she continued, "and she was described as having huge breasts that everyone was gawking at."

"And Ms. Hartman? You are right. I worked that case, and I seem to recall she was a well-to-do society-type.

Well-dressed to the nines, and hair impeccable. Have you actually seen Ms. Hartman, Ms., … Oops, … excuse me, Detective Lawler?"

"No, but a person can do wonders with makeup."

"Perhaps, but I'm not sure you can turn a 35 or 36 B-cup into a woman with huge, floppy breasts with makeup," Delarosa said.

The other men in the room chuckled at the picture Delarosa was painting with his hands as he spoke.

"Well, I've got a theory on that, too. Dr. Phil says there is a guy there at the Retreat who is a Hollywood makeup artist. And he is recovering from the murder of his son. You probably remember Peter Levenson, whose son was murdered by a sports star a few years ago."

"T-Rex. He was acquitted, - by a California jury, I might add - even though everyone knew he was guilty as sin," O'Reilly said, implying 'everybody knows that'.

"Uh oh, News Flash," Delarosa said. We better get an All-Points Bulletin out on T-Rex. They are probably gunning for him next."

"Interesting," said Chilcote. It certainly is a possibility, Detective, and when Delarosa takes a breath he will probably admit it too. Reciprocal murders involving perfect alibis for the people who would otherwise be the prime suspects for the crimes."

"Maybe someone has been watching too much television," Delarosa muttered.

"What is the description of the vigilante murderer, Detective?" Chilcote asked.

"Most people saw a white man leave the alley on one end, but some saw a black man leave the alley on the other end. The white man was described as at least 6'4" by the person who saw him best. How tall is Foster?"

Lawler looked at her notes, "His driver's license shows him to be 5'11" even."

"Well, you know, they can do wonders with makeup nowadays," Delarosa said to loud laughter ... from everyone – except Lawler and Agent Chilcote.

Chilcote came to Lawler's defense. "I think Dr. Stan might have an interesting point, Delarosa. Your killer acted with military precision, the reports say. Well, Ryan Foster is an expert marksman, and he's been police trained. It's a good enough lead that when Detective Lawler called me, we agreed to follow up on it, so we brought her here to talk to you about the possible connection."

Chief Moran spoke up. "So you want to put a career cop away for killing his daughter's murderer?" After pausing just long enough for that thought to sink in, he continued. "You don't like Foster, on a personal basis, do you Lawler?"

"No, not really. We didn't hit it off too well in our first meeting."

"Imagine that," Delarosa said, pushing his chair back and looking up for emphasis.

"He was very cocky and arrogant," Lawler continued. Then, looking directly at Delarosa, she said, "If he's guilty, I don't care if he's a cop or not."

"Nor do I, and nor does the FBI," Moran said. "But, let me tell you this. If you're going to hang a murder on a cop in my task force, you'll need iron clad evidence, and lots of it. I'm not going on a cop witch hunt just for your pleasure. And the same goes for your search for the mystery woman. What kind of follow-up have you done on your end to see if they were even in the areas to commit the crimes?"

"None, yet. I'm just presenting it as a theory. I'll be happy to interview Ms. Hartman in connection with my crime, and I think you should interview Ryan Foster in connection with yours."

"Wait a minute. 'Ms.' Hartman? I thought you didn't like 'Ms.'?" Delarosa interrupted.

"It is fine for others; I don't like it for me," she said, staring at him over her reading glasses. "Other than that, did you understand the rest of the conversation?"

"I'm just curious. How come you, of all people, get to interview the woman with the big cha-chas?"

"Me? 'Of all people'? What are you getting at, Detective? Do you have a problem with…?"

Agent Chilcote interrupted the conversation. "I think it is worth a try. I'll be happy to interview Mr. Foster about his whereabouts during the vigilante murders. Elizabeth Hartman lives here in New York, why don't you and Detective Lawler interview Ms. Hartman together, Delarosa?"

"Oh, no …," Delarosa protested.

O'Reilly smirked and jumped in and said, "Great idea. Tony, you two can do that today."

Delarosa cringed and glared at O'Reilly, who could hardly contain his amusement at the pair working together. Lawler grimaced from her end of the table.

"What do we have on the other vigilante murders?" Chilcote said.

"The copycat murders are being worked by other precincts and appear to be just that; copycats, and not very good ones at that. Ours was like a military operation. The Detectives working the other cases say they are more one on one, sloppy shootings, evidence left behind, different descriptions, etc. They have suspects in mind and hope to make arrests soon."

"As for our vigilante murders, forensics show the handguns carried by the gang members were involved in over a half dozen cold case gang shootings in Bed-Stuy and vicinity, dating back to 2007, another murder during a robbery like Travis', and two liquor store robberies where shots were fired."

"Relevant to our case, the autopsies on the bodies from the scene show three different weapons were fired. Most were from north to south and deadly accurate from a .40 caliber; cartridges were all over the scene."

"One wild .38 caliber shot was removed from the wall in the north end of the alley, a south to north shot which matches one of the gang members' weapons. The other gang members' guns hadn't been fired at the scene."

"One of the deceased gangbangers had two .38 caliber slugs in him in addition to two .40 caliber slugs. The Forensics Pathologist thinks the .38 slugs were fired from a different angle into the perp's back while he was on the ground. That means, gentlemen, there may have been a second shooter."

O'Reilly interjected, "Which the surviving gang member says is wrong. He insists there was just the one shooter he described."

"Maybe the shooter had a second, backup weapon."

"Or the black man seen running away from the scene?"

"One white man, 6'4", and a black man around 5'11" or 6'0"."

"Speaking of that, did he ever turn up at a hospital?"

"No. And we looked in every borough and in Jersey. Also, we found no blood along the sidewalk he was supposed to have ran down. Both disappeared like ghosts into the night."

CHAPTER 38

It was early afternoon when Detectives Delarosa and Lawler arrived at their appointment with Elizabeth Hartman. As they got out of the car, Delarosa said, "No shit. You got a pan head? What year? You got a picture?"

For the next few minutes, they were standing on the street leaning against their undercover car sharing photos of Harley Davidson motorcycles like a couple grandparents bragging about their grandchildren.

"Maybe you are okay. You ride a Harley, after all," said Delarosa.

"Yeah, and maybe you're not such a hetero dirtbag after all, yourself."

"Don't bother coming on to me like that, lady, you still aren't my type."

"I'm not sure what type that would be. Have you tried the Bronx zoo?"

"Let's go do our job."

As they walked up the steps to the expensive townhouse, only a few blocks from the deserted alley where Travis Hartman had been murdered two years earlier, and where the four youths suspected of the crime were themselves murdered only a week ago, Elizabeth Hartman opened the door before they rang the doorbell.

"Please, come in, she said." Turning to Delarosa, "I remember you Detective Delarosa, from Travis' murder. Thank you for accommodating my job schedule today. It is always a hectic time catching up every other week."

"Yes ma'am," he said, seizing the opportunity to take a verbal jab at Lawler, he said, "It's okay to call you ma'am, isn't it?"

"Of course. It is actually polite; why would I mind?"

Delarosa glanced at Lawler, who shot a stern look back at him.

"No reason. This is Detective Lawler from California. We had some questions regarding the shooting of your husband and, I'm sure you have read in the papers about the recent shooting of four young men suspected of being the shooters in your husband's death."

"Yes, I heard about it when I was in California. I just returned from there on a short vacation. I've been out of town

227

for most of three weeks. Last week they had me kind of sequestered, so I was only aware some men were shot near our subway station. I didn't know there was a connection to Travis' shooting until yesterday when I read some of the last week's newspapers. Have they made a positive connection?"

"We're ninety percent sure, ma'am."

"Good. What do you need from me, then?"

"Actually, as you probably know, the shooter hasn't been caught, and he's being hailed as a vigilante, or some kind of Don Quixote hero or something. We're contacting everyone we could find who had been a victim, or spouse of a victim, to ascertain if they know anything about the latest shooting. We have some indications it might have been a revenge shooting."

"Really? And ... and you think I might have had something to do with it? I'm not losing sleep over them being killed, Detective, but I had nothing to do with it, if that's what you think. Besides, don't they have a description of the shooter?"

"Of course, you couldn't have done it. But we're asking previous victims and families where they were when the shootings occurred."

"Well, let's see. That was last Tuesday night or Wednesday night, wasn't it? Either way I was in Los Angeles on vacation."

"Timely," Lawler said barely audibly, as she looked out of the big picture window overlooking the tree-lined parkway.

"Excuse me?" asked Elizabeth glancing at Lawler's back.

"Excuse my partner, she's new in town. It was Wednesday night, ma'am."

"Wednesday night? Oh, yes. I was in the studio audience for the Jay Leno show in Hollywood. Did you really think I could kill four young strong men, Detective Delarosa?"

"No, ma'am."

"I suppose one of their victims could have hired someone, is that what you think?"

"No, ma'am. We just have to ask a few questions. I think we're done now, right partner?"

"Almost," Lawler interjected. "Where were you on September 9th of this year?"

"When?"

"September 9, 2013, it was a Monday."

"I don't recall. I'd have to check my calendar. Why?"

"We'll wait," said Lawler.

Elizabeth frowned. Delarosa was being appropriately cordial, but she could see the contempt in Lawler's piercing glare. "Sure," she said, as she turned around and picked up her cell phone. She looked at the calendar and calculated that it was the day Danny Lemos was killed. She was shocked and puzzled that Lawler had pulled that date out of the air, and was glad her back was to the Detectives, in case her surprise and concern showed. She took a deep breath and turned around. "September 9th," she said as she walked casually back to them. Addressing Lawler, she said, "Why do you ask about that particular date? Excuse me, who did you say you are, and where are you from again?"

"I'm a Detective from Santa Rosa, California. I'm investigating another crime on that date. Did you find out where you were?"

Turning to Delarosa, she said, "I'm a little confused. We were talking about Travis' murder, then we got sidetracked about the other murders, the 'vigilante' murders, I think the paper called them, and now I'm being questioned about an unrelated crime in California? What kind of crime do you think I committed in Santa Wherever, California?"

"Can you answer the question?" Lawler demanded.

"Of course I can, but before I answer any other questions, I think you need to tell me what this is about."

"I'm investigating a murder that happened in Santa Rosa on that date, and I want to know if you have an alibi for that time."

"You must be really new, Detective. Are you going all over the country demanding an alibi from everyone you meet? Why me? Do I fit the description of someone you are looking for?"

Delarosa jumped into the conversation. "Yes, Detective Lawler, does she meet the description of the woman you are looking for?" With that, he tacitly motioned with his hands cupped in front of him in what was clearly a reference to Elizabeth's breasts, which, although adequate and nicely proportioned, were certainly not the size of the woman believed to be a person of interest. "Why don't you remind us of the description of the female person of interest in your homicide?"

"Okay, she doesn't match the description exactly, but I don't understand why she won't answer the question."

"Doesn't exactly match?" Delarosa said, "Not exactly? Well, I guess for one, she's a woman. Actually, that's pretty much all she has in common with your person of interest, who actually might not even be involved."

Elizabeth looked back and forth at Delarosa and Lawler. "You two don't like each other, do you?" Before they could answer, she continued, "As to your question, Ms. Lawler, …"

Again, Lawler cringed at the 'Ms.' reference.

"… I find it intrusive and offensive. I resent your random intrusion into my business. But since you asked, …, if, hypothetically, of course, a young single woman, such as myself, decided to spend a few days at a seaside resort with a prominent married man who wouldn't want to be identified, is that automatically your business? Why don't you go knock on my neighbor's door and ask her if she has an alibi? She's a woman about my size. In fact, she's quite busty if that's what you are looking for."

Delarosa jumped up from the couch. "We are sorry to have offended you." He motioned for Lawler to follow. "We are done here, so we'll be leaving. Thank you for your time, ma'am."

After being escorted out the door, Tony started to walk toward their car, with Lawler following a close step behind. Without breaking stride, he said over his shoulder, "Well, I'd say that went pretty well, wouldn't you, ma'am?"

"Fuck you, Delarosa. You're a real asshole."

Delarosa laughed loudly all the way to the car.

CHAPTER 39

By the next morning, when Lawler arrived at the task force meeting, the story of the interview the night before had already been told to everyone's amusement. As they straightened up their papers on her arrival, it was obvious they had shared a good laugh at the expense of the inexperienced Detective.

Lieutenant O'Reilly said, "Good Morning, Detective Lawler. How did the interview go? Did you get the information you were looking for last night?"

"Not as well as hoped. Nevertheless, I still believe there is a possibility she is the mystery woman involved, but she wouldn't establish an alibi for us."

Delarosa rolled his eyes and shook his head side to side as he repeated the gesture with his hands cupped in front of him and snickered, and then Chief Moran and Lt. O'Reilly laughed. Agents Chilcote and Logan did not openly respond.

"You ever heard of makeup and costuming, Delarosa? Don't forget, one of the guys at the Forgiveness Retreat is a world class makeup artist."

"Looked to me like she did a pretty good job of putting on her own makeup," he said, raising his eyebrows to the other men.

Lieutenant O'Reilly spoke up. "Okay, gentlemen, … and lady … I mean Detectives … let's talk about what we are going to do moving forward. NYPD is going to continue to pursue the military angle in connection with every robbery and assault on the Red Line and A Train around Bergen and the entire Bed-Stuy line for the past four years. We've scoured the alley for prints and blood evidence. Forensics is working all angles. We've re-interviewed the witnesses and the papers have established a tip line. Maybe they'll turn up some new info."

Turning back to Lawler, he continued. "Lawler, I'll be blunt. You have an interesting theory. In fact, it would make a good Hollywood movie, but so far, we have NOTHING that would indicate the theory has legs. If you want to pursue your theory, maybe you need to go back to Dr. Stan and get some facts together to convince us it's more than a hypothetical theory. Good luck with your murder case. I'm not sure a dead dirtbag-gangster-rapist-murderer is worth the time you've already invested, but that's just my opinion, and you may not have the caseload we do."

Agent Chilcote spoke up. "At the FBI, we have learned a long time ago not to laugh off any theory that is even slightly plausible. Agent Logan and I will go to California and interview Foster about the crimes. This is a high national priority case, so we have all options at our disposal. We'll do some follow-up on his phone calls, texts, and maybe his e-mails to see if he keeps in contact with Ms. Hartman, and we'll look at her records also."

"So, all that shit is true about knowing everything we do," Delarosa asked.

"This vigilante thing is directly tied to national security", Chilcote said. "Can you imagine if people all over America started taking the law into their own hands?"

"We might not need as many prisons?" Delarosa responded, looking toward O'Reilly for approval.

"In New York, Detective, right now we are about one more high-profile vigilante murder spree away from being all the anarchy you can imagine, much less handle."

CHAPTER 40

Ryan Foster was bent over his putter, intently lining up his first opportunity for a par on the day, on the sixth hole at Cobb Mountain Golf Course, when his cell phone started playing the theme from the old 'Highway Patrol' TV show on his golf cart. He tried to ignore it, and softly stroked the ball toward the cup. Too softly, it turned out, and it rolled to a stop six inches short of the hole. *"Damn. That call just cost me a skin. I hope it was important."*

By the time he putted out and walked to his cart, the phone beeped, indicating that he had a new phone message. As he and his playing partner pulled their carts toward the seventh tee, he dialed the number to retrieve his voice mail.

"Lieutenant Foster, this is Agent Eric Chilcote with the FBI. Please call me at your earliest convenience. It is quite important. We need to meet with you and go over some details on a case we are working. Again, please call me at the cell phone number on your screen. Thank you and I look forward to meeting with you."

"The FBI! What would the FBI want with me? I covered all the bases in New York and Munich. Did

Elizabeth or Peter screw something up? Danny Lemos isn't worth the FBI's time, and the dirtbags in New York shouldn't involve the FBI. They would only get involved if they are looking at interstate crimes and criminals. We are guilty of an interstate conspiracy to commit murder, but how would they know? If they had anything, they'd be here arresting me now, not setting up a meeting. They've got to be just fishing."

Ryan's golf game went all to hell for the next twelve holes as he tried not to look worried, but couldn't get the FBI out of his mind. After the round of golf, he cancelled lunch with his playing partners and drove toward home. But his curiosity was too great, and he stopped at the first available wide spot in the road and called the number.

"Agent Chilcote," the voice said.

"Agent Chilcote, my name is Ryan Foster. I got a call from you a little while ago. It might have been a mistake. Did you mean to call me?"

"Yes, sir. We are looking into a mass murder that occurred in New York City about two weeks ago. Maybe you heard about it. Four young men, who had extensive criminal records, were gunned down in a dark alley by a man they were apparently attempting to rob. They are calling it a vigilante murder. Are you familiar with the case?"

Ryan swallowed hard. "Vaguely, from the news coverage on TV. What does that have to do with me?"

"Probably nothing. But we are acting on an anonymous tip that you are quite friendly with a woman whose husband was murdered, apparently by the same gang, a year earlier. Do you know the case I'm talking about?"

"Dr. Stan! That bastard," he thought. *"He put Elizabeth and I together, and must have told the FBI we might be involved in the murders. He probably tried to tie Elizabeth into the Lemos murder, also. Either way, that would be a conspiracy and qualify for FBI involvement."*

"Actually, Agent Chilcote, I wouldn't say we are 'quite friendly', but there is a case similar to that which I heard about recently. As you probably know from Dr. Stan, I am attending a Forgiveness Retreat to get over the murder of my daughter. There's a lady at the retreat whose husband was killed somewhere in New York City under circumstances similar to those you described."

"Elizabeth Hartman?"

"Yes, that's her name."

"So, we are following up on anyone who would have a motive to kill the street gang, and her name came up. Then there was this anonymous tipster who thought you might have a reason to help her commit such a murder. I know it sounds like a stretch, but, you're a cop, you know when we get these tips, we have to follow up. Would you be willing to meet with us so we can clear this up quickly and move on?"

"I think I know who your anonymous tipster is. It must be ratings season, and Dr. Stan, the TV Doctor, has quite an inflated imagination. We are in a class together, her husband's killers are murdered, and I own guns; of course it had to be me. I think he's been watching too many of his own reruns. But of course, we can meet and clear up his overactive imagination. By the way, when did those murders occur?"

Chilcote checked his notes. "September 25th."

"Well, I can make this easy for both of us. I was in Munich, Germany at Oktoberfest on that day. You ever been there?"

"No."

"It is the world's biggest street party. Fifteen days of beer, frauleins, more beer, more frauleins, and schnitzel. A half-million people every day. Unbelievable. You ought to go sometime."

"Can we meet tomorrow and look at your receipts and statements? That should clear it up quickly."

"Sure. Come by my house tomorrow at 10:00 AM. I'm sure the FBI already knows where I live."

"Yes. We do." Chilcote smiled, leaving Ryan wondering if he meant it proudly, or sheepishly.

CHAPTER 41

The doorbell rang at promptly 10:00 a.m.

Ryan opened the door and looked at the two men dressed in suits on the steps.

"Lieutenant Foster, I'm FBI Supervising Agent Eric Chilcote. This is Agent Jim Logan."

"Pleased to meet you both. Come on in." He took them directly through the living room and sat at the dining room table, on which three cups of hot black coffee were placed on placemats.

"There's milk and sugar if you are interested."

"No, thanks for me. Three cups. How did you know there would be a third person?"

"I've worked with the FBI before. If they think it's an important case, they always come in pairs."

"I didn't realize we were so transparent."

"Nothing personal. Just an observation."

"I see," Chilcote said coyly. "Do you think this is an important case, Lieutenant?"

"Call me, Ryan. Not to me, but I read up on the case last night. Reverend Al Sharpton and Jesse Jackson are both in New York City to fight over the media spotlight. It's not my first rodeo, gentlemen. I know you guys are jumping through hoops to put a lid on this and the other similar murders in the area, so they need a suspect. And, Dr. Stan never missed an opportunity for publicity either, so here you are."

"Very observant and cognitive. So, can you help us eliminate the tipster's imagination, Ryan."

"I can. Here are the originals of the flight receipts for my vacation in Munich from Sept 23 through the 28th. And here are photocopies of the hotel receipts in Schliersee, and here are a few photos with my Cousin from the trip. I've made photocopies of each for them, after you've had a chance to compare them to the originals. He laid the items in front of the men. As you can see, a person can't be on two continents at once."

"Perfect. Can we take these with us?"

"I'll keep the originals, but I made the copies for you."

"Thanks. If you don't mind, Agent Logan will compare them to the originals?"

"Certainly."

While Logan looked over the papers, Chilcote continued. "If I can change the topic, Ryan, please accept my condolences for the murder of your daughter."

"Thank you."

"Have you been following the Danny Lemos murder investigation?"

"Not at all. Someone hated him more than I did, and they did me a favor. To be honest with you, I'm afraid to ask about it. There is a Detective for the PD who really would love to pin the murder on me. I don't know why, but she can't believe I didn't do it, even though I proved I couldn't have."

"Would that be Santa Rosa Police Detective Lawler?"

"Yes. You've met her?"

"Yes. But you are apparently out of her crosshairs now. Now she's looking at Elizabeth Hartman as a person of interest, even though she was apparently 3,000 miles away from the crime scene."

Ryan tried not to look shocked at the mention of Elizabeth's name. "Elizabeth? Amazing. How in the world did Lawler ever come up with Elizabeth as a suspect?"

"Same anonymous tipster."

"The FBI is looking at Elizabeth for the Lemos murder? Seriously?"

"No, she isn't in our jurisdiction. It's a local case. Lawler's on her own on the Lemos case."

"Be careful. That's why I avoid her. She's dangerous."

"Have a nice day, Ryan. Thank you for this information."

As Ryan was showing them to the door, Chilcote turned at the foyer and said, "Oh, by the way, Lieutenant Ryan, I did have one other question."

Ryan smiled at the tactic. "Sure, Agent Columbo, go ahead."

"Columbo?"

"Surely you remember Lieutenant Columbo? On TV. Columbo? That was his patented technique. Just when the bad guy thought he was safe and let down his guard, Columbo would spring 'one more' pointed question at him to get his reaction. I used it myself on more than one occasion. Works great. You ought to try it. But I digress. You had a question you wanted to ask?"

"No. No, actually. I got caught up in your story and I forgot. I'm sorry to take up your time."

As they cleared the walkway in front of the house, Agent Logan, who had been silent the whole time, suddenly snickered and said, "Wow. That was pretty good. He out-Columbo'd us. This guy is going to be a tough one if he's involved."

"Hmmm," was all Chilcote said.

CHAPTER 42

Ryan arrived early for the Retreat that Sunday Night, then went looking to confront Dr. Stan. His secretary said he wasn't there and wouldn't be on campus until Tuesday. "He's doing a Good Morning America taping in New York, but he'll be here tomorrow."

Ryan stayed away from the Reception get together so he missed all the gossip about Dr. Stan's revelation about the 'mystery suspect', although several attendees speculated it must be Ryan.

Instead, Ryan went to his cottage and removed the washer from the faucet, which created a large leak that spilled onto the floor. He then called maintenance and arranged to be moved to another room for the week.

After moving into his new room, he went back outside and waited alongside the perimeter path outside Elizabeth's and Peter's rooms for their arrival. After a short cordial conversation, he advised them to meet him at the new room later that night.

When they convened for the evening, Ryan turned up the music channel on the TV, and they sat down and began to talk.

"What's with the loud music?" Elizabeth asked.

Ryan motioned for them both to lean closer.

"Let me start," Ryan said in a low voice, leaning toward the others, "We need to be very careful what we say around here from now on. We need to take a whole new approach to our planning and strategy discussions. Dr. Stan has begun to take a keen interest in our actions during retreat weeks. He is in constant contact with both Detective Lawler in Santa Rosa and FBI Agent Eric Chilcote, who is assigned the New York Vigilante Task Force. I believe it is possible that our rooms here might be bugged by the FBI. That is why I got my room changed for the week. We need to keep up our routine, so plan to meet as usual in my room each night. We might have to play Dominoes since we are probably monitored."

Peter began to look around nervously. "Bugged? Really? You think they are on to us that much?"

"Quiet, Peter."

"Oh, right. Sorry." Then, in a quiet voice, he whispered, "But, do you?"

"They are certainly pursuing the thought I am involved, but they don't seem to have you tied into the mix yet, so just be cool and we'll be okay. Remember, we are all in this together, and we have nothing to hide."

"Once we get home on Friday night, we'll use the single use phones to talk about future plans, but for this week, we don't give them anything to talk about; 10-4?"

"Oh, and I suggest you talk in a private place outside when you get back to your homes, which might also be bugged. It depends on how much they think each of us are involved."

"When do you think we'll move on the other guy?" Peter asked.

"We need to lay low for a while, but I have a plan. T-Rex is a big NASCAR fan, and we might pull it off on race weekend in Daytona in February. I'll explain my idea later after some details are worked out."

CHAPTER 43

On Tuesday morning, Ryan was up early and tracked down Dr. Stan on the exercise room treadmill preparing for the day.

"Morning, Ryan. My secretary said you were looking for me."

"Good morning, Doc. I'll get right to the point. Do you really think I'm a mass murderer? How in the hell did you come up with me as a suspect in the New York Subway murders?"

"What? I'm afraid I don't know what …," he began, but then he realized his denial would be futile. He turned off the treadmill and stepped back off the platform.

After an awkward look at the anger in Ryan's eyes, he began again. "No, I don't think you are a mass murderer. I'm really sorry, Ryan. I just got caught up in the gossip from the FBI and Detective Lawler."

"Lawler put you up to this?"

"Not exactly. I got the call from Lawler asking about how you might have been involved in the Lemos murder, then I caught Elizabeth coming out of your room, and then I heard about the New York gang members who got killed right where Travis was murdered, and I put them together in my mind, and I thought I'd better let Chilcote know, like he asked me to."

"Chilcote? Chilcote asked you to report on me?"

"Not exactly, either." By now Dr. Stan was squirming. He took a deep breath and tried to answer Ryan without sounding like he'd been watching too much television. "Well, kind of. First Lawler asked me to keep an eye on you about the Lemos murder. Then when I told her about the subway murders, I got a call from the FBI, and Agent Chilcote said to tell him if I saw anything suspicious. When I caught Elizabeth in your room, it all seemed to fall into place, so I let him know."

"And of course, you had to let America know about the mysterious man who might be the New York Subway vigilante murderer. Thanks for not giving them my name, by the way."

"You're welcome," he said sheepishly, "We're always looking for sensational stories for the show, and I guess I got carried away. I really thought the FBI ..."

"I think you need to shut up now, and listen to me. Unless you want me to go on your competitor's show and ruin your show's credibility, you are going to have to back off on this whole 'mystery man murderer' and let the FBI do their job. I expect a retraction immediately, or I'll blow the lid off this thing, and you'll have all the publicity you can handle."

Dr. Stan stiffened his posture and looked Ryan in the eye. "I'm not sure I have done anything I need to be worried about like that."

"Really?"

"Yeah, really. I didn't mention you by name. My attorneys say there's been no slander."

"Think about it. You are a renowned Doctor. You, and the American Medical Association, are only as good as your reputation for credibility and confidentiality. Ask your lawyers this; if I were involved in some conspiracy to commit murders, which obviously I'm not, but if I were, wouldn't anything I have said in this setting be covered by the Doctor/Patient confidentiality laws?"

"I don't think so, Ryan. We aren't in a doctor and patient relationship. This is just a retreat, kind of like a seminar."

"Really? I just thought that since you are a doctor, a Psychologist in fact, and we have all been invited here to your place of business to share our burdens, and gain the benefit of your professional assistance, you might have crossed that line."

Dr. Stan frowned. He looked worried as he mulled the thought over in his mind.

"What would happen to Dr. Stan's TV reputation, and his medical reputation as well, if it came out he violated doctor-patient confidentiality and went public on national television with pure speculation gained from private, privileged information obtained from a doctor-patient relationship? And, what would the AMA say if a lawsuit was filed against you for violating doctor-patient confidentiality just to boost ratings for your TV show?"

Dr. Stan stared straight ahead at Foster. He didn't like being wrong, but he didn't dare admit he screwed up.

Ryan continued, "Think about it, sir. I can't afford this bullshit. I'm fighting to keep my career in California. Your potential liability for that alone is huge. Television careers like yours have been destroyed for less than this. Neither of us wants to see this get out of hand. You need to fix this, now!"

Dr. Stan suffered for several agonizing seconds about how to broach what were clearly huge potential consequences on his part.

He took a deep breath as he stalled before answering. "Hmmm," he said as he let the air out of his lungs. "Okay, I'll concede you may have a point about our doctor-patient relationship. Neither of us needs this grief in our lives. I'll go on my show tonight, and Good Morning America tomorrow, and say that the mystery man was only a possible theory of my own imagination, and that the NYPD and the FBI are working the murder, and I will not address it further. I promise you; you will hear no more from me on the matter. I'm going to stick with what I know best. Helping people cope with tragic losses. Will that fix your concerns?"

"10-4," Ryan nodded. "That's cop talk for 'message received'."

"I know 10-4, Ryan. Everybody does."

"See you in class."

CHAPTER 44

"Are you kidding me? Fly to Germany?"

"Eric, let's be clear. This is bigger than both of us. The President has made it clear to the Director that he doesn't want to leave any stone unturned on this case. Have you read the morning papers?"

"Yes, I know. Reverend Al is conducting a candlelight vigil in the alley where those fine young men were tragically gunned down on their way to choir practice, by a white vigilante probably connected with local White Supremacy groups. And Reverend Jackson, not to be outdone, is conducting a subway sit-in on the Bed-Stuy line to protest that almost 100% of the subway robbery and mugging arrests are young black men; obviously due to 'racial profiling' by NYPD, who he claims just might actually be involved in the vigilante crime spree."

"Don't forget that Dr. Stan, since his name was leaked as an anonymous informant, came out on Good Morning America Monday with his story of a mystery man, known to the FBI, who may be part of a much bigger murder conspiracy."

"But he recanted it today, didn't he?"

"All I know is that America heard the accusation, and they don't believe the recantation, and now every radical and publicity hound is saying the FBI is behind the cover-up of the mystery man."

Chilcote slowly shook his head and looked toward the window. "When do I have to leave?" he said resignedly.

"Tonight, on the red-eye. We want the interview done by tomorrow, their time, to head off the media if they hear about the cop in California. You just need to interview the cousin and make sure everything the cop, -- what's his name, Foster? -- showed you is confirmed by an independent source."

"10-4, boss."

"Call me as soon as the interview is over."

"Okay, but that will be somewhere around midnight or later our time?"

"OK, you know what I mean. I'll talk to you when you get there in the morning, before the interview, and I'll see you when you get back, Eric."

CHAPTER 45

Ryan took a double-take as he walked into the classroom on Friday, the final day of the Retreat. The room was laid out in precisely the same configuration as it was on that first day of the Forgiveness Retreat some 3 months ago. Again, there were twelve black overstuffed leather chairs organized in a perfect circle, three feet apart. And again, there was the one larger and slightly more grandiose white one, in which Dr. Stan sat during their introductory meeting in July.

Again, Ryan was sure he was the last to enter the room, other than Dr. Stan, of course, who would certainly make his grand entrance once Ryan was seated. But now there were four empty chairs, reminding the attendees of the three fellow classmates who had dropped out along the way, and the young lady whose husband died in a car crash following an argument, who committed suicide after the third week. Someone had placed a single red rose on the chair she had occupied earlier.

As soon as Ryan was in his seat, the attendant left the room for a brief moment, and Dr. Stan swept into the room with his usual flair. But this time there was no applause as he strode across the room and sat in the white chair.

"Good morning, ladies and gentlemen. Before we start, let us offer a prayer to the one who guides us in our lives, in the name of Valerie, whose burdens were too great for her to bear, and who left us to be with her beloved husband in heaven. And let us also ask for continued guidance to the other three missing mates, who weren't ready to face their personal demons and dropped out along the way. We pray they will regain the strength that brought them here in July, and they will return again, stronger and more prepared to seek the forgiveness we have all found in these seven weeks."

Ryan glanced at Peter and raised his eyebrow almost imperceptibly, while Peter quickly glanced away.

"Amen," Dr. Stan continued, and the others repeated, "Amen."

"Today brings us to the end of a long and eventful journey. We've all had success, in our own way, of course, in confronting our losses in a new light, and we've all had some measure of success in achieving our goal of forgiveness."

This time it was Peter who looked at Ryan without expression, then glanced at Elizabeth, who was pretending to be enthralled by the words of Dr. Stan. Most of the other attendees weren't faking it, and nodded in unison in agreement.

Dr. Stan continued, "We are going to have a short meeting this morning as we reminisce about our time together. Collectively, in these seven weeks, we have laughed together, cried together, healed and forgave together. As we celebrate our successes together, I want to go around the room one last time, and have each of you tell us what you have gotten out of these seven weeks of healing and forgiveness. Let's start with you, Elizabeth."

"Well …," Elizabeth paused a moment as she collected her thoughts. "I'm probably not the best to start with, since I had a big boost to my ability to move on when the New York vigilante provided a measure of 'street justice' by killing four members of the gang who took my husband's life. That event immediately brought significant closure to my suffering, even though not a day goes by that I don't miss Travis as much as ever. But I have to admit …" She paused and looked at the floor, then looked around the room, "… that that event did more to help me heal than being here at the Retreat. I don't want to take anything away from your work, Dr. Stan, and I probably would have greatly benefitted from it anyhow, but that event …" Her voice tailed off as she didn't finish the sentence.

"I understand what you are trying to say, Elizabeth. Sometimes fate jumps in and plays a big role in the healing process, even if forgiveness isn't in the mix. Fate and events out of our control can sometimes be more important in healing your grieving than forgiveness. Ryan, you had a similar experience. How did it affect your ability to forgive and help to heal the pain of the loss of your daughter?"

"Events out of our control?" thought Ryan. *"Is he playing some mind game with us? Still trying to get a reaction for the FBI? Why start with Elizabeth and I? Certainly, he didn't want to begin this conversation with two 'downers' regarding the Retreat, unless he wanted to solicit some indication for someone else, as to whether we were involved."*

He was certain the room was bugged and they were being videotaped. He was also certain that by this very afternoon some phycologist at FBI Headquarters would be poring over the tape of this conversation for body language and voice inflections and intonations, hoping to find a tell-tale mannerism indicating guilt.

Ryan glanced around the room. The only new piece of furniture he didn't recognize was a large Frederick Remington western-style lamp on the buffet table along the wall. *"That must be the camera,"* he thought.

Looking in the direction of the lamp, he sat back and said, "I'm afraid I'm with Elizabeth on that point, Dr. Stan. Nothing will ever settle or heal the loss of Marcy. I'm certain this whole healing and forgiveness process here at the Retreat would have helped somewhat, but the rage I felt was hard to get past, so thankfully 'fate, and events out of my control' intervened and resolved my feelings of rage and revenge." He looked around the room and gestured with his hands as he spoke. "I don't know how the others in the Retreat have coped in that regard, but I hope your guidance has helped them get through their own tragedies and find peace on the other side, like I have." He smiled at Dr. Stan.

"Thank you, Ryan, for your kind words. He also glanced in the direction of the lamp on the buffet along the wall, as if to say, *"Did you get that? Can I go on with my meeting?"*

"Now let's continue with some of the other graduates and hear about their stories of success here at the Retreat."

For the next two hours, Peter and the others each heaped praise on Doctor Stan and the Forgiveness Retreat, and gave testimony about how it helped them cope with and begin to heal from the losses they had endured. Ryan was greatly impressed with, and more than slightly amused by, how Peter conveyed his gratitude to the Retreat for introducing him to 'a new way to cope with grief'.

Finally, Dr. Stan had endured more praise than even he could stomach, and he announced, "There is no point in having further discussions today, since I know you are all anxiously looking forward to getting back home and celebrating with your loved ones, so I have decided to end the Retreat on this positive note, and wish you all the greatest continued success as you reclaim the glory of your lives and move forward with that new 'healing feeling' of forgiveness in your hearts."

Following a brief chorus of applause, the attendees filed out of the room and many of them grabbed their suitcases waiting at the door and headed for the shuttle bus to take them to the airport for their return flights home.

A few lingered behind to visit with Dr. Stan and each other, while Ryan, Peter and Elizabeth headed for their rental cars to rendezvous at their previously agreed location, some fifty miles away. As Ryan was walking away from the group, one of the other men in the class approached Ryan and said, "Hey, Ryan. Some of us are getting together for a few drinks to celebrate our graduation at the Brick Oven Pizza. We'd be happy if you'd join us."

"Sorry, I won't be able to. I have an errand to run before heading to the airport." At that moment, Ryan realized that he had been so engrossed in the murder plot that he hadn't even bothered to learn the man's first name in seven weeks. The best he could muster up was, "Best of luck to you for the rest of your life."

"Thanks, same to you, Ryan. Maybe if I'm lucky, the same thing will happen to my daughter's killer that happened to yours."

"Yeah, that was pretty lucky."

CHAPTER 46

Peter walked into the Bunkhouse Pub in Fort Collins, Colorado, and pulled out a chair at the table with Ryan and Elizabeth. "I thought this Friday night would never come," he said, as he sat down hard into the chair.

Before we start, are either of you carrying anything you got from the retreat? Any parting gifts that could hold a transponder or microphone?"

Elizabeth and Peter both shook their heads, leading Ryan to conclude that this carefully chosen location was secure from listening bugs, and they could converse freely.

"It couldn't come soon enough for me either, said Ryan, raising his glass in Peter's direction to emphasize his point."

"It sure feels good to be away from the Retreat campus. Ever since you told us we might be recorded, I didn't feel comfortable anywhere on the campus," Peter said.

Elizabeth was barely listening. She was obviously elated at being done with the Retreat and Dr. Stan's narcissism. She had arrived first at the meeting location and appeared to have a head start at the bar.

"Listen. Isn't that a great new song?" Elizabeth interrupted as the jukebox began to belt out a new tune. It's someone called Avicii, singing 'Wake Me Up When It's All Over'.

"What's an Avicii?" Peter asked.

Without answering, she began rocking out to the beat in her chair while Peter watched and realized he didn't care what an Avicii was. When Ryan walked up to the table with another round of drinks, he also paused and watched until she felt uncomfortable and stopped.

"Sorry," Elizabeth said, "Being out with the boys and enjoying good pub beer takes me back to my college days."

"I can't wait 'til it's all over'," said Peter.

"The song?" Elizabeth asked.

"No. I'm thinking about our 'thing'."

"We are too close to blow it now, Peter," Ryan said. "By tonight, we have to have everything down so that we don't have to contact each other for a month or two, unless we have to."

"Seahawk Sally, are you clear on your Twitter accounts and how to use them?"

"Yes, I am, Harry Smith."

"How about you, Bridget Brown?"

"Yep, I've been studying the Seahawks and even watched a couple episodes of 'General Hospital' just to get in character."

"Great," Ryan said.

He then passed out a small thumb drive to each of them, saying, "Here is the scripted game plan for the takedown of T-Rex. It is a lot more complicated than before, and you have to be spot-on for your parts or it won't work. Sorry it's not on toilet paper, but it is too long. Guard this as if your life depended on it if you get caught with it, because it does. Open it only on your special computer. Watch the Seahawks site for messages from me about tickets and travel changes. Otherwise, be there and be ready to follow the script exactly as I've written it."

"I can't wait to read it. Are you sure it will work, Ryan?" asked Peter.

"I'm pretty sure I have T-Rex pegged correctly. He's just a dumb petty criminal who can play exceptional football, and isn't smart enough to take advantage of his skills, get rich, enjoy life, and stay out of trouble. I can't emphasize enough; I'm expecting Academy Award performances from each of you."

He then handed Elizabeth a throw-down phone marked 'American Rent-a-Car' in tape on it. "Save it in a safe place until I tell you. Don't use it for anything except exactly as written in the script."

"Okay," she said as she put the phone in her purse and fastened the zipper. "What about disguises? Do I have to wear fake breasts again?"

"No, Elizabeth."

"Darn."

"Just be your own sexy self and it will work out fine. You'll see what I mean when you read and follow the script."

"After the New York subway caper, I trust anything you come up with," said Peter.

"What about the risks?" asked Elizabeth.

"If you follow the script, there is no way you can be implicated in it. I'm the only one at risk if you stick to the script and your story. This is important. If, somehow it goes all to hell, don't try to contact me. Just ignore everything and go home on your scheduled flight, and never look back.

Remember; admit nothing, deny everything, and demand proof."

At that time, Katy Perry began singing 'Roar' on the jukebox in the background, and Elizabeth started to rock out again.

"This is so sad. I feel like you guys are the only real friends I have," said Peter.

CHAPTER 47

Munich, Germany

"Thank you for seeing me on such short notice, Mr. Harbusch."

"No problem. What does the great American FBI want from me that they would come to Germany?"

"Have you talked to your cousin, Ryan Foster, about us coming here?"

"Yes. I called him as soon as I heard from you. That is what I don't understand."

"The FBI is looking into a murder, actually a mass murder, which occurred in New York City earlier this month. We received a tip, an anonymous tip, that thinks your cousin might be involved."

"Ryan? A mass murderer? Of course not."

"I don't think so either, but we have to check out all leads, because we have no other suspects."

"If you have no suspects, you just pick someone?"

"No, but someone called us to say they think he might be involved. I spoke to Ryan last week. He claims you were together at the Oktoberfest in Munich when the murders occurred. I have been sent here to confirm his alibi with you."

"What is this 'alibi'?"

"It means he has someone who can prove he wasn't where the crime occurred, when it occurred, so he couldn't have done it. He says you were at Oktoberfest together from September 23rd through the 28th. Is that true?"

"Yes, of course we were." Klaus pulls out a photo album he had carefully put together from the Oktoberfest and pushes it across the table to Chilcote.

Chilcote looked carefully at the mementos, souvenirs and photos in the album. As he turned the last page, Klaus said, "I still don't understand how you think Ryan was in New York when he told me that he showed you his flight tickets and hotel receipts?"

Chilcote ignored the question. "Do you have anything else?"

"What else? You've seen flight coupons, hotel receipts, and now you see all these photos. What else do you want?"

"Can I take these photos and receipts with me? Our experts will verify them."

"You think they are fakes? You think I could have made a hundred fake photos to show you?" Klaus' blood pressure was clearly on a rapid rise. "My cousin told you he was not in New York. Here is the proof he was here with me. Why do you keep trying to say he was in New York? Does this ... this ... anonymous person ... what has he shown you that he thinks shows Ryan was in New York? Here is the proof he was in Germany with me, and you still don't believe him."

"Please calm down, Mr. Harbusch. We aren't accusing Ryan of anything. We just need to verify things. This is a big case in the USA."

"And so the FBI needs to arrest someone? By asking for these items, are you now accusing me of being involved?"

"Of course not."

"It seems to me that you are."

Klaus grabbed the papers from his hand. He was getting more agitated as he spoke. "I'll never understand your American government and your arrogance. I thought you were here to prove my cousin is innocent, but now I see you are here to try to make up a crime on him? What kind of justice … and courts … do you have in America? My niece is murdered and her killer goes free. Where was the FBI when Marcy was killed? You didn't care about the murder of an innocent girl, but when some poor black criminals are shot in New York, all of a sudden it is a 'big case'."

Before Chilcote could respond, Klaus continued, "And when someone who won't even give his name says my cousin is suspicious, now the great FBI gets involved, and comes all the way to Germany to try to make him guilty."

As he spoke, he shook the papers in his hand in front of Chilcote. "Here is the proof you wanted to show he was with me, and you still don't believe it."

Disgustedly, he continued, "You are not interested in the truth. In Germany, we know about this 'big case' in New York from the internet. I know what is going on in your country today. It is all over the news that your President wants someone arrested to stop more violence and to satisfy the minority leaders in New York. You just want an arrest to please your government and you don't care who you arrest. You have no authority here in this country. Get out of my house; get out of my country, and go back to New York and find the real killer, not create one. No wonder no one in Europe trusts you. Get out of my house!"

Chilcote made his way quickly from the Harbusch home and went directly to the airport in Frankfurt. Once he was booked for the return flight and sitting in the lounge, he called his boss at FBI headquarters.

"I'm telling you, boss, we are wasting our time. I saw pictures of Ryan and his cousin all over Oktoberfest. In the Spaten Pavilion, the Tuborg Pavilion, the Beck's Pavilion, and the Lowenbrau Pavilion, – which, by the way looks like the most fun. The guy couldn't have done it. He was thousands of miles away in another country with fifteen million of his newest, closest friends as witnesses."

"Did you get the pictures?"

"No. Harbusch got really mad and threw me out of the house. And frankly, I don't blame him. Foster's clean on this one. We need to look closer at other angles."

"Okay. I admit it sounds like he's clear. I'll see if I can get in touch with Dr. Stan and see if he's really off the soapbox. I wish he'd have given you some of the photos we could show our Technical Analysis guys."

"Maybe Klaus e-mailed some of his favorites to Ryan, Chief. Just have Technical Analysis pull them off the 'cloud', and use them to show Dr. Stan."

"Good idea. We don't like to give that much attention to the 'cloud', but if we can pull some photos off of the internet broadband, maybe the boys in TA can find a flaw in them where they have been altered. Eric, get back here to New York and kick those local guys in the ass. They have to have something from the crime scene, or their military veterans profile search, to lean toward another suspect by now."

CHAPTER 48

The hastily called Task Force Meeting was underway when Detective Delarosa sauntered into the room his usual fifteen minutes late. He stopped just inside the door and looked around. When the conversation stopped, he spread his arms out from his sides he said, "Hey, where's the broad from California?"

"We cut her loose," Agent Chilcote said. "Her murder investigation is a local state crime with no quantifiable national or interstate connection. But she did alert us to the possibility of an interstate conspiracy, which gives us the green light to stay on board for a while."

"That's too bad. I was just starting to like having her around."

"You? Yeah, right."

"No, really. She was interesting. I've never been around a lesbian before. I thought I might learn something. Plus, we found out we had a lot in common."

"What on earth would that be?"

"Well, for starters, we both ride Harleys and we both like pretty women."

Delarosa laughed, until he realized he was the only one. "C'mon, guys. That's funny."

"Maybe fifteen years ago," said Chief Moran. "You and I will talk in my office after the meeting; and bring your ass."

Chilcote continued, "As I was telling the other fellows, Delarosa, we checked out Ryan's alibi, and it is rock solid. He was definitely in Munich, Germany, when the vigilante murders occurred. I interrogated him and even flew to Germany to interview his cousin. That didn't go over too well, but that's another story for later. Bottom line, he's got a perfect alibi for the time frame."

Delarosa shook his head. "A perfect alibi? Seems to be a common theme in all these murders. To me, whenever a prime suspect has that perfect of an alibi, it's usually a bright red flag. Maybe we shouldn't be too quick to write him off just yet."

"Whatever," Chilcote said. "We think he is clear on this one. What have your detectives come up with on the previous victims with a war veteran background? I think that is our best direction to focus on."

O'Reilly took up the discussion, "We checked every known victim of these dirtbags, and no-one stands out as ready, willing, and capable of pulling off this type of job."

"Maybe it was never reported," said Agent Logan. "If the guy is really that committed to vigilante justice, maybe he just decided to handle it himself."

Chilcote passed over his partner's comment without appearing to give it any consideration. "I strongly believe that the location, that particular alley, is important to the killer for some reason."

"Possible," continued O'Reilly. "And the military precision of the killing has to be important also. NYPD has checked their files for trained veterans who live in the neighborhood, especially focusing on those who were victims along the Bed-Stuy and other nearby subway lines. Your FBI headquarters just gave us their list of all commando-trained vets known to live in the area. We're checking them out, but no-one appears to fit the case so far."

Delarosa was sitting with his feet up on the desk, looking past the other men in the room and tapping his pencil on the side of the desk.

"Something on your mind, Sergeant?" Chilcote asked.

"Yeah. I'm still thinking about Ryan Foster's perfect alibi for our case. Seems to me the Santa Rosa Detective used the same word, 'perfect', to describe his alibi when the dirtbag who killed his daughter was murdered."

"And don't forget, Elizabeth Hartman had a pretty good alibi for the time of our murders. She was on national television," said O'Reilly.

"Pretty good? I'd say 'perfect'. If they are, in fact, involved, we're going to have our hands full proving it," said Delarosa. "You fellows aren't going to believe this, but I'm beginning to think the detective broad may be onto something and we shouldn't be too quick to exclude her."

"Now I've heard every God damn thing," said O'Reilly, shaking his head and throwing his hands up in the air.

Chilcote pushed his chair backward, stood up and began to pace back and forth. "Let's not get carried away. I spoke to Dr. Stan and showed him some photos of Ryan and his cousin at Oktoberfest, and he seems to have backed off his suspicions altogether. They finished the Retreat, so he's not going to see them anymore. He gave us a video of the last session where they talked about the murders. We have our psych guys looking at them for clues that might help us. In the meantime, we need to keep looking at the 'similars' and combat-trained military veterans with an axe to grind with street thugs."

"What street thugs?" O'Reilly chuckled. "Muggings are down about 100% on and around the Bed-Stuy subway line."

"Okay, let's get back on track, gentlemen." Chilcote said. Turning his attention to a middle-aged man who had just slipped into the room and sat in one of the chairs behind the task force members, he said, "I would like to introduce you to Dr. Edwin Bichner, one of the FBI's premier profilers. He's been looking at the New York subway shooting case for impressions of the killer, and has some conclusions we'd like to share."

Dr. Bichner stood up and stepped toward an easel in the corner. Delarosa rolled his eyes. Bichner wore an open collared well-travelled wool blazer, coffee stained around the right sleeve, and frayed at the elbows. His unkempt full beard screamed of perhaps an Ivy League academic background, above average intelligence, unconcerned with appearance, yet obsessed with the substance of his expertly cultivated field of expertise.

"Gentlemen. As Agent Chilcote said, I have studied the clues from your killer and I have some conclusions which might assist you in finding him."

"Clues," thought Delarosa, *"If there were clues, we'd have him by now."*

"Let's start with a basic primer of a vigilante murderer of this type. He is not a serial killer, at least not yet, but the audacity and planning of the crime itself suggests the characteristics of one. This might be just the first, especially if he's pleased with the result. If he was going to become a serial killer, I think he would have been in touch with us to taunt us in some way."

"The first profile characteristic we look for is - was the killer organized or disorganized? This usually tells us a lot about the killer's personality. And the personality of the killer is a leading predictor of behavior."

"From this crime scene, we can assume the answer to be … 'very organized'. He planned the execution extensively, taking advantage of his knowledge of how his victims would act. This guy is very good." Bichner couldn't contain his enthusiasm and admiration for the killer, as he methodically recalled the precision of the attack. "Cleverly, he lured them into the very trap they were laying for him, and he used their 'home-field' familiarity to catch them unexpectedly off-guard. He liked his odds, even though he knew he was badly outnumbered; they were well-armed and about to strike on their own."

"To do so, he almost assuredly had an accomplice. To catch them so off guard, there must have been someone acting as 'bait', upon whom the killers were totally focused. Hence, the other man described by witnesses who left through the opposite end of the alley. The forensics guys tell us that evidence appears to indicate the accomplice may have even shot one of the victims while he was on the ground."

"But the only eye-witness says he acted alone." Delarosa said.

"Witnesses lie, or get confused," said Chilcote, "Forensics point to the scenario that he wasn't alone. We think the surviving gang member may have lied to save his life. If so, in order for us to get the real story, we'll have to make him more afraid of us than he is of the killer. That's going to be a challenge, since he witnessed what the killer can do first hand. Please continue, Dr. Bichner."

"As I said, he was organized and had a calculated plan, carried out to apparent perfection. This was not the work of an irrational psychotic man. The typical 'psycho' is sloppy, acts somewhat spontaneously, and leaves evidence, and acts without conscience or care for the outcome of his acts. Your killer planned the crime carefully, acted violently and maliciously, …" Again, Bichner's voice teemed with excitement as he spoke. "… and without remorse, but … he left behind one of the attackers as an unharmed key witness, and he left the gang's guns behind for the police to find and tell his side of the story. He wanted to watch the gang suffer and die in front of him, yet he wanted the full story told, his way. He has GOT to be connected with a previous crime by the gang or some connection with other gang crimes in the neighborhood. It is my understanding that the task force is planning to re-interview the survivor and see if he holds to his 'one man acting alone' story."

"Yes, sir," said Chilcote. "The task force decided that if he's not intimidated by NYPD, maybe the FBI can evoke some fear in a young sixteen-year-old looking at hard time for a federal offense; so Logan and I will be interviewing him next week."

Bichner rubbed his forehead and said, "Good luck with that. Continuing, your killer has military or at least quasi-military experience. I strongly think he has to have 'black ops' training, but even if he is only an avid paintball fanatic, he is familiar with guerilla war type tactics and has a 'black ops' mentality. He has some connection to this gang, or similar subway gang tactics, evidenced by telling the police to compare the guns to unsolved crimes of this type."

"Could it be a former gang member with a grudge?" asked O'Reilly.

"Not likely, at all, for several reasons," Bichner continued. "First, it's not their style to lay a trap in an alley where they might get cornered and killed in a shootout. No 'O.K. Corral' shootings for these guys. They do drive-by shootings, anonymous, often random, surprise ambushes from a moving car so they can get away quick before they can get shot at. This was more Mafia-like or military."

"Second," he continued, "these gang-banger types never act alone like a lone wolf type assassin. They need courage, support and witnesses; someone who can vouch for their bravado during bragging rights back in the 'hood."

"And third, there would have been active gang war repercussions by now. In fact, the opposite is true. There are virtually no gang activities going on, indicating that all the street gangs in Bed-Stuy are scared they may be next."

"So, … bottom line, who is our killer?" asked Delarosa.

"Our killer is most likely twenty-five to forty-five years old, judging from his experience and his athleticism..."

"You keep saying 'he'," said O'Reilly.

"I believe it was a man because of the macho nature of the crime, the strength needed, and the military nature of the attack. Women tend to murder more out of passion and spontaneity, seldom kill more than one person in their crimes, and rarely, rarely, act as methodically as this. When a woman does show this level of planning and discipline, they almost always use poison."

"Poison? Did you say poison?" asked Delarosa, almost knocking over the chair next to him as he sat up sharply.

"Yes. Why?" said Bichner.

"I'm just thinking about another murder case I had in mind. Go on."

"Lastly, most serial and mass killers think rules are there for others, not themselves, and most act without remorse. Our guy is doing what he thinks he has to do, he knows it is wrong, but he is driven by something stronger than conscience."

"Like revenge?" asked O'Reilly.

"Exactly like revenge." Bichner said.

"Like revenge for the murder of your daughter, your son, or your husband. Back to our threesome from the retreat …," Delarosa said resignedly. "Revenge. Poison. I'm telling you, guys, Lawler is looking smarter than we gave her credit for."

CHAPTER 49

Reggie Bennau was already seated at the table with his attorney in the interview room at the Crossroads Secure Juvenile Center in New York City. The lawyer, a clean cut African American wearing a tailored $400.00 pinstriped suit with matching vest, was a stark contrast to his young client. Yet, to Chilcote, Reggie looked remarkably more at ease in his orange jumpsuit.

Chilcote and Logan walked behind Reggie and the lawyer, circled the table and sat down in their most intimidating style. Reggie looked at his lawyer, who didn't blink.

Before either could speak, Reggie's lawyer began, in a thick African accent, "I can make this quick and painless, gentlemen. I'm Kanye Matumbe, and I am an attorney from the Youth Innocence Project. Reggie is not going to discuss this matter any further with you or NYPD. He stands by his story, which we maintain was taken out of context."

"He isn't a member of that or any other gang. He happened to be walking by the alley when the gang members came in from the other end, following a white man, who turned and shot them all. The shooter obviously recognized that Reggie wasn't involved, and that's why he didn't shoot Reggie, also. Reggie, being a good citizen, stayed behind as a witness to the crime, and even helped the police by pointing out that it might be a good idea to check the guns against other local street gang activities. In short, Reggie isn't a criminal, he is a hero being persecuted as part of a systematic pattern of racial bias by the New York Police Department."

Chilcote and Logan were startled and visibly taken aback by Matumbe's statement, and stared at each other in disbelief at this shocking change of Reggie's story.

Matumbe continued. "If Reggie is charged with any crime, The Youth Innocence Project looks forward to proving his innocence in court, while exposing the injustices being perpetrated against young men of color by the NYPD."

"Is that right, Reggie? That's your story now." asked Chilcote.

Reggie looked down and gave a shrug with a slight nod, without making eye contact. Matumbe said sternly, "I just told you, he isn't going to answer any questions."

"Wow," said Chilcote. "First you get used by the gang for their purposes, and now these guys show up in expensive suits and are going to exploit you for their own agenda. When do you get to act on your own, Reggie?"

Reggie looked over at Matumbe, taking the time to size up the suit. Then he looked up at Chilcote and Logan. They thought they could discern fear and confusion in his eyes.

Matumbe jumped to his feet. "That's an outrage. This meeting is over, right now. Let's go Reggie."

As Reggie pushed the chair back and started to obey his lawyer's command, Chilcote decided to pose a theory to get Reggie's reaction. He said, "Very well. If that's how you want to play it, Reggie. But don't forget about the deal you made that night with the shooter." Gesturing at Matumbe, he said, "Do you think this guy is going to hang around to protect you when you get back on the street?"

Reggie stopped in mid-movement, and for a moment stood half bent over, frozen in thought. He slowly straightened up and stared at Chilcote, questioning whether the man actually knew about the conversation, or was just bluffing.

Seeing the reaction, Chilcote saw that Matumbe was becoming extremely agitated, so he pressed further. "I guess you aren't going to worry about what he'll do if you don't go through with the deal?"

"Open this door immediately!" Matumbe shouted. "Pay no attention, Reggie. It's a trick." Turning toward the glass one-way mirror panel, he shouted, "Now, gentlemen!"

"Of course. We are done here." As the door opened, Chilcote said, "Good luck, Reggie, when you get out, call me if you change your mind about helping us."

CHAPTER 50

After the Forgiveness Retreat, the conspirators were back at their previous lifestyles, except for Ryan. News that he was mentioned as a potential suspect in the New York Subway murders had reached the California Highway Patrol, and that department, always wary of potentially bad publicity, decided to delay his reinstatement as Commander for the Clear Lake CHP Office. They offered him a ninety-day 'temporary' assignment at a desk job in Sacramento Headquarters, pending an in-depth Departmental investigation into the new allegations, and a required psychiatric examination to determine to their satisfaction that he was again fit to command the Clear Lake CHP Area.

Within the next few weeks, the New York media headlines shifted away from the murders, helped greatly by a sex scandal involving two members of the New York Knicks and their wives.

Eventually, Al Sharpton and Jesse Jackson milked the murders for all the publicity they could glean out of it, and then left town just as quickly as they arrived, heading for

Atlanta, where a young black armed robber was shot dead during a robbery attempt by a white liquor store owner.

And back in California, the Santa Rosa murder of Danny Lemos produced no new local leads, and was soon set aside by other fresh crimes, keeping Lawler and her fellow Detectives busy. Every Detective hates to lose his or her first murder case, so, every once in a while, she called Chilcote to see if there were any new developments.

In the meantime, the Subway Shootings Task Force continued to monitor Ryan, Elizabeth, and Peter's lives and on-line activities. The task force met by phone every week, then every other week, while the FBI and NYPD followed up on the scores of anonymous leads that came in from the tip line established for that purpose.

During one such conference call, Agent Chilcote briefed the members on the results of the FBI's evidence, follow-up, and ballistics investigations.

"Every piece of garbage in the alley was gathered and dusted for fingerprints. Nothing was revealed that might assist the investigation."

"All potential persons-of-interest leads; military, prior victims, even local paintball devotees were investigated,

Steve Davis

categorized and compared with the profiler's report, to no avail."

"There are actually four parts to the FBI Ballistics investigation. First, we were able to convince the California Highway Patrol to order Ryan to surrender his .40 caliber departmental-issue handgun for testing against the cartridges and bullets that killed the street gang. The test-fired bullets and expended cartridges from Ryan's CHP handgun did not match those found at the New York City crime scene."

"Secondly, as for the dead street gang's weapons that Reggie Bennau collected and turned over to us at the scene, they were all dusted for fingerprints, and the prints matched the dead men and Reggie, as you'd expect."

"Next, they were all test fired. The bullets from those weapons, as we expected, had striations and barrel markings which matched slugs recovered from several other unrelated and unsolved crimes and gang shootings dating back to 2007."

"Seems like our shooter did us all a favor by ending a six-year crime spree," said Delarosa.

"He's still a mass murderer, and possibly guilty of hate crimes," Chilcote quickly pointed out. "If I may continue ..."

292

"Sorry, sir," said Delarosa, "I was just sayin' …"

"And finally," Chilcote continued, "There is the third set of ballistics, which led to a fourth; the analysis of the cartridges found in the alley at the ambush scene from the killer's gun, identified as a .40 caliber Glock, and the bullets recovered from the bodies of the deceased gang members. They were compared against our database of known criminal investigations. The .40 caliber shell casings from the murder scene had all been wiped clean before being placed in the gun, and they produced no prints as we had hoped for."

"That report did provide another unexpected twist however; the .40 caliber slugs that killed all of the gang bangers also matched an unsolved gang-related homicide in Brooklyn Heights in 2010, involving a separate street gang. And, get this, … the .38 caliber slugs in one of the dead men matched another unsolved crime, also in Brooklyn Heights in 2011."

"Doesn't that kind of remove Ryan from the suspect list, unless you think he was in a Brooklyn Heights street gang in 2010," O'Reilly asked. "Now it's starting to sound like a gang war."

"It would seem so, but here's the twist. NYPD narcs and informants in Bed-Stuy and the Heights are saying there is no gang-war talk. Both gangs are running scared of the killer or killers and not looking at each other."

Chilcote took a deep breath to let that sink in, then said, almost excitedly, "But wait, it gets better. Their informants are telling an interesting story that's being spread on the streets. According to the story, a couple of days before the vigilante shootings, on the other side of town, two Brooklyn Heights gangsters allegedly got shook down by a solo male they thought was a cop, in the middle of a drug deal, and their weapons were stolen. Let me repeat that. Just before the vigilante shootings, the guns used in that crime were possibly stolen from a rival gang by someone acting like a cop. We are trying to get more information on the gun shakedown, but no-one is offering specifics because the guns were 'white hot' and they were in the middle of a drug deal."

"Yeah," O'Reilly said, "What are they going to report? 'Officers, we were selling some illegal drugs and some guy stole our illegal guns that would implicate us in some murders and robberies over the past six years!' You almost have to admire the guy, he's a genius and he's got balls to pull that off."

"And Ryan? Could he have been in town at the time?"

"It doesn't look like it. We checked him out right away, and he was …"

"Let me guess," Delarosa interrupted. "He's got a 'perfect alibi', right?"

"Afraid so," Chilcote said. "He was in Germany."

"Gentlemen, if it's Ryan, he's like a fucking ghost, and he's playing with us, which really pisses me off," said Chilcote. "I want that son of a bitch."

CHAPTER 51

The Invitation; Mid December, 2013.

"I'll have a blue, blue Christmas without you, …"
Ryan crooned to himself as he opened the inside door from
his kitchen to the garage and approached the storage locker in
the corner. He unlocked it, opened it, and pulled out his dive
bag, removing the dive vest from inside the backpack type
cloth bag. He unzipped it and pulled out the computer he had
hidden inside. *"Can't be too careful, especially now,"* he
thought, as he went back into the house.

A half hour later he was sitting in the Coffee Loft, a
Ukiah Coffee house, enjoying a white chocolate coffee
mocha, a cinnamon roll, and the free wireless, 40 miles from
home.

As he sipped his coffee, he turned on his computer
and signed onto the Ticket Master website.

An hour later, he entered the cash pool credit card
number and clicked on the 'Buy Now' button. He sat back
and smiled as he received confirmation of his purchase.

"Four tickets, Richard Petty Tower for the Daytona 500," he murmured softly to himself. *"That should get the rat to come out of his hole."*

He then went onto Twitter, logged in as Harry Smith and left a message on the Seattle Seahawks page, writing, *"Man, am I stoked. Just scored four top tier tickets to the last Seahawks home game. Wonder who I should take with me."*

The next morning, he returned to the Coffee Loft and logged on. Among the several dozen responses to the posting, each one suggesting he take them, were the two he was interested in; Seahawk Sally tweeted, "Just let me know and I'll be there", and Bridget Brown responded, "Me, Me, Me. I'll make it worth your while."

"You are such a slut, Bridget," he thought as he closed the computer and stuck it into his briefcase.

CHAPTER 52

Almost exactly one month later, Ryan opened the pool computer and opened Word. He began to type the invitation that he hoped would entice T-Rex out of his lair to attend the Daytona 500 next month.

He created some very official looking stationary and printed it out, then reprinted the letter of invitation and put it in a matching stamped envelope and sealed it.

Then, as he had done four weeks earlier, Ryan drove to Ukiah and sat at a corner table at the Coffee Loft. After he got his cinnamon roll and white coffee mocha, he sat down at the computer and logged into the Wi-Fi.

Opening Twitter, he sent a post to Seahawk Sally and Bridget Brown saying, *"Mom's birthday this week. Sent her four tickets from all of us to the next home game. You can expect a thank you call."*

Soon after, Seahawk Sally responded, *"Waiting for the call. Thanks for handling it."*

Bridget Brown re-tweeted, *"Looking forward to it. Hope the Seahawks follow the usual script."*

Just over a week later, Elizabeth was getting ready for work when she was startled by the ring from the cell phone in her purse at her dressing table. She let it ring again while she opened the drawer and removed a piece of paper. *"Show time,"* she breathed, as she took a deep breath and picked up the phone. "American Rent-A-Car, this is Jessica, how may I direct your call?"

"This is Tyrell Rexford. I'm responding to a letter I got from Mr. Gerald Maxwell about some tickets he sent me."

"Certainly. I'll put you through to his extension, Mr. ... did you say Rexford?"

"Yes, Rexford, but he probably remembers me as 'T-Rex'."

"Okay, Mr. Rexford. Please hold a moment and I'll tell him 'T-Rex' is on the phone."

Elizabeth waited for ten seconds and spoke again. "I'm sorry, Mr. Rexford, he is on the other line. Would you care to hold a few minutes?"

"Sure," T-Rex said.

After thirty seconds, she picked up the phone again and said, "I'm so sorry, Mr. Rexford, but Mr. Maxwell is running late for an appointment with Fox TV about advertising during the upcoming NASCAR race. He said to give you his personal cell phone so you can call him direct while he's en route. Is that okay?"

"Yeah, sure. I want to talk to him about the race anyhow."

After she gave the number to him, Elizabeth said, "Will that be all, Mr. Rexford?"

"Yes. Thank you, Jessica."

She hung up and immediately called the number she had given T-Rex. When Ryan answered, she said, "It's on," and hung up.

Instantly, as Ryan hung up, the phone rang. "Maxwell," he said casually.

"Mister Maxwell, this is Tyrone Rexford."

"T-Rex. My man. Did you get the tickets I sent you?"

"Yes, sir. Thanks a lot. Those are great seats. What's the deal? Have we met? Do I know you?"

"You probably don't remember me. We met a couple times when I was a junior assistant here at American. I was certainly awestruck to meet the greatest football player ever." Ryan glanced down at his Google notes. "Your contact was with Chuck Heathley, who used to be the Head of Corporate Sponsorship, wasn't it?"

"Yeah, Chuck. He was a good guy."

"Yep, he was. Shame about his passing a couple years ago. But … he used to always tell me, 'Jerry, if you ever get to the top, you take care of T-Rex. We'd be nothing today without him.' Well, I finally made it to the top, and I thought I'd make it up to you, like I promised Chuck I would."

"Yeah. Sorry I couldn't make the funeral, but you understand?"

"Sure, sure. By the way, just between me and you, I've always been a huge fan and I think you got a raw deal and I'm glad the jury saw through it, too."

"Thanks. What do I gotta do in return, Mr. Maxwell?"

"Nothing, man. Just enjoy the race. I remember how you used to love NASCAR. Chuck used to say how you made this company what it is today. Hey, I'd love to make you Grand Marshall and do some promos, but I hope you understand, the company bigshots are worried about being 'politically correct'; afraid of potential 'negative publicity', so we can't acknowledge you officially, but that doesn't mean we can't show our appreciation in some small way, for the old times, right, T-Rex? It is okay if I call you T-Rex, isn't it?"

"Yeah, Sure. I thought you guys had forgotten about me."

"No, never. You'll always be included as long as I'm at American Rent-A-Car. It'll probably cost you an autograph, though. If it's okay with you, I'll drop by and get an autograph at the race."

"Sure, buddy."

"Hey, you've got my cell phone. If anything comes up or you have any questions, call me direct. The big shots don't know about it. It's just between you and me, … and Chuck's memory."

"Got it. It's good to know there is some loyalty left in the world, Gerald."

"Please, T-Rex, call me Jerry."

"Okay, Jerry. Thanks again."

"See you at the race."

Moments later, Harry Brown left a message on Twitter for Seahawk Sally and Bridget Brown, saying, *"Mom called to confirm. She'll be happy to be there."*

"I guess we should plan on that weekend," said Sally.

"Going to be a great game," said Bridget.

CHAPTER 53

"This is the ATT operator. Mr. Chilcote, all conference callers have checked in and are on the line. Thank you for using ATT for your conference call needs."

"Welcome to the conference call, everyone."

"I'll start by saying welcome back to the task force, Detective Lawler," Agent Chilcote spoke into the microphone in the middle of the conference table at the FBI's New York Office. "As I told you earlier, Delarosa here seems to think your suspicions may warrant your continued involvement in the task force. You know the usual players here in the room with me; Delarosa, O'Reilly, Moran, agent Logan and myself. There are a couple others who I will introduce as this conference call progresses."

"Welcome back," the others chorused.

"Thank you for the call the other day, Agent Chilcote. I'm not as sure about a conspiracy as I was when we last met, but anything you come up with might have a bearing on my case, so I welcome the opportunity to be involved and learn from the pros."

Before Chilcote could continue, Lawler said, "Hey Tony, how's that Harley running?"

"Just fine, ma'am," Delarosa said, to the collective gasp of the others in the room as they collectively cringed at the 'ma'am' reference."

"Good. I'm glad. I figured a fair-weather rider like you would have crashed it by now."

The others laughed, and Delarosa just smiled.

Agent Chilcote, caught off-guard by the banter, began to cough, then said, "Okay everyone, shall we get back to the business that brings us together?"

"We don't have a lot of new developments to report, so we figured we could accomplish just as much on the phone. For openers, what is the status of your investigation, Detective Lawler?"

"We are at a dead end. The mystery woman hasn't been identified and may never be. We don't have anything to ID her. We can't afford to waste any more time looking for her, since we don't even know if she was involved. We re-contacted all the witnesses, and they recall seeing her talking to him, but she apparently never had access to his cup of coffee, which was laced with arsenic poison."

"Poison." Delarosa thought to himself.

Lawler continued, "The coffee shop was shut down for a few days while the health department looked for the source, but there was nothing. Someone had to have slipped it in his drink at the counter before he picked it up. The baristas have all been questioned and cleared. No-one remembers anyone else in the shop. Everyone was looking at her. I've been assigned two other priority homicides right now, but we are open to any new developments that would tie Ryan, Elizabeth, or even the makeup guy, Peter Levenson, to the case."

"Levenson," Chilcote pondered aloud, "We don't find any connection to him, although we can put him in Baltimore for no apparent reason during the time of the New York vigilante murders. He was at Camden Yard for the whole home stand of Orioles' baseball games when the murders occurred. He was even on TV several times."

"Wow," Lawler said, "He must be quite an Orioles fan to fly from California to Baltimore to watch a baseball series."

"Actually, two series."

"Really? Does he do that often?"

"Never before, according to the 'cloud'. He seems to have developed a new interest in Baseball. And why the Orioles? We can't find any previous interest in the Orioles or any other Baltimore sports team."

"Why don't you just ask him?"

"We don't even have enough to ask him any questions. We have nothing to remotely tie him to the Lemos or vigilante murders, except that he kind of knows the other two, who may or may not be involved either, from the Forgiveness Retreat, and, of course, we know he'd like to see T-Rex dead."

"He's sure acting strange all of a sudden," said Delarosa.

"Here is another interesting tidbit. Levenson apparently has taken an interest in all kinds of sports. I asked Dr. Stan to call all three of them last week, just to supposedly see how they are doing after the Retreat, and guess what? He tells me that Peter told him he was going to the Daytona 500 in February.

"So now Levenson's a NASCAR fan? I don't think so. Sounds like another alibi trip," said Delarosa, "Now we just have to figure out what he's distancing himself from."

"Or getting closer to," Logan said, "Remember, T-Rex lives within a hundred miles of Daytona Beach. If Levenson is heading to Daytona Beach, maybe we should notify T-Rex he might be on a hit list."

"I think we'll need more than that to start notifying people they may be in danger."

"We might be jumping ahead on this, but maybe we should casually inquire as to Ryan's and Elizabeth's whereabouts that weekend. Detective Lawler, do you think his friend in California could feel him out?"

"Detective Atkins is a loyal cop, and wouldn't condone any criminal activity by Ryan, but I'm not sure if he is willing to be a spy or informant unless we have something firm to go on."

Logan was on his computer, when suddenly he about jumped out of his seat and said, "Whoa!"

Chilcote interrupted the conversation. "Hang on a minute. What do you have, Logan?"

Logan leaned close to the microphone. "We may be closer than we thought. I just checked T-Rex's Twitter page, and guess what, here is a post from a couple days ago;

'Good to know some people still remember how much money I made for them before everyone else

abandoned me. One of my old sponsors, who asked that I don't reveal their name for potential negative publicity reasons, just comped me four prime tickets for the Daytona 500 in February. Me and my posse will be enjoying one of my favorite sports from the best seats in the house.'

"The Daytona 500? It looks like Levenson is going toward the crime, not making an alibi like we thought. Maybe he's finally decided to do something about T-Rex himself," Delarosa said.

Chilcote looked out the window of his office for a moment, then he said, "I think we do need to notify T-Rex about the possibility, and use the situation to set a trap for Levenson and the others."

After a few more minutes of conversation, Logan announced, "This is it, gentlemen, I think we've hit the jackpot for their next collaboration for murder. I just looked at Elizabeth's Google calendar and guess what? ... "

Delarosa interrupted, "Wait a minute. You can do that? How did you get her password?"

"Password?" Logan said incredulously, "This is the FBI, remember? Now, do you want to hear the news, or not?"

"Yeah, sure."

"Okay. As I said, I just looked at Elizabeth's Google calendar and guess what? She has the week of February 19-24 blocked out, marked 'Vacation in Florida.'"

"Really? I wonder what part of Florida? I'll bet it's not far from Daytona Beach."

Delarosa sat up in his chair. "Crap! I didn't know you could do that. Remind me to delete my online calendar and shit," he said, while the others wondered if he was kidding.

"Too, late, Tony," said Logan with a chuckle.

"So, Elizabeth and Levenson are converging on Daytona Beach for race weekend, just when T-Rex gets some anonymous free tickets. Lawler, get in touch with Ryan's people out in California and see if he is planning a trip to Florida that weekend."

Chilcote turned away from the window he was looking out of and walked slowly back to the ongoing conversation. "I don't know. We've been waiting for months for them to screw up, but I've got a funny feeling about this. I keep thinking they are smarter than that."

"I agree. How did they know right where to find T-Rex?" Delarosa asked.

"They are smart. They must have been the anonymous donor for the tickets."

"Delarosa, why don't you do some follow-up with Elizabeth, and when you are chit-chatting, see if you can get her to talk about her Florida vacation plans."

Turning back to the table, he said into the microphone, "Finally, this looks like the break we've been waiting for. If we play this right, we've got the opportunity to get our conspirators and prevent a crime. We've got one month to spring the trap."

CHAPTER 54

Detective Atkins picked up the phone on his desk. "Detectives. Atkins here."

"Darrell. This is Ryan Foster."

"Hey, Ryan. What's up? When are you going back to work?"

"Looks like I've been cleared for March 1st. I can't wait to get back to the office. That's the reason I called," he continued, "I'd like to brush up on my shooting skills. Can you contact your range officer and get permission for me to use the range this Wednesday? I'd call myself, but he might not recognize me since I've been gone."

"Sure, Ryan. I don't see why not. Any day and time in particular?"

"Thursday would be perfect. That way I can get it out of the way before I travel this weekend."

"Travel again? I'd have thought you'd be ready to stay home awhile."

"Oh, I will. But first I'm going to take one last weekend off, and go to the Daytona 500 in Florida. I always wanted to go see that race, and I decided I'm going to do it while I still have time before I go back to work. It's this Sunday."

"Daytona? Florida, huh?" he paused for a brief moment. "Okay, I'll call him and let you know ASAP."

Detective Atkins hung up the phone and looked at the floor and shook his head slowly; a deep frown of concern etched into his forehead. He had become quite friendly with Ryan through this ordeal, and he didn't want to think about what Ryan might be planning. *"I could just ignore my suspicions,"* he thought, *"but that wouldn't be the right thing to do."*

He went directly into the Sheriff's Office. "Sheriff, I just got a call you should know about."

Gleason looked up from the paper he was reading. "What's up, Darrell?"

"Ryan Foster just called. He's been cleared to go back to work on March 1st. He called to ask if he can use the range this week to brush up on his shooting skills."

"What's unusual about that? I'd do the same thing if I'd been off as long as he has."

"Nothing. Normally. But he also mentioned he was going to Florida this weekend to the stock car race in Daytona Beach."

"Shit. Florida." Gleason didn't need any further explanation of Atkins' concerns. "Damn. I hoped and prayed he was over all that. They're still considering him a 'person of interest' in the New York vigilante murders, and Detective Lawler still thinks he had Lemos killed, and now he's brushing up on his shooting skills before he goes to Florida this weekend, where T-Rex lives. God damn him!"

"I thought the same thing. Since Lawler has been working with the task force looking into the murders, I think I should tell her. She probably has a direct task force contact with the FBI. They need to get involved if something's going down this weekend."

"Yeah, call her. And then call that FBI guy and notify him yourself. We need to be sure we cover all the bases." He slammed his fist firmly on the desk. "Damn him."

"What about the range?"

Gleason thought a moment. "Arrange it. It's okay. If he's really just getting ready to go back to work, it would be normal to do. If he's not, he'd be suspicious if we refused."

A few minutes later, Atkins was on the phone to Detective Lawler.

"Lawler," she said as she picked up the phone.

"Detective, this is Darrell Atkins. I have some information you should know about."

"Atkins. I was going to call you this week. What's up?"

Atkins proceeded to tell her about the conversation with Foster, during the middle of which she interrupted him. "That is the final piece of the puzzle. The FBI Task force just found out that our three suspects are all converging separately on Daytona Beach and the Daytona 500. And ... T-Rex is also a guest at the race. It is definitely on for this weekend. Thanks for the tip. I've got to call Agent Chilcote right now. We've got to move on this, now. Thanks again. Goodbye."

Lawler put in an urgent call to Chilcote, who was at the New York FBI office.

"Great work, Detective Lawler. Looks like it is definitely going to go down this weekend in Daytona as we suspected. We need to get the task force together as soon as possible. Can you make it Wednesday? We'll meet Wednesday, or Thursday at the latest, at Daytona Beach PD."

"Yes, sir. I'll be there."

"All right, I'll see you there. Got to go now. I'll contact you later by e-mail. I've got to let Daytona Beach PD, Delarosa and the others know. Goodbye."

"Good …" The dial tone told her he was already off the line.

"Yes!" she shouted out loud, "I knew it!"

CHAPTER 55

As scheduled by Atkins, Ryan showed up at the range at the assigned time on Thursday morning. He looked quite relaxed, wearing a brand new long sleeve denim shirt with a Jeff Gordon logo on the chest. He and the range officer discussed NASCAR for a while, and it turned out both were Gordon fans.

After qualifying with his handgun, he also practiced with a rifle he had brought along. "Nice shooting, Lieutenant," said the range officer as Ryan was cleaning his pistol afterward. "It's almost as if you weren't gone at all. I wish all our Deputies could shoot as good."

Before he could respond, he heard a familiar voice behind him. "Yes, you've got a nice pattern there, Ryan."

Ryan turned and was met by Darrell Atkins whom he hadn't noticed standing in the shadows behind him.

"Well, hello, Darrell. I didn't see you there behind me."

"I just dropped by to see how you are doing."

"Great. I'm starting to really look forward to coming back to work on the first."

"Say, Ryan. I've been thinking. I've got a friend who has a fishing boat over in Fort Bragg. I thought maybe instead of going to the race this weekend, how about you, me and him go out deep sea fishing this weekend. I'm sure you'll have a great time – better than at the race – and you can record the race this year, and go to the 500 next year. Hell, if you'd like company, I might even go with you next year."

"That's a real nice offer, Darrell, but I think I've kind of committed to going to the race. Maybe later in the year. I'd love to go."

"Committed? Oh. I didn't realize you were meeting someone there."

"Actually, I'm not. But I've got the race ticket and the flights all lined up and all, so I'm pretty committed. Another time?"

"Yeah. I'm really sorry. I just thought …" his voice tailed off.

"… thought…?" Ryan paused as if to draw the rest of the sentence out of Atkins.

"Nothing. I just thought you could use the diversion."

"Diversion?"

"Yeah. You know. From the stress you've been through. People suspecting you and stuff. I thought maybe a day on the ocean might help."

"Really, I'm doing fine. I think after this weekend I'm going to be even better. I'm really looking forward to this trip as exactly what I need before I go back to work."

"Okay," he said. *"I tried,"* he thought to himself. "Good luck, Ryan." He reached out and gave Ryan a bear hug, as if to say goodbye to a friend he wouldn't see again."

"Hey, Buddy. I'm only going for the weekend. We'll do that fishing trip soon."

"Yeah."

"I better go now. See you soon." Ryan grabbed his gear bag and walked out the door.

Atkins watched him walk away and stared at the door long after it closed. *"I tried. I really tried to save him. There goes a good man down the path of destruction."*

Steve Davis

CHAPTER 56

It was 0905 Daytona time on Friday when Agent Chilcote called the meeting to order. "Gentlemen," he paused as his eyes spotted Lawler, "and ... uh, Detectives, please be seated."

As the task force members were seating themselves around the conference table, Lawler leaned over toward Chilcote and said in a low voice, "It's okay sir. I'm over that ma'am thing."

"Oh, I hadn't noticed whatever you are talking about," he said as he turned back to the group. "Some of us know each other, but since there are several more FBI Field Agents that have been added to the task force, as well as Daytona Beach Detectives, let's go around the room for introductions. Also refer to your Task Force Team assignments, on the table in front of you, to get to know your fellow team members."

After introductions were completed, Chilcote continued, "Here is what we know so far. The proposed intended target for this crime is Terrell Rexford, the former pro football player known as T-Rex, who was acquitted of murdering his estranged wife and her boyfriend, Sean Levinson, even though everyone knows he did it.

"T-Rex has been advised of the possible plot to shoot him, and he has decided to go ahead and attend the race as planned. He is adamant that no-one, especially Levenson, is going to intimidate him and his entourage of bodyguards. He is staying at the posh Hotel DuBoise while in Daytona Beach. His entourage is sited in the rooms on either side of his sixth-floor suite at the DuBoise. He doesn't want FBI protection – he doesn't trust us – thinks it's a trick. He insists his team of bodyguards are more protection than we could give him. Nevertheless, Task Force Team One, led by Detective Lawler, is assigned to protect T- Rex at all times, at the hotel, restaurants, and at the racetrack, as necessary, as long as the threat is viable."

"Our prime conspirator-suspect is California Highway Patrol Lieutenant Ryan Foster. Memorize the dossier on him that you will find in the packet in front of you and note that he is a law enforcement officer and he is an excellent shot with a handgun and a rifle. He's basically a good guy, but the murder of his daughter changed him. His only suspected malicious intent is toward T-Rex, but he should be considered armed and potentially dangerous if cornered. Once a crime is attempted, do not let down your guard, just in case. He is not likely to commit the crime where other innocent bystanders could be hurt."

"Why not just stop him and disarm him like any other suspect?" a Daytona Beach Detective asked.

"Because he's got his bases covered. He hasn't threatened anyone, including T-Rex. He hasn't committed any crime that we can even remotely pin on him, even though he might have, I repeat – might have - been the shooter in the New York Subway gang massacre a few months ago."

"He's a law enforcement officer," he continued, "so he can legally carry a concealed handgun in Florida, even in the vicinity of T- Rex, except, of course, he can't legally carry it at the racetrack, which is private property, and posted to that effect."

"We have to re-iterate this. Even though the task force thinks they are up to no good, Ryan, Elizabeth and Peter have not violated any laws, and all we can do is follow them and be prepared to stop anything if they attempt it."

"Task Force Team Two, headed up by Detectives Delarosa and O'Reilly, has been assigned extra people and will take over the Ryan Foster surveillance. We need to account for Ryan's every move 24-7!"

"Ryan arrived in town Wednesday night on the evening flight. He checked into his room at the Daytona Legends Hotel at 9:35PM, and we've already had a glitch in our stakeout. While the first stakeout team watched the lobby, and assumed he was sleeping after the long flight, he may have slipped out, because he came strolling into the lobby around 2:00 PM Thursday. We're not sure when he slipped out, and we have no idea where he was during that time."

"Since then, we have had a team on his floor where we can watch his door, and I just talked to them a few minutes ago, and he has been hanging around his hotel all day, catching up on his lost sleep out by the pool."

"Conspiracy Suspect number two is Peter Levenson. Team Three, led by FBI Field Agent Barkley, and Daytona Beach Police Detective Cochran, is assigned to him. They, and four other DBPD Detectives, will monitor him in teams 24/7."

"You will note in his dossier that he has not been directly linked to any crime so far, but he is the one who has the direct motive to kill T-Rex. It may be 'his turn' to commit a crime in this conspiracy. He is a disguise master, so be prepared for that. He could look like anyone, even a female. If he does, indeed, attempt to kill T-Rex, he is not likely to show poise in the act, because of inexperience and his hatred for T-Rex, and may inadvertently injure others in his way."

"I don't believe he is the potential killer because of his obvious personal involvement with T-Rex, but if not, we aren't sure why he is even here. In the other cases in which we suspect these conspirators, the person with the motive for the murder has had a perfect, foolproof alibi, far from where the crime was committed."

"Levenson has not arrived in Florida yet, but his Delta Airlines Flight is scheduled to arrive on Saturday night at 5:45 PM. Barkley and Cochran will meet his plane and Team 3 will monitor his whereabouts 24-7. He has reservations at the Hyatt in Daytona Beach through Sunday night. His departure flight, also on Delta, is on Monday morning at 8:05 AM."

"Our third Conspirator-suspect is Elizabeth Hartman, a well-to-do New York realtor who may be the money behind the conspiracy, even though surveillance of her bank accounts shows nothing out of the ordinary. Ironically, they would have us believe, Elizabeth has chosen to spend this week in Daytona Beach on 'vacation'. Also, 'ironically', at least we hope, she is also staying at the Hotel DuBoise, but in a different wing of the hotel from T-Rex. So far Task Force

Team Four, led by Agent Logan, has reported she mostly shops and lounges around the pool."

"I should mention that, adding to our problem, is this. Even with the FBI's best surveillance efforts in the past few weeks, we haven't been able to show any conversation between them, no social media posts, blogs, or tweets, – nothing. For all appearances, they don't even know each other are in town."

"Agent Chilcote, if you have all these suspicions that they are truly co-conspirators, as you suspect, why don't we round them up for Conspiracy to Commit a Federal Crime. That's a Felony good for many years in Federal Prison, and we can probably get them to roll over on each other," the Daytona Beach Detective said.

"Well, there are three major problems with that. First, in spite of lengthy investigations into five murders, we can't tie them to even one crime. Secondly, we have no evidence, no phone tap, no e-mail, no tweets, twitters or anything to show they have conspired to do anything. All we have is five dead dirtbags and the collective hunches of about a dozen Detectives from across the nation and in the FBI, and the hope they will screw this caper up and we can catch them red-handed before the sixth murder. And lastly, our FBI profiler says that due to the unique relationship of the conspirators - they are all victims whose loved ones were murdered - they have a very deep commitment to the relationship with the others, and therefore the chances of any of them rolling over on the others is extremely small."

"We all have each other's cell numbers. We'll keep everyone posted as the week progresses. Don't overlook even the slightest clue as to when and where it will go down and let us know any developments that make you suspicious."

"Don't worry, sir," said Agent Logan, "they can't possibly pull off a crime against T-Rex with this net around them."

CHAPTER 57

Ryan went to the track for the Friday Sprint Cup practice session and sat in the bleachers away from the crowd. The only other 'fans' nearby were two men, neither of whom was wearing any NASCAR memorabilia, a dead giveaway they were Detectives tailing him.

Soon, the cell phone in his pocket – the one marked with a 'T' for T-Rex - rang. "Hello. This is Jerry," he answered, knowing the caller had to be T-Rex. "What? I can barely hear you with this noise from the race cars. Hold on a minute, while I find a quiet place."

He quickly made his way down the stairs and ducked under the grandstands behind a concession booth where he couldn't be watched, and said, "I can hear you now. Who's calling?"

"Mr. Maxwell, I mean, Jerry, this is T-Rex."

"T-Rex! What's up, my man?"

"I was just checking on something. Hey, is something going on? I got a call from the FBI, saying I might be targeted if I went to the race Sunday. Do you know anything about it?"

"Hell, no. You and I are the only people who know you are going to be here. I haven't told anybody. Even my boss doesn't know I did it. It was just between you and me, in Chuck's memory. What do you mean, 'targeted'?"

"Killed, man. Murdered." Then, he sheepishly added, "I might have tipped 'em off."

"What do you mean?"

"Well, I might have mentioned it on Twitter. But don't worry. I didn't mention you or American Rent-a-Car by name."

"I can't see why that would be a problem. That's outrageous, man. Who'd want to kill you? And why here? It's got to be a prank. You will be in the middle of 100,000 fans at the most famous racetrack, and on national TV. No-one could get to you here, even if they wanted to. You still have your bodyguards, don't you?"

"Yes."

"They are good at what they do, aren't they?"

"Of course."

"I wouldn't worry about it. It's gotta be a prank from someone who is still sore about the verdict. But hey, listen buddy, if you aren't going to use those seats, let me know now. I've got lots of people who'd love to use them. So, let me know now, okay."

"Don't worry, Jerry. I'm sure it's a prank. I'll be there, don't worry about those seats. We are using them. Okay, man?"

"Okay, good. Enjoy the race, T-Rex, and don't worry about it. I'm still going to drop by and get that autograph. Okay?"

"Right on."

"It should be a good, exciting race. Hey, I've got another call coming in. See you there. T-Rex."

"Bingo. Just like I figured," Ryan thought as he hung up.

As he walked back up the stairs toward his seat, he passed one of the men who had been tailing him going the opposite direction to check on him. As he passed the man, he talked into the cell phone, "Okay, Bill, I'll see you at the front gate at the New Smyrna Raceway tonight at 5:30. Later, dude."

As he passed, the man turned around and headed back up behind him. *"Enjoy the race at New Smyrna tonight, fellows,"* Ryan snickered to himself.

On his way back to the hotel, he stopped for dinner at a Barbeque Restaurant. After ordering, he went into the rest room. He pulled the battery and SIMM card out of the phone. He stomped the phone into small pieces and flushed them down the toilet along with the battery and SIMM card.

CHAPTER 58

Peter Levenson walked down the covered gangway from Flight 1111 and into the lobby of the airport. He looked around the room with anticipation. As he expected, as soon as he emerged through the doorway, a man whom he spotted as an obvious undercover police detective was seated in the boarding area holding a newspaper in front of his face. After Peter passed, the man got up folder the paper under his arm and made his way down the walkway about fifteen feet behind him. *"Just as Ryan predicted. Just be natural and quit looking around. Act like you don't see them, Peter,"* he said to himself. As he ducked into the restroom, he glanced back at the man, who made brief, inadvertent eye contact, but kept on walking.

"Maybe not," Peter thought as he walked to the urinal. When he emerged a few minutes later, the man was not in sight. He continued down the walkway toward the Baggage Claim area. When he turned left at the main terminal, he noted another man, dressed more casually, with a polo shirt, watch him walk by and fall in behind him as he walked.

Steve Davis

"Did he just talk into his wrist watch, or did I imagine it?"

At the Baggage Claim, he looked around for 'polo shirt', who was not in sight, but, there in the crowd to his right was the first man who had followed him.

"Leapfrog. They're playing leapfrog. I hope Ryan knows what he's doing. These guys are following me like I'm public enemy number one. I'm sure Ryan and Elizabeth are getting the same treatment."

From the airport, the taxi drove straight to the Daytona Hilton. As he got out, he noticed a plain sedan pull into the driveway, but stopped far behind the taxi. 'Polo Shirt' got out and began to walk in Peter's general direction. Peter stepped into the hotel and pulled his luggage straight for the Registration Desk.

After Peter checked in, he made his way to his room on the third floor. He felt like he was being watched as he slipped the card into the key slot, so he glanced in both directions but saw no-one. He dropped off his luggage and went to the hotel restaurant for dinner, where he was soon joined, six tables away, by his new shadows, 'Polo Shirt' and the other detective.

CHAPTER 59

Sunday Morning; The Daytona 500

Peter was the first to arrive at the track on Sunday morning, the day of the Daytona 500. In fact, he was there when the gates opened at 8:00 AM, followed by Agent Barkley and Daytona Beach Detective Cochran, working as Team Three. They seemed a little surprised that he was easily recognizable, with no attempt to disguise his appearance.

Once inside, he made his way around the outside walkway to the concession stands adjacent to the ground floor entrance to the Richard Petty Grandstand. He ordered some food and coffee at a nearby concession and sat at a table with a good view of foot traffic approaching the Petty Tower.

At 9:25 AM Barkley reported that Levenson seemed to be extremely nervous and had not moved from his position for over an hour, as if he were waiting to meet someone.

Another hour passed, and Barkley reported once again that Levenson hadn't moved from his location, even though probably 15,000 people had passed by his location.

"Stay with him. It's obvious he's there at that location for a reason," said Chilcote.

CHAPTER 60

"Two eggs, ruined, with hash browns – smothered, covered, topped, and scattered!" yelled the Waffle House waitress who took Ryan's order to the cook twenty feet away,

"Two eggs, ruined, 'browns smothered, covered, topped, and scattered!" the cook hollered back without looking up from the grill.

"A Gordon fan, huh?" she said as she turned back to Ryan.

"How'd you guess?" Ryan asked.

"Not too hard. You are wearing a Gordon shirt."

"Oh, yeah," he said as he glanced down at his Jeff Gordon denim shirt.

"I'm a Junior fan, myself," she said, referring to driver Dale Earnhardt Jr., "Gordon whines too much. But it's okay, as long as it's a Chevy driver. Even Johnson would be fine with me."

"Earnhardt would be okay with me, too. Junior has earned it and has a huge fan base down here."

"Good luck," she said as she walked away, "Gotta work."

It was just after 9:00 AM when Ryan replaced the menu into its slot and leaned back in the well-worn counter stool at the Waffle House near the Daytona Legends Hotel. He glanced over his right shoulder and confirmed that Delarosa and O'Reilly, the two men he had observed tailing him from the hotel, were still hanging out nearby.

Delarosa leaned across to table to O'Reilly, "He's smaller and less buffed than I expected him to be. I expected the guy to look like Schwarzenegger, since he took down four men by himself in a dark alley."

"Yeah. But he looks like an okay guy to me. I still can't help but think about his daughter getting killed and then they want to put him away for murdering her killer, when he was nowhere around. I kind of hope we're on a wild goose chase down here?"

After breakfast, Ryan walked down the block and stood at the bus stop for the Speedway Special bus to take him the short distance to the race track. Delarosa stood nearby while the crowd gathered and waited, and then shortly later a 'conspicuously unmarked' car pulled up and Delarosa got into the passenger seat. It remained illegally parked a short distance away until the bus arrived.

At the end of the short bus trip, at the Speedway bus stop, Ryan got off the bus in the crowd and looked for the men following him. He had to stall and hang around for a couple minutes for the trailing Detectives to illegally park their unmarked police car and catch up to him.

"Thought we'd lost him there for a minute, O'Reilly said."

Across the street from the race track, Ryan stopped at a souvenir trailer and bought a Jeff Gordon DuPont Racing #24 jacket and cap. He made sure the Detectives trailing him had plenty of time to see him slip into the jacket and cap, and casually walk toward the track entrance.

Near the entrance to the track he spotted a ticket scalper trying to be inconspicuous as he worked the crowd. "Tickets? Anybody need tickets?" he said in a voice that only those walking nearby could hear.

"What do you have for one ticket?" Ryan asked as he approached the man.

The man looked him over, up and down. "Over here," he motioned as they stepped off to the side.

"Man, it's your lucky day. I got the best seat in the house, near the top of the Allison Tower, coming out of turn 2 with a view of most of the track. VIP section; they even have waiters to take your order. Just $300.00." He placed the ticket in Ryan's hand, as if to say, *'Of course you're going to jump at this bargain',* as he turned his head to the side as if to watch out for cops.

"Not so fast. What's the face?"

"The face? What's that got to do with it? This race has been sold out for a year. Nobody buys tickets for face value."

"Yeah, yeah. What's the face?"

"$185.00. But you can't touch it for that. Tell you what. I'll let you have it for $250.00."

"What else you got?"

"What's wrong with this ticket, man? This is a great seat. A brother has to make a little profit, doesn't he? How much you want to spend?"

"$150.00."

"No way, man. How can I sell it to you for less than I paid for it?"

"Well, for starters, you didn't pay near that much for it. Look here. See this name? NAPA Auto. This was part of a huge block of tickets bought by NAPA Auto for their distributors. The ones they don't sell or give away, they sell to you guys for pennies on the dollar. You probably paid about $80.00 or less for it."

"No, man. You got it wrong. How much you want to give me for it?"

$150.00. Listen, it is a single ticket and no-one, except me, comes to the race alone, at the last minute, that can afford a top-level ticket. So, you'll probably get stuck with it. Oh, you might sell it at the last minute for almost nothing, but you can't afford not to double your money right now."

"Forget it, man. $220.00. Last offer."

"Okay, here is what else I know. It is illegal for you to sell this ticket over face value."

"What are you, a cop or something

"No. not in Florida." He nodded over his left shoulder. "But you see those guys just hanging out over there watching us."

The scalper looked over Ryan's shoulder at Delarosa and O'Reilly, who immediately looked away conspicuously. "Yeah, I see them. Who are they?"

"They are cops, of course. I saw them bust a guy in the parking lot for scalping. As soon as you sell me this ticket, for $150.00, which is below face value and therefore legal, of course, you better haul ass and get away from here." He was still holding the ticket in his left hand. He discreetly extended his right hand with a hundred and a fifty-dollar bill. "Here's my $150.00. Deal?"

"Okay. Deal. Thanks for telling me about the cops."

"As soon as I walk away, they're going to come over here, so get out of here now."

The scalper turned and walked away from Ryan and the other men. Ryan turned and nonchalantly walked toward the men to keep them from chasing after the scalper. After he believed the young scalper had a good head start, he turned and started walking directly toward the entrance gate.

O'Reilly followed Ryan and directed Delarosa to stop the scalper to find out where Ryan was going to sit. The scalper took off jogging into the crowds coming from the parking lot. Delarosa walked briskly after him, trying not to arouse Ryan's attention, but soon gave up as he lost him in the crowded entry.

Ryan walked straight to the entrance gate and passed through it. He glanced at his watch; 10:35 AM. He turned east, away from the Allison Tower, and joined the growing crowd, trailed by O'Reilly.

O'Reilly crowded into the front of the line and flashed his badge at the ticket agent. "Police Officer. Where's that guy's seat?"

The ticket agent looked at him skeptically. "Yeah. Like I memorize everyone's ticket in case some cop wants to know. Did that badge say New York? C'mon. Nice try. Where's your ticket, buddy."

O'Reilly watched Ryan getting further away. "Forget the fuckin' ticket. Police business." He pushed his way through the gate and took off in Ryan's direction.

"Cheap ass!" the ticket agent yelled at him.

Agent Chilcote was seated inside the Task Force Command Post when the radio crackled. "Task Force Team 2. This is Delarosa. Ryan just bought a ticket from a scalper who lost me in the crowd. We don't know where Ryan's seat is located, so keep him in sight at all times. Where are you now, 2-A?"

"Don't worry, I've still got a good visual on him," said O'Reilly. "I'm inside the gate, heading west. Command Post, he's wearing a Jeff Gordon jacket and cap. Looks like he's going into the restroom. Catch up with me here 2-B. I'll keep him in sight till you get here."

"This isn't starting very well," Chilcote said to no one in particular at the Command Post.

Ryan entered the crowded restroom and walked to the urinals side of the full-length divider, then ducked back against the back side of the entry wall. O'Reilly entered the restroom, then had to choose which side of the divider to check. He glanced first to the urinals side of the divider, and not seeing Ryan, went to the sinks and stalls side. As he moved through the crowded room, surveying the sinks area, and straining to see shoes in the closed stalls, Ryan ducked back out of the entrance side and scurried into the crowd.

O'Reilly ran outside and looked in both directions. "Crap. This is Team 2A. Other members of Team 2 converge on this location. Keep an eye out for Ryan. I lost him at the rest room by the main gate. He might still be inside in one of the stalls. I'm going to go back and check the stalls, but I'm pretty sure he slipped out. He's wearing a multicolor Jeff Gordon DuPont jacket and cap."

Chilcote grabbed the microphone. "All posts. Be on the lookout for Ryan. Wearing a Jeff Gordon jacket and cap. He may be headed anywhere, stay focused on your own target, but be looking for him." He put down the microphone and slammed his fist on the desk, "Shit!"

"How in the hell could that happen? They've only been tailing him for fifteen minutes."

"Do you realize how many Jeff Gordon jackets there are out here?" a voice asked anonymously.

"I don't care if you stop Jeff Gordon himself. Find Ryan!"

CHAPTER 61

At precisely 11:15 AM, Elizabeth exited Room 430 at the Hotel DuBoise and closed the door behind her. She wore a white Hotel DuBoise bathrobe and matching slippers and carried a large beach towel as she walked to the elevator. She was joined by another man she hadn't noticed before in the hallway, and, without speaking, they descended to the ground floor.

She confidently strode through the hotel lobby and headed toward the huge glass sliding doors which separated the lobby from the hotel pool in the open courtyard. As she did so, she pretended not to notice Agent Logan, whom she did not know, who got up as she crossed the lobby and followed her into the courtyard.

She went straight to a lounge chair in the front row at the open end of the courtyard. She slowly and seductively removed her robe, revealing a skimpy hot pink bikini. As she did so, she shot a quick glance over her shoulder to see Agent Logan, who was joined by his partner, Daytona Beach Detective Hoskins, whom she rode on the elevator with. She noticed that both were watching her every move from the opposite side of the pool.

She couldn't resist a smile as she enjoyed the attention. Sliding a pair of oversized sunglasses on, she arched her back flirtatiously as she adjusted the chair back into a semi-reclined position and sat back, keeping a watchful eye on the men, but more importantly, the windows of rooms 600 and 786.

"All in all, this just might be my favorite stakeout of all time," Logan whispered to Hoskins. He pulled out a deck of cards and began to shuffle them. Their casual Tommy Bahama beach shirts blended into the pool scene in a strangely conspicuous way as they both tried to look like they were also just relaxing around the pool.

"What's not to like for a New York-based Agent?" he continued, "It's snowing in New York, and I'm sitting here in the Florida sunshine, at a five-star hotel, beside a beautiful pool, assigned to watch a gorgeous woman in a bikini, while the others are trying to keep up with Ryan in a mob scene at the race track."

"Hard to think of her as a cold-blooded murderer, if she is," the Detective said.

"She's getting up."

The men watched intently as Elizabeth walked over to the pool and stepped into the water up to her neck, paused a few seconds and went back to her lounge chair. She bent over to spread out a towel on the lounge, then she held the front of her bikini with her right hand, loosened the rear strap with her left, and laid face down on her blanket, tossing the straps to the sides. Every once in a while, she would raise up just enough to change the page of the magazine she was reading. Each time she did so, she revealed a little more of her bare breasts, causing the men to stop their game of Rummy and lean forward each time in anticipation.

Elizabeth looked up and saw the curtains of room 600 part for a moment, then open fully. She smiled at the thought that another man had joined the Elizabeth show.

Logan sat back in his chair and fanned out his cards. "If this is a conspiracy to kill T-Rex, why is she even here if she is just going to lay around the pool. T-Rex left for the race track forty-five minutes ago with his entourage. I just heard Team One say on the radio that T-Rex and his boys were at the track already and on their way toward their seats."

"Maybe the attack isn't going to be at the track at all. Maybe it's here later, or at a restaurant."

"That's their problem for now. Let's relax and enjoy the view. By the way, here's three nines, the two, three, joker, and five of clubs, discard the king, and I'm 'OUT'. Count them up partner."

CHAPTER 62

As soon as Ryan slipped away from the officers at the restroom, he went directly to a nearby Tony Stewart souvenir trailer and bought a Tony Stewart jacket, backpack, cap and sunglasses. He slipped around the side of the trailer, slipped into the Tony Stewart jacket and cap, and stuffed the Jeff Gordon jacket and cap into the backpack.

Keeping close to a large group of fans outside the grandstands, he made his way toward the east gate of the race track. Shortly later, while the Task Force, Detectives and local Police were searching for him at the track wearing a Jeff Gordon Jacket and cap, he had his hand stamped and slipped out of the east entrance wearing the Tony Stewart paraphernalia and dark sunglasses. He walked a short block across Midway Avenue and into the nearby Daytona Beach International Airport Long Term Parking Lot and approached the Chevy rental car which he had rented and parked at that location during the time he was unaccounted for on Thursday night and Friday morning.

He pulled a pair of skin colored latex gloves from his pocket, put them on, and got into the car. He glanced at his watch as he pulled onto Midway Avenue and headed north. *"11:20,"* he thought, *"Driver introductions start in about an hour."*

Steve Davis

CHAPTER 63

"All task force units," Chilcote spoke into the long silent microphone, "Anybody have anything to report on Ryan or Levenson?"

"This is Team 2," Delarosa said, "We've got our members fanned out all around the track. Nothing so far. It's easy to hide among 120,000 of your closest friends. But T-Rex should be alright. We've assigned extra members to hang around T-Rex's location in case Ryan tries to make a move on him."

"This is Team 3A. Levenson has been sitting at the same table watching everyone passing by his location since 0830. I've watched everyone who passed by here, probably 50,000 people, and I've been especially looking for Ryan, and I think maybe Levenson was supposed to meet Ryan, but the plan fell apart and Ryan isn't going to show up. I'm pretty sure he made us back at the restroom, and Levenson is wasting his time waiting for him."

Detective Lawler said, "This is Team 1, with T-Rex. Where did you say Levenson is sitting?"

350

"At the concession stand near the tunnel entrance to the Petty Grandstand."

"Okay, get ready. Our guy, T-Rex, is approaching that area now on his way to his seats in the Petty Grandstand," Lawler responded, "You should see him soon. He's got his fedora pulled low with a full-length coat, with three bodyguards on all sides like a frickin' rock star."

"Team 3 here. Levenson just spotted T-Rex's entourage coming toward us and perked up. He's getting up and hiding his face and waiting for T-Rex to pass."

"Team 1 here. We have your subject in sight. He's definitely locked in on T-Rex. We are turning into the tower entrance now, passing your subject's location."

"He just got up and is following you about 25 feet behind you. Looks like he's moving in on your guy. We are closing in on him."

"10-4."

"He has quickened his pace catching up to you. We're practically running to keep up. He's right behind you now. Reaching into his pocket. He's got something ... possible gun in his right hand! Move in on him! It's going down. Now!"

Suddenly Peter was swarmed front and rear by officers from both Teams, who grabbed at his right arm.

"Freeze! Police!" yelled the agent in charge.

"What the …," Peter yelled. Before he could react, the first man to reach him tackled him and pinned his right arm behind his back, causing him to drop the object from his grasp. The others held him down until he was safely handcuffed.

Two men pulled Levenson up to his feet while Lawler reached down and picked up the dark object, Levinson's wallet.

A small crowd gathered around to see what was happening, including the T-Rex entourage, who looked back at the commotion occurring behind them. One of the bodyguards pushed his way back to the scene of the fracas and took a close look at Peter. "That's him alright, officers," he said, "I've been carrying his photo in my wallet for over a year. Let me at that fucking punk. I'll teach him to mess with T-Rex."

"We've got it from here. You and your group can go on and enjoy the race. He won't be a problem, now."

"You goddam right. I told T-Rex this morning we'd handle it. But he didn't believe me. Let's go see the race, fellas."

"What the hell is going on?" Peter asked. "What's this all about."

"Stopping you from doing something stupid."

"What are you talking about?"

"Your attempt to kill T-Rex. You have the right to remain silent ..." He stopped as Lawler tapped him on the elbow and showed him the wallet.

"Are you crazy?" Peter said. "I'm just going to my seat to watch the race."

Another agent who had searched Levenson said, "He's clean. No weapons."

"Look in my wallet. My ticket is in there. I was just getting it out to check the row and seat number. The race is about to start soon, you know."

"Check his wallet," said the man holding his arm. The disgust that this might be a mistake was now becoming increasingly apparent.

"Here it is. Petty Tower, row 45, seat 27," said Lawler.

Lawler sidled up to Peter, like an old friend, "What are you three up to, Peter? This can't all be a coincidence. Seats in the same tower as T-Rex, your timing, Ryan losing us. Come on. It's over. Tell us what's going on so we can stop it before Ryan gets all three of you into big trouble over your head."

"Who are you? Do I know you? …, T-Rex? Ryan? What do they have to do with this … this unprovoked attack?" Peter said.

"You know what I'm talking about, Peter. We know all about what you, Elizabeth, and Ryan are planning. You might as well call it off. It's not going to work."

"Elizabeth?" Peter asked incredulously.

"Peter. We are here to keep you from ruining your life. Come on. Work with us while you still haven't broken any laws."

"If I haven't broken any laws, why am I handcuffed?"

"Uncuff him," said the agent in charge.

After the cuffs were removed, Peter rubbed the wrists where they had been. "Thanks. Now, if I haven't broken any laws, am I free to go? I have been looking forward to seeing this race for a long time, and it's about to start."

Lawler looked at the other lead Detective from Team 3, who gave her a frown of resignation and a slow head shake. "Okay, Peter, you can go," she said. "But we'll be watching you all day and night until your flight leaves tomorrow morning. I guess officially I should apologize for knocking you down and handcuffing you, so consider this an apology, even though we still know you are up to something."

"Apology accepted." He took a step or two and then turned around. "And, if someone does kill T-Rex today, or any other day, please, by all means, tell them I said 'Thank you'. Good bye lady and gentlemen."

As Levenson walked away, Agent Chilcote approached the group, having ran down from the Command Center.

"What the … ? Why did you let him go?" he said.

After he was advised by Lawler what had happened, he shook his head in disgust. "We're screwed. I've got one team watching Elizabeth sunbathe, and now two more teams just got set up and were 'had' bigtime by Peter. This is all a ruse to keep us away from the real plot involving Ryan, and we've lost him in this crowd. Two of you continue to follow Levenson, but we need to redouble our efforts to locate Ryan.

Steve Davis

The rest of you fan out and find Ryan. He's somewhere out there, and he's got something planned. And put two extra men on guarding T-Rex."

CHAPTER 64

Ryan parked in the west parking lot at the Hotel DuBoise. He took off his Tony Stewart jacket while still in the car, and the Gordon denim shirt. He opened a bag next to him on the seat and took out, and put on a lime green golf shirt. Also from the bag, he retrieved a mustache and goatee beard disguise, and put them on. He looked around to assure there was no-one watching, then doffed a Daytona Shores Golf Course hat. Pulling it low on his forehead, he popped open the trunk, and exited the vehicle.

He retrieved a golf bag from the trunk of the car and walked to the rear side door of the west wing of the hotel. Using his room key card, he opened the door and went up the back staircase to the 7th floor. He opened the door to room 786, and entered the room.

He took off the golf shirt and pulled out the Jeff Gordon denim shirt that he had worn to the range on Thursday and put it on. He went to the window and looked down at the pool area and saw Elizabeth sunbathing on a deck chair. Just as he planned it, he couldn't see the men watching Elizabeth from below his location. He looked across to the east tower and smiled when he saw the curtains opened to room 600. *"I knew it,"* he said.

He pulled a screwdriver from the golf bag and unscrewed the window hinges and carefully swung it all the way back into the room. He picked up a roll of thin transparent painter's window covering, and carefully taped it over the open window and curtains. Then he dragged the desk over in front of the window, and pulled a shower curtain out of the golf bag and spread it over the desktop.

"That should contain most of the gunshot residue."

Next, he unzipped the golf club cover on the golf bag and pulled out a sniper rifle with a folding tripod and a scope attached and carefully unwrapped it. He snapped on a polarized filter to diminish any glare from the room 600 window, then screwed a long silencer onto the barrel. He carefully placed the tripod on the desk with the muzzle still well inside the open window, so as not to be visible from the outside, and aimed it in the direction of the window of room 600.

Ryan went to the bathroom and grabbed a roll of toilet paper and wrapped his entire face and neck with it, leaving a small gap for his eyes, which he covered with his sunglasses. Next, he wrapped his arms with toilet paper, covering them from the top of the gloves to the shirt sleeves.

Stepping toward the window, he took a mirror out of his pocket and held it so that it reflected a beam of light onto the ground in front of Elizabeth's lounge chair. Seeing the beam of light dancing across the open page of her magazine, she closed the cover and glanced up to the window of room 786. Another flash of light confirmed Ryan was in position. She acknowledged him by removing her sunglasses and putting them back on, while looking in the direction of Logan and Hoskins, indicating they were in position and occupied.

CHAPTER 65

Within minutes after the failed takedown of Levenson, the Task Force had stationed one extra man at each end of the row T-Rex was sitting in. Another was posted at the foot of the stairs in case Ryan showed up and made an attempt on T-Rex.

T-Rex's bodyguards kept looking at the men and talking amongst themselves, until it appeared they were more interested in the men than the upcoming race. Just before driver introductions, the lead bodyguard got up and made his way across the crowded row to speak to the agent at the end of the row.

"Officer, me and the boys hate to see you guys wasting your time just hanging around watching us."

"It's what we do. There was a threat to T-Rex and we have to act on it, no matter what we think of the person involved, or whether he believes it or not."

"Yeah, we know about the threats and we know how you feel about T-Rex, but it's not necessary."

"Look. I know you guys think you got him protected, but we have to sit here and make sure he's safe."

"That's what I'm trying to tell you, man. You are wasting your time. He's not here."

"What are you talking about? I can see him right there," he said, pointing to the group of men.

"That's not T-Rex. It's his double. T-Rex got nervous about the threats and decided to send his double, Michael, instead. He's safe back at the hotel. I've been watching you guys and thought I better tell you. I hate to see you waste your time."

"Are you fucking kidding me?" the agent said as he leaped to his feet.

The bodyguard motioned to his friends, and the man posing as T-Rex removed his hat and opened his coat. Close in appearance, but clearly not T-Rex.

The agent shook his head in disbelief and hurried down the stairs to the man guarding the foot of the stairs, while he yelled into the radio, "Command Post, this is Team 1. I just found out the guy we've been guarding as T-Rex isn't him at all. T-Rex is back at the hotel."

Steve Davis

"God damn him," said Chilcote as he reached for the microphone and keyed the switch. "Are you sure?"

"A hundred percent. If Ryan's here he's stalking the wrong man. What do we do now?"

CHAPTER 66

Elizabeth held her bikini to her bosom with one hand as she stood up and looked around as if looking for assistance. Finally, she looked at Logan and Hoskins and walked over to them. Logan cringed as to what she might be up to.

"Pardon me, gentlemen. Could I impose upon one of you to tie the back of my swimsuit for me. I can't seem to reach it."

In room 786, Ryan squeezed the trigger slightly and whispered, "Come to papa, you miserable coward."

Logan jumped up to help Elizabeth, as the radio blared, "Team 4, come in. Team 4."

"I'll handle this, Hoskins. You get the radio."

As Logan slowly began to tie Elizabeth's bikini string, Hoskins stepped to the side out of Elizabeth's earshot, and answered the radio page, "Team 4-B. Go ahead."

"Be on the lookout. We just learned that T-Rex isn't even at the track. He's in his room at the DuBois. He's there with you. Have you seen him? Or Ryan?"

"Copy, boss. Negative on Ryan or T-Rex."

"What about Elizabeth, do you still have her in sight?"

"Yes, we've still got Elizabeth in sight." He raised his eyebrows at how closely she was 'in sight'. "Do you want us to go check on T-Rex in his room?"

"Yes. Suite 600."

At that moment, there was a loud, yet muffled, 'POP' that echoed around the pool foyer, accompanied by the sound of a shattered window glass from the west wing of the courtyard.

"Goodness! What was that?" Elizabeth jumped back excitedly, catching her still untied bikini and holding it loosely in place.

Both men jumped at the sound and ran out into the open where they could see the broken window on the sixth floor, in time to see a small puff of dust come from inside of room. "Crap! Quick. Room 600. T-Rex may be in trouble," Logan shouted. "Let's go." He keyed the radio mike and yelled "Shots fired at Hotel DuBois. Room 600. We're checking on T-Rex."

Elizabeth held onto the untied bikini and stepped back as they ran around her. After they fled, she walked back to her lounge chair. She put on the robe and slippers and headed for her room.

At the Command post, Chilcote slammed his fist on the desk, and threw the radio across the room, hitting the back of a chair and bouncing onto the floor. "Shit. He did it right under our noses," he screamed, "How? He was just here at the track. How could he have figured out that T-Rex chickened out?"

He went quickly across the room and picked up the radio. To his relief, it worked when he keyed the microphone. "Team 1, all members respond to the DuBois. Team 2 and Team 3; stay at the track and keep an eye out for Ryan. Lawler, you are the only one who actually knows Ryan. Check the stands at the track and look for him. Find him! Ryan, damn it."

"100,000 people here, sir."

"I don't give a damn if you have to frisk every one of them, find Ryan if he's here."

"10-4, sir."

He paused a moment to gather his thoughts. "Get Daytona Beach PD on the scene as soon as possible to lock down the DuBois. He may be on foot or traveling by bus. We've got to pin Ryan's location down right now. Put out an

All-Points Bulletin to all law enforcement agencies to be on the lookout for Ryan Foster.

"What description do I give them, boss," his aide asked.

"Give his physical description, WMA age 45, six feet tall, 185-195 lbs. Last seen wearing Levis and a Jeff Gordon jacket and hat."

"That narrows it down to only about fifty thousand people here this weekend," the aide murmured.

CHAPTER 67

As soon as the shot was fired, Ryan ripped off the painters covers over the window and curtains and stuffed them into the golf bag. He picked up the screwdriver and re-attached the hinge to the window, closed it and closed the curtains. Tearing the GSR-stained toilet paper from his face and arms, he ran to the toilet and flushed them in several flushes. Moving as fast as possible, he removed the silencer and wrapped the rifle in the shower curtain used to cover the desk. He shoved it into the golf bag.

He took off the Gordon shirt and put the golf shirt back on. He threw the screw driver and the Gordon shirt into the golf bag, moved the desk back into position and glanced at his watch as he paused before opening the door. Two minutes and 5 seconds had transpired since the shot. The first responding officers, the men assigned to watch Elizabeth, would be approaching T-Rex's 6th floor room in the west wing.

He left the room and walked to the east tower elevator, which he took to the lobby, turned left and calmly walked to the side lobby door. He could hear a siren approaching in the distance.

Exiting the building, he walked out to the parking lot wearing the golf shirt and hat and golf bag over his shoulder, appearing like any other hotel guest, unaware of what transpired, and en route to his tee time.

He got into the rental car and pulled out of the lot as the first police car was visible about three blocks away. He drove a safe distance toward the beach and stopped in a McDonald's parking lot. He could hear sirens in the distance, as he took off his latex gloves and wadded them up in a used hamburger bag, and put on new gloves which were not covered with gunshot residue. He disposed of the bag in a McDonalds trash can and pulled out onto Mason Avenue and headed toward the beach and away from the track.

CHAPTER 68

Two minutes after the shots were fired, Logan and his partner were standing outside T-Rex's 6th-floor room, knocking on the door, normally at first, then louder. Getting no response, they summoned a maid from down the hall and had the door opened.

"Aaack," she screamed as the men burst past her and saw the lifeless body of T-Rex on the floor next to the shattered window. The back of his head was split wide open from the exit wound. A pair of binoculars lay on the floor to his side. The TV in the next room was blaring with the early laps of the Daytona 500.

Logan grabbed his radio, "All teams and Control, this is Team 2A. T-Rex has been shot and killed at the Hotel DuBoise. We need to get the PD and others to the DuBoise ASAP for lockdown and search. Lock down the hotel and don't let anyone out."

Trying not to disturb the glass and any other evidence that might exist, Hoskins looked out the window to try to determine where the fatal shot was fired from. The entire east wing appeared normal, some curtains open, some closed, but all of the glass windows appeared in place. He looked at the roof and hoped it hadn't come from there.

The Hotel manager was now standing at the door looking at the scene in disbelief.

Logan ran up to him. "Grab your pass key, we need to check all rooms on the fifth through seventh floors across the courtyard that have a clear view of this window. Have someone meet us at the fifth floor with a guest list."

Hoskins," he yelled. "Get up on the roof and see if there is anything to indicate the shot came from there. Also, shut down the elevators and lock down the east wing and the courtyard. Nobody leaves until the police arrive and screen them."

CHAPTER 69

Ryan was already long gone from the Hotel by that time. He drove a half-mile further down Mason Avenue heading toward the beach. The local highways were nearly deserted, as everyone who wasn't at the track seemed to be watching the race at home. Turning off of the main highway, he drove to a light industrial area and stopped at three separate locations, a half mile apart, with large curb-level storm drain openings, which he had scouted out earlier on Thursday. He disposed of parts of the rifle in each one, each wrapped in a sealable plastic bundle with a corrosive agent to speed the corrosion process. The silencer was similarly placed in yet another drain in another area.

Having disposed of the gun, he drove to a previously located dumpster and disposed of the plastic table cloth, and the painter's covers. Next, he drove directly to a Goodwill donation box he had also scouted out on Friday. He wiped down the inside and outside of the golf bag, and put it in the box, covering it from being visible from the outside with donated clothing.

371

He changed out of his golf shirt and put on the Gordon denim shirt covered by the Tony Stewart hat and jacket. He then drove back to the race track and parked outside the east entrance. He carefully wiped down the interior of the car, removed the gloves, and stuffed them in his pockets until he passed a trash can in the east parking lot and disposed of them deep into the garbage.

With collar up and hat pulled down low, he re-entered the track using his ticket stub and the hand stamp, and headed toward the Allison Tower. Along the way, he stopped at the first restroom and went into a stall and changed back into the Jeff Gordon jacket and hat, leaving the Tony Stewart hat and jacket in the backpack hanging on the inside of the door, knowing someone would help themselves to them when found.

He scrubbed the re-entry stamp from his hand, and headed for the Allison Grandstand. *"It would be fine if they see me now,"* he thought, *"I've been here all day."*

CHAPTER 70

The first arriving Daytona Beach Police officers quickly cordoned off the hotel and the surrounding blocks, but Ryan had already slipped away un-noticed.

T-Rex was pronounced dead at the scene and Evidence Technicians were already on site and beginning to diligently process the crime scene.

Chilcote arrived at the DuBoise about twenty-five minutes later and began to grill Logan and Hoskins. "What about Elizabeth? Have we accounted for her exact whereabouts at the time of the shots fired?"

Logan and Hoskins looked at each other sheepishly and Logan said, "Yes, she's clear."

"Clear? What exactly does that mean? Did you have eyes on her at the time?"

Hoskins giggled.

"What's so fucking funny about this?" He waved his hand toward the body of T-Rex on the floor.

"Well, our job was to keep her under surveillance, right?"

"Yes. What aren't you telling me?"

Logan looked at Hoskins, then Chilcote, and said, "I was tying her bikini for her down by the pool when the shots were fired." He took a step back, looked down and away as if he thought Chilcote would explode.

Chilcote took a step back and yelled incredulously, "You were tying her fucking bikini when T-Rex was murdered? What the fuck is going on around here? Are we the fucking FBI or the Keystone Cops? They not only killed our man that we were supposed to protect, but they are mocking us while they do it. Peter got us to jump him at the track, and Elizabeth has you tying her fucking bikini while T-Rex is shot by a sniper, who I assume has to be Ryan. They are playing us like a fucking fiddle."

He turned to the radio and keyed the mike, "All Teams. This is important. Keep looking for Ryan. Bring in Peter and Elizabeth to Daytona Beach Police station, now!" Turning away from the radio, he said, "We'll see if the weak links of this conspiracy can hold up to a little scrutiny and interrogation by the FBI and Daytona Beach Detectives."

Spinning around to face Logan and Hoskins, he said, "You guys, don't just stand there, find out where the shots came from."

"Hey, cool your jets, boss," said Logan. "Take a deep breath. We've been working on that since the crime occurred. We traced the probable trajectories for the fatal shot and narrowed it down to about ten rooms across the courtyard. Hoskins and the manager have narrowed it down to one of five rooms with an unobstructed shot at this window."

"Five rooms. You can't do better than that?"

Logan continued from his notes as if Chilcote had said nothing. "Room 686 is occupied by an older couple, who were in the room when the shots were fired. Rooms 688 and 788 have been cleaned from last night and are vacant, waiting for the next occupants to check in. Room 784 is occupied by three guys who appear to be at the track for the race. Room 786 is the most likely, Hoskins and the manager looked at it just now. It was rented but doesn't look slept in, but it does look like someone was there. It was reserved several months ago, and rented to a single man who checked in Thursday night around midnight. The card used to hold the room was a prepaid card. The lab guys are at the room now going through it for prints, GSR or other evidence. Hoskins says he checked each room and saw no evidence of powder flashes, GSR, or anything to indicate a gun had been fired inside."

"What about the vacant rooms?"

"They are being held vacant and have been sealed pending inspection by the lab."

"What about the roof?"

"Probably not. Hoskins has been up there. It is very inaccessible. It would take a Navy Seal Team to get up there and back down un-noticed."

"I'm beginning to think …," his voice tailed off. "Have someone go up there and make sure the lab guys check it out when they are done with the rooms."

"Already done, sir."

CHAPTER 71

Elizabeth was dressed in her room relaxing on the bed and enjoying a drink when there was a firm knock on the door.

She threw the book down and got up and walked to the door. She peeked through the peep hole and saw it was Logan and Hoskins. *"Right on time, just like Ryan said they would."* She opened the door and said, "I hope you aren't here to finish tying my bikini. You guys left me half undressed by the pool."

"No ma'am. This is official business." Showing their badges, Logan continued, "We are going to have to ask you to come down to the police station. We need to talk to you about an incident that happened here in the hotel a little while ago."

She leaned forward and lowered her voice as if she were asking to be let in on a dark secret. "Was it about that noise we heard?"

"Yes ma'am. A hotel guest by the name of Tyrone Rexford was murdered." Logan watched her closely, looking for a reaction to the mention of T-Rex by his real name, but there was none.

"I don't know any Mister Rexford. What has he got to do with me? I've never heard of that name?"

"You may know him from his professional name, T-Rex."

"T-Rex? Isn't that some kind of dinosaur?"

Logan stared at her for a long moment.

"Actually, she's right," chuckled Hoskins, "Tyrannosaurus Rex was the biggest dinosaur."

Logan glanced annoyingly at his new partner. "This was a football player, Tyrone Rexford, who went by the name of T-Rex."

"I think I've heard the name somewhere before, but I still don't get what that has to do with me?"

"We just want to ask you some questions down at the station."

"But you know exactly where I was, unless you think I killed him while you were tying my bikini by the pool, which you didn't even finish doing, by the way, leaving me half-exposed to the world."

"Sorry, ma'am. Can you please come down to the station with us?"

"Do I have to?"

"Yes. We have Peter Levinson down there now, and we will have Ryan Foster soon. Please let's do this the simplest way possible." Again, he looked for a response, other than surprise, to hear her friend's names mentioned in connection with a murder.

"Peter and Ryan are here in Daytona?" she asked incredulously.

"Please? Can we just go."

"Very well," she shrugged as she put down her drink, "I'm curious to see Peter and Ryan, and see what it is you think we've done?"

CHAPTER 72

Back at the speedway, Peter was sitting in his seat at the end of the row, enjoying the race, when he was approached by the same Detectives who had accosted him earlier. "Hello again, fellows. Have you come up here to beat me up again?"

"No, we hope not. But we are here to take you downtown to the police station and ask some questions about the murder of T-Rex."

"Murder of T-Rex? He's right up there in the section behind me. Remember, we kind of went through this earlier?"

"I'm afraid not. That person is an imposter. T-Rex has been murdered back at his hotel and we've been asked to bring you downtown for questioning about a conspiracy to commit his murder."

"That bastard is dead? Really? ... Dead?" Peter began to tear up at the news that the man who murdered his son was now dead, and secretly he was pleased that he had some small part in it, albeit indirectly. "Thank you, gentlemen, that's wonderful news."

"Whatever. We've still got to take you down to the station."

"But, why?"

"We've got Elizabeth down there and we'll have Ryan soon enough, and the FBI wants to talk to all of you about an interstate conspiracy to commit murder."

"Elizabeth? Ryan? I'm really confused. I can't imagine …. But certainly, if it will help, I'll be glad to go with you. I'm just sorry I'm going to miss the end of the race. Can't you wait till it's over. This is my first race and it's very exciting."

"No, sir. It has to be now. So, if you'll just come with us."

As he got up to leave, he said to himself, aloud, "I can't believe it. That no good bastard is really dead?"

CHAPTER 73

On the other side of the speedway, Ryan sat down in his seat in the Allison Tower and enjoyed the race for two hours or more, until, just ten laps from the end, he heard a familiar voice coming down the row toward him saying, "Excuse me, folks, excuse me." He looked up to see Detective Lawler flash her badge at the fellow sitting next to him and say, "Police business, sir. You'll have to make room for me here."

As the annoyed fan moved to his left to make room, Lawler sat down next to Ryan and said in a calm voice, "Hello, Ryan."

"Detective Lawler? I had no idea you were a NASCAR fan, too?"

Lawler ignored the question. "You did it, Ryan. Your little gang really pulled it off. I've been thinking about it while I looked for you for the last hour or more. I'm actually impressed."

"Did it? What do you mean?"

"Seriously, Ryan. I've been scanning the crowd for over an hour looking for you, but that shouldn't surprise you, it's just the way you planned it."

"Really, Detective? You've been looking for me? Here? At the Daytona 500? You came all the way from California to look for me at the Daytona 500? You should have called." He patted his pocket to emphasize his point. "I've got my cell phone. I could have saved you the trouble."

"Enjoy it, Ryan. Part of me says you deserve to gloat. You pulled it off. I mean ... you really pulled them off ... all of them! At least it looks that way for now, anyhow."

"I'm not sure what you are talking about, ma'am?"

"That ma'am shit doesn't even bother me anymore, Ryan. I've grown as a person, actually, thanks largely to you. You see, I've earned my stripes on this one. Here I am. Just a couple months ago, I was just a scared new Detective from Santa Rosa, California, working my first murder. Now, I'm in Florida, working with the FBI, New York PD, and Florida Detectives, and they haven't gotten any closer to you than I could."

"How can I possibly feel bad that I can't pin Danny Lemos on you when the three of you just made fools of the FBI and all of these big name police organizations, right under our noses. If this works out for you, and it looks like it just might, some day I'm going to say I'm proud to have been fooled by the best gang of amateur assassins ever assembled. There might even be a book in it for me down the road."

"Still not a clue what you're talking about."

"Sure Ryan. In case you weren't a hundred percent sure, T-Rex is dead. A sniper took him out at his hotel today. That should be all of them, right?"

"All of them? What do you mean, Detective? Still no clue. But if, in fact, T-Rex is dead, the guy who killed him should get a medal. If you expect me to feel bad, it isn't going to happen. I just hope my friend, Peter Levenson, has a good alibi, or they'll probably try to blame him."

"I agree. We'll ask him when we get downtown."

"Downtown?"

"You know, Ryan, that we are going to have to take all of you downtown to talk about this, right."

"I'm not sure why. Look around, Detective. Isn't this a good enough alibi to eliminate me? Unless you think I shot him from my seat here."

Lawler scanned the crowd and nodded. "It's a pretty good alibi, all right. Maybe perfect, in fact. But there are too many 'loose ends' the FBI will want to talk to you about. It shouldn't be a problem, just 'loose ends', like GSR tests and the like. And that shouldn't be a problem either, because I already know you were at the range this week wearing that same Gordon shirt, so if the residue tests are positive, they won't mean a thing. Genius, Ryan. You used us against ourselves. So, why don't we just go down there now and get it over with?"

"Okay, Lawler, but let's enjoy these last few laps first. I've been waiting for a long time for this race, and my favorite driver is in position to win it. See that bright car down there that is painted like my jacket, that's Jeff Gordon, and he's in fourth place. Watch closely, these last few laps are always the most exciting. I think you might even enjoy it."

"I guess there's no harm. No reason for him to run, he's covered every base, it appears." "It sure is noisy." As she sat back in the seat, she thought, *"I can't believe I'm sitting here watching the end of the Daytona 500 with a guy I'm taking in for conspiracy to commit interstate murder as soon as the race is over."*

The track announcer called the final lap; "They're coming out of turn four! Earnhardt leads coming to the checkered flag! They are bouncing off one another! Any one of them could win it!"

"Come on, Jeff!" Ryan yelled.

"Harvick tries to make a move on Busch … they hit …they're both into the wall, collecting Edwards and Sorenson. Up front, coming to the checkered flag, Keselowski gets around Gordon for third, as Earnhardt holds off Hamlin to WIN the Daytona 500!"

CHAPTER 74

When Lawler and Ryan arrived at the police station they walked down a hallway where the police had conspicuously located Elizabeth and Peter in waiting rooms so each had the chance to see the others.

"Why are Elizabeth and Peter here?" Ryan said as he waved to each of them in a friendly, reassuring manner.

"Agent Chilcote will explain."

Chilcote was waiting for him in the interview room. "Hello, again, Ryan." Without waiting for a response, he continued, "I'm sure you remember me. We met at your house in California a while back."

"Sure, I remember you."

"We have already obtained and executed a search warrant of your room, luggage, and person. These men here are going to test your hands for GSR ..."

"Gunshot residue?" Ryan interrupted, "I don't know if you are aware of it, Agent ...uh ... Chilcote, isn't it? I don't know if you are aware, but I was at the shooting range Wednesday before I came down here to Daytona."

Chilcote acted unfazed by the information he already knew, continuing his thought, "… then we are going to talk about murder … Interstate Conspiracy to Commit Murder."

"Murder? Who? You guys still think I murdered someone?"

"We'll talk in a minute. We'll need your clothing now."

Two men in lab coats helped him to take off his Jeff Gordon Jacket and denim shirt and swabbed his hands thoroughly for GSR. When they were finished they scurried out of the room.

While Ryan changed into a jumpsuit Chilcote provided, he was advised of his rights by Chilcote. When he concluded, Ryan said, "I have nothing to hide, so I'll answer your questions, but for the record, I refuse to waive any rights to which I may be entitled. If this is an official interrogation, and you guys are going to try to pin a murder on me, perhaps you should get me an attorney."

"The FBI is taking this murder very seriously. I can assure you that that you haven't covered everything. You left a few errors along your path; every crook does, and you are all three going to fall for this, and the other previous murders, under the Federal Interstate Conspiracy statutes. You are talking about several lifetimes of federal prison time."

"We are also interviewing Peter and Elizabeth about the same interstate murder conspiracy. They seem like nice people who are pawns in this case. Is there anything you want to tell us to save your friends, before they get themselves in over their heads?"

"Wow. Are you 'scapegoating' us, Agent Chilcote? I can't speak for Peter or Elizabeth about their whereabouts when whatever crime you are talking about occurred, but they never seemed to me to be Bonnie and Clyde types. Do they seem that way to you?"

"You know how this works, Ryan. I ask the questions, you answer them."

"Okay, ask me."

"Where were you after you dodged the agent's following you at the track?"

"Dodged the agents at the track? Was I being followed at the track? If I was, they had to have told you, I was just enjoying the Daytona 500 for the past four to six hours."

"I'm talking about the time after you left the track?"

"Left the track? Wrong again, Agent Chilcote. I was there all along. Say, did you say something about 'previous murders'? What are you talking about?"

There was a knock on the door and one of the men in the lab coats stepped in and handed a piece of paper to Chilcote. He glanced at it;

Hand Examination:
Subject tests 'very weak; possible, but inconclusive' for GSR, possibly contaminated from clothing.

Clothing Examination:
Weak GSR present from the sleeve of the Jeff Gordon denim shirt.

Chilcote looked up and said confidently, "First mistake, Ryan. You tested positive for GSR. Tests reveal you've recently fired a gun."

"Really? I suppose you could have gotten a reading, but it would have to be very weak. Like I said, I qualified at the range the day before I flew to Florida for the race. Does it say how strong of a reading they got?"

"I told you, I'll ask the questions."

Again, there was a knock and two men entered the room. They held a brief conversation with Chilcote and shook their heads as if in resignation while they spoke. Chilcote waved them out of the room with no comment.

Chilcote sat in his chair and stared at Ryan for a very long time without saying anything.

"More bad news, Agent Chilcote?"

Chilcote stared back, expressionless.

"Sir, are you trying to intimidate me? Because, if you are, it isn't working really good. Did you have any more questions?"

Chilcote shifted in his chair, then sat back. "You are all pretty smug right now Ryan. Your co-conspirators are both claiming complete innocence also. Do you expect us to believe you all coincidentally showed up here at the same time? And all with perfect alibis while the murder of T-Rex goes down?"

"You all may be on top of the world right now, but you are amateurs. You hear that? Amateurs!"

His voice increased an octave or two as his anger and frustration began to surface. "This is the FBI you are dealing with, and we don't like to hold empty bags. You are good. I'll even give you 'very good'. But, somewhere you fucked up. Everyone does who thinks they can get away with murder. We aren't going to quit looking until we find that screw-up, then I will get to look you in the eye again, and we'll see how smug you look them. You got that, Ryan?"

"Yes sir. Please save this videotape and don't destroy it. I'll have an attorney ask for a copy of it, and the threat you just made."

"What videotape? This is the FBI, Ryan. We haven't accused you of anything yet. We're just chatting, right?"

Across the hallway, they continued to interrogate Peter and Elizabeth to no avail.

The official police report concluded that Peter was "just one of 100,000 race fans who attended the race that weekend, except he was under FBI surveillance the entire race including the time of the murder, and apparently didn't even know Ryan and Elizabeth were 'coincidentally' there in Daytona" The report didn't even mention that Peter was tackled and detained while walking to his seat.

The same report also showed that Elizabeth, who was also under 24-7 surveillance, did little more than shop, eat alone, have one nightcap in the hotel bar, and sit by the pool sunbathing during the day. The timing of the bikini strap incident was particularly embarrassing to the FBI.

As for Ryan, unless they could prove otherwise, they were forced to concede that he was at the track when they lost sight of him and was still at the track and enjoying the race when Lawler finally found him again. They could only speculate on his whereabouts during their surveillance lapses. Security cameras back at the Hotel DuBois showed many people, but none showed a clear image of Ryan or anyone who fit the description of Ryan's clothes.

When Ryan was released at about 6:30 PM, Peter, and Elizabeth were waiting. "T-Rex is dead. This calls for a toast, and I know just the place," he said.

Forty minutes later, they were enjoying dinner and toasts at the 'Old Beach Course Barbeque Restaurant', located on Highway A1A, close to the long extinct stock car beach race course south of town. After dinner, they walked a mile or more down the beach and back, where FBI audio and visual surveillance teams reported they laughed and spoke in hushed tones among the roar of the ocean and out of earshot of listening devices.

They ended the evening with meaningful long hugs and each went to their respective hotels. The next day, they boarded their respective flights and returned to their homes, vowing to never contact each other again.

CHAPTER 75

Even though Ryan was never charged or questioned again in the murders, the CHP looked at the preponderance of evidence and determined that Ryan would be relieved of his command for public relations reasons, and re-assigned. He promptly filed for early retirement.

A month later, the Clear Lake CHP office staff and officers had a cake and coffee retirement reception for him at the afternoon briefing. At the conclusion, when there were only a few close friends around, an officer asked, "C'mon, boss, you can tell us, did you do it?"

"Of course not. Do you think I did?"

"Yeah, we kind of 'do' think you did. We think you pulled off a perfect crime."

"Well, if you think I did, you are cops; aren't you supposed to read me my rights?"

A few snickers, which broke into laughter, a shrug of the shoulders, and Ryan said, "That's enough screwing around. You guys and gals need to 'hit the road'. Be careful out there; it can be dangerous."

One by one the officers filtered out of the room and resumed their day.

Ryan drove home, contemplating what life would hold for him as a recently divorced man who was suddenly retired and out of work. When he got home, he poured himself a drink and went out to sit on the porch and relax looking out on the lake below him.

He reached over and picked up the mail he had picked up off the kitchen table, and began to sort through it.

He stopped abruptly and his heart froze when he spotted a large manila envelope marked 'City of Daytona Beach; Traffic Enforcement Division' addressed to him. He tore open the envelope and pulled out the contents. A self-addressed envelope fell into his lap.

He turned over the top piece of paper and saw a red light traffic enforcement photo, clearly showing him, wearing the Tony Stewart jacket and cap that would destroy his alibi for the time of the murder, as he ran a red light on his way back to the track, just blocks from T-Rex's hotel. It was time stamped shortly after the murder, at the time he claimed to be at the track.

The accompanying letter from the Traffic Enforcement Division invited him to pay a 'red light enforcement mitigation fee' of $98.00 to avoid any further action on the part of the Police Department.

He quickly stuffed $98.00 in cash into the self-addressed envelope, drove to the Post Office and dropped it into the mail slot.

THE END

WANT MORE ACTION FROM STEVE DAVIS?

"22E ... Officer Down!"

The first novel by Steve Davis. Here is the storyline:

> Casey Tyler was only nine years old when his father,
> California Highway Patrol Officer Sonny Tyler, was gunned
> down in 1970 while on patrol in the early morning hours on a
> lonely highway on the rural California north coast.

> Murders just didn't happen in Eureka in the 1970's, and the
> murder of a cop was especially unthinkable. But even more
> unfathomable was the thought that the case would remain
> unresolved, which meant that someone in the community had
> gotten away with such a heinous crime for seventeen years.

> It wasn't for lack of effort, or even lack of suspects.
> Humboldt County Sheriff's Detective Sergeant Don Regan
> pursued the case with pit bull intensity, but over time, every
> clue, every theory, and every suspect was exhausted, and the
> file became a 'cold case' with no resolution.

> But, unthinkable or not, here it was, 1987, and Rookie CHP
> Officer Casey Tyler found himself working in the same
> office, patrolling the same highways upon which his father
> was murdered by someone he had stopped for a routine traffic
> violation.

> When Casey and the soon-to-retire Sergeant Regan began to
> look into the case again, things heat up quickly. Soon Casey

found himself and his loved ones directly in the crosshairs of the killer. An attack on his fiancé and the attempted murder of his mother begin to unravel Casey's personal life, adding anguish and urgency to the investigation.

Then an attempt on Casey's life proves fatal for a local hired gunman, and reveals new information which sends the case spiraling full circle, until Casey finds himself staring into the eyes of the killer, separated by the barrel of the biggest gun Casey ever saw.

"Snap Judgement"

The first in a planned series of novellas (short novels) by Steve Davis, under the pen name 'Lt. Steve Davis'. The series follows fictional California Highway Patrol Officer Corbin 'C. D.' Dixon as he investigates crimes originating from traffic accidents that don't pan out to be what they seem at first glance.

Here is the storyline of '*Snap Judgement*':

Officer Dixon is assigned to investigate a hit-and-run accident near the mountain community of Cobb, in which the wife of a prominent defense attorney is killed.

As the clues reveal, the victim, a pedestrian on a deserted road, was actually struck by two vehicles, the first of which mortally injured her, and the second vehicle, which killed her outright. CD must find them both to unravel the case.

During the investigation, CD begins to suspect the first 'accident' may have been intentional, with the husband the prime suspect.

A carefully orchestrated of cat-and-mouse ensues, in which the husband uses the court system to destroy or exclude every piece of evidence until Casey is down to one final scrap of cloth upon which the entire case may hinge. When the court orders that scrap of cloth to be destroyed, the case appears lost.

Then CD devises a trick to save the evidence, but will it work? Just when it appears the trick may have worked, the case is blown wide open by the most unexpected game changing witness imaginable.

"22E ... Officer Down!" and *'Snap Judgement'*
are available at www.DavisMedia.com,
or on Amazon.com in paperback or Kindle E-book,
or may be ordered through any bookstore
using the ISBN# 9780991442003.

Steve Davis

Made in the USA
Columbia, SC
09 April 2018